An
Enemy
Like Me

The differences
that spark us are
nothing compared to the
similarities that bond us
together! ♡ TerriBrown

An Enemy Like Me

TERI M. BROWN

atmosphere press

Published by Atmosphere Press

Cover design by Matthew Fielder

atmospherepress.com

To my grandfather who fought in the war and to my dad who lived with the consequences. Thank you both for your service to your country.

Chapter 1

WILLIAM: Spring 1944

For the first time in his short life, William heard his parents yelling at one another. It wasn't like the time his mommy barked "NO!" when he walked into the street without holding her hand. That had been quick and sharp, and over as fast as it had started.

What penetrated the walls of his small bedroom flowed like a river swollen with too much rain. Loud, meaningless words raced back and forth, first from his mother and then from his father. Try as he might, his mind could not catch the sounds and turn them into comprehensible sentences. Perhaps they were using the words Oma used when she sang songs from something she called the Old Country. Except sprinkled among the unfamiliar words were those he understood. Words like "father" and "please" and "Jacob" were all tangled up with syllables powerful enough to change his world.

On this night, the first of what would be many nights, the soothing sounds of whispers and laughter that always helped him drift off to sleep turned harsh and frightening. His mother was the machine gun he saw the time his parents took him to the picture show downtown. Bullets flew from her mouth, a staccato spray that hit his father squarely in the chest. He imagined his father slumping to the floor, dead like the soldiers who plagued his dreams for weeks, convincing his mother to never let him see the news reels again.

Then, without warning, his father spoke in a roar of thunder like the summer storms that sent William scampering into his parent's bedroom in the middle of the night. With each boom, William imagined flashes of light streaking across the kitchen, lighting up his parent's faces.

His mother no longer had soft arms, hair as warm sunshine, and a smile that made William warm inside. His father was no longer taller than the forest trees, yet gentle as the wind that blew his kite on a spring afternoon. Instead, they were cold, hard, and unsmiling, like the monsters hiding under his bed.

He wanted to stand up to determine what was happening, to try to understand the words, but his legs would not move. With no place to turn for comfort, he sunk deeper into his bed, pulled the covers up close to his chin with arms as wobbly as his lower lip, and held tightly to his birthday present. Brelli, though nothing more than the fake fur of a stuffed bear, would have to do. Eventually, the war in the kitchen ceased, and with another squeeze of his stuffed companion, he fell into a fitful sleep.

The sunlight danced on his eyelids, waking him to a quiet morning. Had the machine gun bursts and thunder been his imagination? Padding into the kitchen, he found his parents talking quietly, nothing out of place except his mother's smile. She crouched low and wrapped her arms around his tiny shoulders in a good morning hug. Then she helped him into his chair and pushed a bowl of warm oatmeal across the wooden table.

Silence reigned, except for the scrape of chairs on the floor and the small boy's spoon hitting the side of the metal bowl. His father sat with his head bent low over his hands. William straightened in his chair, struggling to identify what his father held that captured his attention so completely, but there was nothing except two calloused hands clasped tightly together in his father's lap.

Before William finished his oatmeal, his daddy muttered "Goodbye" in a voice sounding like a radio show announcer instead of his own father. Then he left the room without any kisses or hugs. William couldn't remember a time when his daddy hadn't kissed them both goodbye. He pushed his oatmeal away, unable to swallow, and studied his own hands like he had seen his daddy do.

That night, after being tucked into bed, the sounds began again. Rapid machine gun fire from his mother followed by thunder and lightning from his father. This time, however, the voices stopped abruptly when a door slammed so forcefully that his bed shook. He held his breath, the silence surrounding him, until a small noise that sounded like the hurt bunny they nursed back to health last spring seeped under the door. He couldn't have known it was the sound of his mother crying.

During the day, William's world continued like normal. He would eat and play. His mother would dote on him. His father would come home from work in time for the evening meal. They would spend time together before he went to bed with a goodnight kiss. But at night, his world turned upside down as he tried to block out the noise and the monster-like visions of his parents.

Then, one morning, instead of the usual breakfast followed by his father's daily departure, William's parents sat him down on the living room sofa. The corners of William's mouth tugged into a grin. He rarely got to sit on the sofa with its white and gray stripes dotted with hundreds of pink flowers because mommy didn't want him ruining the pretty material. William dreamed of driving his cars from flower to flower, but, as he learned, sofas were for sitting and sitting only.

William glanced around the room, looking for the reason for the unexpected treat. When he realized there were no visitors, and he had not been instructed to wash his sticky fingers after his pancakes, his heart thumped in his chest as though he had been running instead of eating breakfast.

He didn't know what was happening, but everything was wrong, exactly like the loud voices in the night. Tightening his fingers into balls, he glanced sideways at his parents, fully expecting them to transform into the monsters he imagined them to be in the night.

But instead of turning into a monster, his daddy simply began to talk. With each passing second, his mommy's face puckered, and tears leaked from her eyes, making two tiny trails across her cheeks, down her neck, and onto her soft pink sweater. The sight of his mother crying was worse than imagining her with a machine gun and made it difficult to focus on his daddy's words.

"I'm leaving...fight in the war...Show I am a patriot... Japanese...It is up to me to keep us free..." The more his daddy talked, the more his mommy cried, the wet spots growing larger on her sweater.

What did his daddy mean? What was Japanese? War? Patriot? Freedom? Why was his daddy using those powerful words of the night? The only thing he understood were the words "I'm leaving," and there was nothing else for a boy of almost four to understand. He, too, began to cry, creating his own wet patches on the shoulders of his plaid pajamas. Before long, his daddy joined in as well.

William was never quite sure how much time passed since their talk on the floral sofa and the day his father left for the war. In many ways, life went back to normal. Mommy and Daddy no longer argued in the night, and, like before, they kissed each morning as Daddy left for work. But his mommy's soft smile was still missing, prompting him to climb up onto the bathroom sink to look at himself in the tiny square of a mirror. With solemn eyes, he noted his smile was missing, too. He wondered if their smiles were going to war with Daddy.

Without warning, William woke one morning to voices in the kitchen. He recognized Uncle Otto's voice and went racing out to say hello and receive the treat his uncle never failed to bring with him. A piece of root beer flavored stick candy appeared out of his pocket after he swung William in a wide arc that made his breath stick in his throat.

As he unwrapped his candy, he looked around, surprised so many other people gathered in the kitchen before breakfast. Grandma and Grandpa Phillips were there. He didn't know they were coming from their home far away for a visit. But before he ran to them, his Oma Elisabet came into view. Despite living around the corner, Oma never came to their house. Instead, he went to her tiny apartment which smelled of chocolate and marzipan.

The smile on his face scampered back to its hiding place. He spied his father sitting in a chair with a bag at his feet. Then he understood. Today was the day his father left for the war.

Although his mommy made a delicious breakfast with sweetbreads, eggs, and bacon, all his favorites, William was not hungry. He pushed food around with his fork, watching everyone cautiously. He still didn't understand how long his daddy would be gone. He had been told "Not long," or "Until the war ends" but never an exact number of days.

When Grandma and Grandpa Phillips went home after a visit, Mommy would say they would be back again before long. "Before long" usually lasted from Thanksgiving time until the apple tree in the yard blossomed. Is that how long Daddy would be gone? Would he miss Christmas and his birthday like his grandparents?

After breakfast, Uncle Otto leaned down toward William. In a quiet whisper, he said, "Your daddy needs you to be the man of the house while he is gone. It is going to be up to you to take care of your mommy." Then he said, "Don't cry, William. Your daddy doesn't need to see you cry as he goes off to war. You need to be a big soldier."

William was an obedient boy. He would not cry. He would be the big soldier like he was asked.

With a bit of jostling and maneuvering, they piled into the car and headed to the train station. William had never been in a car with so many people, nor had he ever ridden in his daddy's car with Uncle Otto driving. Grandma and Grandpa sat in the front with Uncle Otto, and Mommy, Daddy, and Oma crowded into the back with William. He sat on his daddy's knee, pressed against his mommy, while the buildings flew by the small side window.

He had been to the train station many times before. The squat green building next to the track was always full of people with suitcases scurrying from one place to another. However, his favorite parts of the station were the shiny black steam engines and the long cars trailing behind. He would point to trains carrying loads of lumber from the lumberyard where Daddy worked and others carrying stone from the quarry. He would count the cars as they passed, but once he reached 12, William would let his daddy take over because all the numbers after 12 confused him. He longed for the day when he would be able to count as high as his father.

Today, as Otto parked the car and everyone piled out of the open doors, an unidentifiable emotion planted itself firmly in William's gut. All around them, people hugged and cried and said goodbye. Smiles mingled with tears and 'I love yous.' Patriotism mingled with heartache. Loyalty mingled with selfishness. Soldiers, fathers, brothers, sons stood amid the fluttering American flags strung between the platform's timbers.

William was too young to understand the emotion

that permeated the train station. How does a four-year-old describe grief, uncertainty, fear, longing, and a smidgen of 'patriotic soldier' all rolled into one little boy's heart? From that day forward, trains would forever be linked with the sorrow of goodbye and the American flag would remind him of his father.

He regarded a boy about his age holding his own father's hand. As his father picked him up, both began to cry. William's mouth opened and his eyes widened. Didn't the boy know that crying was not allowed when you sent your daddy off to war? He wanted to tell him the rule, but the sound of Oma crying brought his attention squarely back to his own family.

His daddy hugged Oma, and she tried to talk between her sobs. "Jacob, I don't...want to...lose you the way...I lost your...father...Oh, Jacob!" William wasn't sure what she meant, unless it was like losing one of his metal cars. Tears sprang to his eyes. He didn't want that happening to his daddy. If he lost his daddy like his best yellow car, he would have to cry, wouldn't he?

Next, Daddy turned to Grandma and Grandpa Phillips. He hugged them both tightly and thanked them for taking care of his wife and child. They, too, began to cry.

Tears welled up in William's eyes, but he closed them tightly. "Brave soldiers do not cry. Daddy needs me to be a brave soldier." He opened his eyes again as his daddy turned to Uncle Otto. Both gave each other thumping slaps on the back as they tried to hold back the tears. Both, however, were unsuccessful.

Turning to his mommy, Daddy's tears flowed freely. He held her in his arms and murmured things William could not hear. He wondered if they were secrets, but if so, they were not happy ones because his mommy continued crying. She looked so little in Daddy's arms. Would she be able to take care of him while Daddy went to war? How would she do things that only daddy's who are tall as the trees can do?

He tried to swallow, but something reminding him of a jagged rock from the quarry where Daddy took him swimming was in the way, making his throat ache. His eyes kept threatening to spill over, making it hard to see. But he had promised. Big soldier. Brave soldier. His daddy was going to war. His tiny mother with the sunshine hair needed him to be the man of the house. His tall as the trees father needed him to be a brave soldier. He would not cry.

Finally, his daddy squatted down and scooped William into his arms. He held him so tightly that had the rock not been in this throat, he was sure his few bites of breakfast would have popped out the top. He put his head on his daddy's shoulder, forcing the tears to stay inside his eyes, while his daddy cried into his hair, making streaks on William's cheeks.

He whispered to William like he had whispered to Mommy. He told him secrets, but these secrets were not sad like Mommy's secrets. They were words that made him brave. His daddy trusted him to take care of his mommy and be a soldier just like him.

Without warning, the train whistle blew, startling everyone on the platform. Passengers, mostly men heading off to war, gathered their things and moved toward the train. Without another look at his family, his duffle slung over his shoulder, his daddy handed a ticket to the uniformed man on the train. The whistle blew one final time and began to move slowly down the tracks.

Puffs of black smoke bellowed out of the engine, spilling gray ashes across the brims of the hats and shoulders of the families left behind. Everyone, William included, frantically waved at the train until there was nothing left but a few distant puffs of smoke.

His thoughts, as he walked dry-eyed back to the car with nothing but his father's words echoing in his ears, were that Uncle Otto told the wrong people not to cry.

Chapter 2

WILLIAM: November 2016

He should have worn a thicker coat, not the lightly lined windbreaker he'd been wearing all week. He smiled faintly, remembering something he overheard when he first moved here from Ohio over three decades before. "If you don't like the weather in North Carolina, wait a day." Though this saying wasn't quite true, the weather did shift with a manic propensity. Yesterday dawned as a cool autumn day. Today trumpeted the arrival of winter.

He cursed lightly under his breath as the stiff breeze caught at the wreath he tried to maneuver to the old red Chevy pickup parked in the driveway. Although he wished the wind would settle down and let him start the task at hand, he couldn't help but stop to admire the beauty of Old Glory snapping back and forth above his head on the flagpole he erected shortly after building his home.

William loved the American flag his entire life. From the time he was a small child, his mother taught him songs like "My Country 'Tis of Thee" and the "Star-Spangled Banner." He joined the military for a tour of duty like his daddy, in part because it was the right way to serve the country you love and show your patriotism. Now, when he would spot a flag, particularly one unfurled in all her splendor, his chest would swell with pride, and he would develop tears in his eyes.

The truth was he didn't go anywhere without the American flag. On family beach trips, he hung a flag on the cottage every morning and took it down every night despite the jibes of those who loved him. "One week without a flag, William. Can't you make it just one week?"

It was the same when he went to his beloved antique car shows. He had been restoring cars since he was a teenager and had been attending car shows and swap meets since his kids were little. Sometime after 9/11, he began taking a flag with him, setting it up at the corner of his little lot. He marveled at the number of people commenting on the flag, becoming convinced it drew more attention than his hot rods.

He even owned a lapel pin he wore whenever he went about his day to remind him, and those who met him, that he was, indeed, a patriot. That's because, for William, the flag was more than a symbol of American freedom.

The American flag stood for his father, his father's sacrifice, of a life well led, of pride, and of patriotism.

William's American flag was a powerful, potent reminder of everything he understood about life, from his first fuzzy memories in a train station to the present day. How could a man be expected to leave the house without a flag standing for all that?

So, despite the cold seeping into his arthritic bones, and despite the wind desperately trying to jerk the wreath out of his hands like a toddler fighting for his favorite toy, he paused long enough to recite the Pledge of Allegiance in his mind. '...with liberty and justice for all.' With that, he quickly moved to the passenger side of the old truck, yanked the door open, urgently hoping to find a place out of the wind.

He propped himself between the door and the frame to keep the wind from slamming it shut again. From that awkward angle, he wrestled the wreath inside and then let the wind catch and slam the door shut with a bang. Now, nearly running to the driver's side, he slid into the seat, started the truck, and adjusted the heat to high.

Veteran's Day was more than a great day for clothing sales, though one might not know it from his morning perusal of his small town's paper. Every Veteran's Day since his father passed, William placed a wreath on his father's grave. Sure, he could simply have the florist deliver it, saving himself the trouble, but this was a day to remember his father, a man who remained taller than the trees, in his own mind, his entire life.

William was certain the flag's performance this morning had been for his father, in the same way his saying The Pledge had been. His father would have done so, but in death no longer had the ability. Patriotism was a legacy he left to his son. William held onto it, grasping firmly, like it was his father's own hand.

He had to admit the florist did a good job. The wreath was beautiful. Red, white, and blue flowers and ribbons with the symbol of the 16th Armored Division of the Army in the center – a yellow, red, and blue triangle sporting tank tracks, a single cannon, and a lightning bolt topped by the number 16. At the bottom of the wreath were the dates April 14, 1944 to June 3, 1946 – the days, months, and years his father spent separated from his son. Those extras were not cheap, but William believed his father deserved far more than a generic wreath because his father gave far more than generic service to his country and to his family.

Carefully, he slid the truck into gear and drove down the steep driveway that led to the road out of his tiny neighborhood and headed toward town. He couldn't go down the drive on a morning to visit his father's grave without thinking about his mother, too. Despite being a terrible driver, she would proudly tell everyone she had never been in an accident. William and his father would always mutter that she never looked in the rear-view mirror to witness the thousands of accidents she left in her wake.

No matter how often she tried, she never managed to turn the car around at the top of his drive, but going down the steep incline in reverse left her breathless. He could hear his dad saying, "Bonnie, driving down this hill is man's work." Then she would laugh, a sweet little laugh, and hand him the keys. Their relationship, though not perfect, had been beautiful. There was no doubt they loved one another deeply.

Jacob and Bonnie married in June 1939. William was

born nine months later. The day his mother died in 2000 was the day his father quit living, though he managed to walk the earth for another ten years. Sadly, those years were often empty for Jacob, despite William's best attempts to fill his father's time with love, laughter, and time together. His dad wanted nothing more than to die and be with his beloved wife. Eventually, he got his wish.

William passed through the quaint little town he had grown to love as his own. Though born in Ohio and spending the greater part of his life there, North Carolina and the historic town of Southern Pines became his home when he moved here to start a new business venture. He particularly loved the patriotic holidays in this town with their parades honoring Vets and the flags put up by Boy Scouts that ran down the main thoroughfare.

Southern Pines was a sleepy town with no stoplights when he moved here, and though it had grown considerably, it still had the sleepy town feel. Small shops lined the road divided down the center by a railroad track. Pedestrians walked the streets of town all year long, hustling to the Post Office or window shopping while licking at an ice cream cone. To this day, whenever the train would come through, William would stop to count the cars the way he had done as a small boy. He always smiled when he got to the number 12.

William was thrilled when his parents decided to retire to North Carolina and joined him in Southern Pines. When his father was still alive, they would come into town on these celebratory days for the sole purpose of spotting the flags. Though William's love for flags rivaled his father's, it certainly did not surpass it. Not a July 4th, Flag Day, or Veteran's Day went by in which

Jacob wouldn't observe the line of flags and start to cry.

After going through town, they would stop at the coffee shop, his dad wearing his WWII Veteran ball cap, where many would humbly thank him for his service. While sipping coffee, his father would regale the old-timers with stories about the war. Except, William acknowledged, Jacob never really talked about the war at all. Instead, he would talk about the time after the war as he waited to come home from Germany. The bad memories of killing, cold, hunger, fear, loneliness, and danger were tucked away deep inside and only came out during the now-occasional nightmare.

Today, however, William rode alone down the street, passing the wind-whipped flags with nothing but a wreath and his memories for company. As he pulled into the cemetery thick with pine trees, a solemnness filled his soul. As far as his eye could see, flags snapped and crackled in the morning sun. So many gravestones with flags and wreaths. So many men and women who sacrificed so much.

He pulled the oversize truck over to the side of the small road in front of his father's grave, reading the stone: Jacob Wendel Miller. He then bowed his head, saying a silent prayer for all those who fought in times past.

Chapter 3

JAKOB: 1917 - 1935

September 17, 1917, was a red-letter day for Elisabet and Hyrum. A round, pink-faced baby with dark hair sprouting at all angles arrived after several hours of intense labor for Elisabet and hand-wringing and pacing for Hyrum. Of course, Elisabet had expected so much hair after all the heartburn during pregnancy. The wives' tales she grew up on were rarely wrong.

Hyrum was not concerned with hair or heartburn, though he was elated with his mother's premonition. "Without a doubt, Hyrum, Elisabet is carrying a boy. Do you notice the way her hips jut to the front?" To Hyrum, everything jutted to the front, but his mother's prediction had been right, as always. He wanted to name his son Hyrum Jakob Mueller, Jr, but Elisabet refused outright.

"No son of mine is going into the world with someone else's name. My son...our son will start this life with a name of his very own." However, she consented to giving her son family names, "But only the strong ones." Her son would be Jakob, Hyrum's middle name, and Wendel after Hyrum's father who brought the Muellers to the United States when Hyrum was nothing more than a tiny boy. Her son, Jakob Wendel Mueller, would have to work hard to live up to his name, but Elisabet was sure as a first-generation-born American, he could do so.

The first year of Jakob's life was uneventful. He ate, slept, grew, cried, and gained enough independence to sit and crawl on his own. He spent hours playing at his mother's feet as she tended the house, while his father, like many local immigrants, worked long hours at the lumberyard in town. He was holding on to a kitchen chair with one hand and a red wooden block in the other the day his father threw open the door with a shout.

"Elisabet! Elisabet!"

Elisabet threw a look in her husband's direction as she reached for the baby, now wailing. "Hyrum, what in the world? Have you no manners? And the baby! You've startled the baby with all your shouting." She patted her son, handing him the block in hopes of soothing him, and turned dark eyes toward her husband. "I spend all day working, trying to take care of the house and the baby, and you undo everything the moment you set foot in the door."

Hyrum tried to look contrite without success as a broad smile replaced any semblance of remorse. "But Elisabet," he said with urgency and much less volume, "I've been promoted to delivery driver! I will now drive the team from the lumberyard to the customer." He stood taller, more erect, pushing his chest out as he declared with pride. "This is a massive responsibility for such a young man, but I have proven my worth to the company."

Elisabet, whose eyes were no longer murky, but clear and bright, squealed, "Oh, Hyrum! I'm so proud of you!" At Jakob's renewed squall, they both laughed.

As with most newly married couples, notably those whose roots in America were so tenuous, such news was most welcome. A promotion meant more security and more money. Their dream of having a large family and buying a little house in town moved closer to reality.

With the excitement of a child on Christmas morning, Hyrum declared an evening of celebration. The news quickly spread throughout the neighborhood, and soon, family and friends made their way to the Mueller's tiny home. The woman tittered about houses and babies. The men slapped Hyrum's back and passed around the whiskey. It was long after midnight when a slightly inebriated Hyrum fell into bed.

The arrival of morning is early and harsh to nighttime revelers, but Hyrum was excited to prove his mettle and walked to work as quickly as the pain thudding behind his eyes would let him. After an uneventful loading, Hyrum took the reins and started out across town. The clomping hooves marched in perfect rhythm with his head, but he smiled despite the pain. The celebration had been grand. His family was so proud of his accomplishments. He, a young man from Germany with broken English, was making his way in America.

Hyrum, despite the aftermath of too much celebration, jauntily removed his hat in a wave whenever he encountered someone going about their morning routine. He wanted everyone in town to know of his good fortune.

He carried a load of lumber to build a new barn for the Buffenmouier place at the edge of town. He chose a circuitous route leading through the neighborhood of his youth, despite it being a bit out of the way.

His own mother stood in the yard hanging out the wash as Hyrum passed. "Hello, mother!" he bellowed jovially, trying to ignore the pain the noise caused in his head. She looked up, smiling broadly, so proud that her son, her Hyrum, was a driver at only 22-years-old. She scurried to the front yard to watch him drive down the street, and, of course, to meet the approving nods of the neighbors.

Down 10th Avenue, across to Lafayette and then onto 11th he went, finally taking a left turn onto Liberty Avenue that would take them out of town and to their intended destination. All was going well until the wagon wheels, weighted down with heavy timbers, jammed against the train tracks. Hyrum was thankful to learn he was beyond the sight of those he had been trying to impress.

He ordered the workers riding on top to push while Hyrum urged his horse forward, but the wagon remained cemented in place. Hyrum then tried the reverse, having the men push the wagon back off the track as he hitched up the horse and pulled from the rear. Although the wagon bounced and swayed with their efforts and the wheels groaned, working their way up the incline, each time they stopped pushing, the wagon settled back against the tracks.

Hyrum sent the men back to the lumberyard to find more help. With a bit more muscle, they would be able to move the load backward off the track to take the main road out of town. As he waited with the load, his shoulders sagged under the realization that his vanity was the real problem. If he had taken the fastest route out of town, he wouldn't have failed to transport his first load to the customer. "From this day forward, I will keep my pride in check," he muttered. Then he jumped down from the wagon and began removing some of the lumber, hoping the reduced weight would move the wagon on its way before his boss had to become involved.

Then the train whistled, long and piercing, in the distance. Moving more swiftly than before, and much faster than he thought possible given his celebratory condition, he began throwing lumber off the wagon, urging the horses to move forward.

Nothing. He continued to throw and urge, the train chugging closer each passing second.

Hyrum should have abandoned the wagon, but he didn't want to lose his job. He stayed until the last possible second before jumping out of the way, but it was too late. The impact sent Hyrum flying hundreds of feet down the track to land in a heap of wood, metal, and horse flesh. The last thing he remembered before waking in the hospital was the screeching of metal on metal and a loud, piercing scream. He didn't realize the latter came from his own lips.

The cast began at his neck and covered his body down to his toes. According to the doctor, he broke every bone in his body and was lucky to be alive. Though he doubted he broke every bone, he felt confident he'd managed to break most of them. The recuperation would be long and arduous. According to the medical staff, he was unlikely to walk again.

Elisabet came every day to visit him, always with a smile on her lips and an eagerness in her voice. "The doctors are wrong, Hyrum. I know they are. Think positively. You will walk again. For me. And for Jakob." Her upbeat optimism pained him more than his injuries. Had he kept his pride in check, had he simply done the job instead of showing off, he would be at work, not lying in a hospital bed, unable to move – unable to see his sweet baby boy. The hospital had very strict rules against visitations by minors.

Several days after the accident, Elisabet's smile, the one she planted on her face each time she crossed the hospital room's threshold, drained off her lips at the sight of a roomful of solemn-faced doctors and nurses. She looked from one to another and then at Hyrum, who refused to look her in the eyes.

A tall doctor with graying hair stepped forward, took her by the arm, and propelled her to the green wooden chair brought in exclusively for her visits. "Mrs. Mueller," the doctor began. Elisabet strained to hear the doctor's words above the whooshing of waves against the shore that began in her ears. "Your husband," he lifted his shoulder in Hyrum's direction, "has developed complications from his injuries." Elisabet sucked in sharply and then slowly released the air from her lungs, urging her heart to beat in a steady rhythm. They were a team. They would handle these complications together.

Except merciless words assailed her certitude, leaving no space for teamwork. "Lockjaw...no cure...will not live."

When the room emptied of the unwanted messengers, Elisabet rested her face on her husband's, letting the grief mingle on their cheeks. Then, without speaking, she walked from the room. Less than an hour later, despite the rules, Elisabet sneaked their son into his father's room to say goodbye.

Jakob, days shy of his first birthday, didn't grasp the solemnity of the event. He babbled in his mother's arms and reached for his father who could do nothing more than give him a longing look as tears coursed down his cheeks. Two days later, Hyrum was dead.

Jakob turned seven the year the tetanus shot came into existence, a medical breakthrough that came too late for his father. Elisabet, whose optimism went to the grave with her husband's body, perceived the miracle cure as a cruel joke taunting her with what might have been.

Elisabet had no time to grieve. She had a son to raise, and doing so as an immigrant single mother would not be an easy endeavor. Her first venture was as a laundress, but she soon realized her kitchen concoctions, chiefly her baked-goods and candy, were in high demand among her locals.

Within a few short months of Hyrum's death, Elisabet delivered her treats throughout the German community.

Despite working from before the sun came up until long after it went down, Elisabet found it difficult to make enough money to support herself and her son. Though never without food, Jakob was often hungry – a condition that plagued him throughout his childhood.

By the time he started school, Jakob was taller than the other boys his age and rail thin. Elisabet complained he had a hollow leg he used to store food for future use.

Not understanding his mother's sarcasm, he would examine his leg, hoping to find that extra food.

When Jakob turned 12, the nation plunged into The Great Depression. At first, this national economic challenge did little to change their lives. As Elisabet quipped, "Poor is poor. It is hard to get much poorer than we already are." For her small family, losses in stock markets and savings accounts meant nothing. She would continue to do what she'd always done – work. And the stock market would have to figure its own self out.

Except the financial problems of the country did not work themselves out, leading more and more of her customers to cut back on the extras, including such indulgences as chocolates and truffles. When the Depression no longer lived on Wall Street but on her street, her wares became expendable, making the job of feeding Jakob significantly more difficult.

Now, in addition to baking, she took in ironing, mending, and moved Jakob into her room to offer his tiny space to a boarder. Each night, she pleaded with God. "Dear Lord, please, please help me find a way to feed my son. I don't understand what you want from me. I don't understand why I'm being punished, or why you are punishing Jakob, a boy who isn't old enough to have done anything wrong. Please, please help me." But nothing came of her prayers. Elisabet figured He was overrun with the prayers of hungry, hopeless people, and tried not to hold His lack of concern against Him.

However, she couldn't sit back and let Jakob starve, which led her to make a decision that squeezed her heart and made the breath catch in her throat. If Elisabet couldn't keep her son fed, she determined she would have to find someone who could. She wasn't going to let the only part of Hyrum she had left die of starvation.

Weeks before he turned 14, Jakob packed his few belongings and headed to the Hersch farm amidst a great many tears from his mother. She worked out a deal with Mr. Hersch, a trade of sorts. Jakob would become a farmhand. His pay was room and board. "It's the right thing," she told herself over and over as he turned left and disappeared down the block.

Jakob did not have the same misgivings. He obediently said, "I'll miss you, Mutter," when she would start crying over his imminent departure. Though this was true, he longed for the adventure to begin. He wanted to see more and do more than go to school and help his mother deliver marzipan.

On the day of his departure, Jakob hugged his mother gently, murmuring in her hair, "It's okay, Mutter. I will be fine. Better than fine. The farm is barely eight miles away. I will come home every Sunday to visit. We will spend the day together, and I will have so much to tell you." Jakob followed through on his promise. Every Sunday, regardless of the weather, he walked the eight miles to visit his mother and regaled her with stories of the farm, before heading back to start the process over again. He never missed a Sunday visit.

Though farming was demanding work, Jakob flourished. He loved having a man in his life to teach him the things his father never had the chance to teach. Tools, those beyond kitchen utensils, and animals, those beyond the strays that wandered the streets of the city, made their way into his daily life. While he learned of seeds and planting, he also learned what it meant to be a man and do a man's work.

Four long years later, with no end of the Depression in sight, Jakob decided to find work in the city. He believed the time had come for him to be the head of the household, relieving his mother of the responsibility of caring for them both. He couldn't do that working for room and board on a farm eight miles from town.

His mother put up a feeble protest. However, the truth was simple – she missed her son. It would be lovely to have him home again.

Chapter 4

BONNIE: 1918-1935

If ever a child was born with the proverbial silver spoon in her mouth, it was Bonnie. Her father was an engineer by trade, spending his early years designing products every American needed, or at least wanted. When companies formed to create new and exciting versions of the automobile, Carl found his niche in the world.

Life for Carl's family was easy and gentile. They resided in a mansion in Detroit, Michigan near the water where they moored their 65-foot yacht. Elaine, his wife, accepted invitations to tea, and his children attended the finest schools. Bonnie reached adolescence before discovering not all her friends had a button strategically placed on the dining room floor by their seats to bring the butler hustling.

As with most girls her age and in her station, she was blissfully unaware of the poor and unfortunate. She always had plenty of food on the table, parents who loved her and lavished her with everything money could buy, and good friends with which to share secrets.

When not in school, Bonnie learned how to be a lady, which was something she did well with little instruction. She always piled her blonde hair high on her head and topped it with the most fashionable hat. She adored her mink stole and the jewelry her father gifted to her despite her mother's objections. "You are going to spoil her beyond reason, Carl."

But he responded, and Bonnie agreed, "Pearls and diamonds are exactly what little Bonnie needs."

Bonnie's gift for design, one she inherited from her father, became evident when she was quite young. However, engineering was not something a woman could ever hope to achieve, even if society allowed a woman of her station to work outside the home. Her mother cautiously channeled Bonnie's gift toward home design, a skill without the unseemly connotations of engineer or inventor.

With an expertise belying her years, ten-year-old Bonnie turned her bedroom into a French provincial heaven with marble topped surfaces, claw-footed tables, and dashes of pink and gray amid the white woods and marble. Her favorite piece was a crystal chandelier hanging in the center of the room that danced colors of the rainbow across the ceiling and onto the floor.

As soon as she completed her room, Bonnie turned her attention to other rooms in the house. "Daddy, may I design your study?" Carl, though he adored his daughter, could not imagine his manly study with its dark wood, shelves of books, and hunting paraphernalia discarded in favor of something pink, soft, and floral. He quickly suggested the parlor, a room he rarely frequented, and one that could handle his child's penchant for femininity. Her mother, however, did not show the same enthusiasm. "Bonnie, sweetheart. Your room is lovely. Divine, really. Perfect for a child your age. But I can't imagine me sitting among pink ruffles while having tea with the ladies. It wouldn't be dignified." Bonnie took the criticism framed in a compliment to heart.

Over the following months, Bonnie carefully noted what she loved, and what she didn't, about homes throughout Detroit as she went visiting with her mother. She filled a notebook with descriptions of rooms, color combinations, textures, and materials. She looked at the difference between what men wanted in a study versus what women wanted in a parlor. Then, when she felt confident about what her mother meant by dignified, she sketched out her vision of the parlor.

As her mother looked over the sketches, she said, "It's feminine, mother. Very soft and light. But it's also functional. See, you can easily arrange everything to handle an intimate group of women or host something much larger. What do you think?"

"I think I underestimated you, Bonnie. Let's see what you can do." By the time she completed the parlor, everyone agreed the dining room should be the next to receive a makeover. And so, life would have gone on, from one room to the next, had The Great Depression not come calling.

Prior to any hint of economic collapse, Carl sold his stocks in Cadillac, taking a new position as Vice President of Durant. His long-range goal was to own his own car company, and this was a stepping-stone in the right direction. The initial economic downturn, though not something he worried about immediately, soon changed the automobile market. These luxury items were so new that not having one wasn't too much of an inconvenience. Many of the smaller automobile companies began to fold, but Durant continued to hang on with some major cutbacks, prompting Carl to make a few of his own.

When they went from several butlers and maids to a much smaller staff, Bonnie didn't notice. One afternoon, she babbled on about decorating the dining room. "I have been looking at furniture, mother. This dining room table is so dark. Have you seen the furniture at the McMurray's home? The color is so much lighter than ours. Can you imagine how much larger this room will look if we remove all this dark mahogany?" She gestured around the room, stopping when she reached the far wall. "I want to add a bold striped wallpaper on the wall behind the buffet table, and, of course, this china needs to go. There are so many new patterns available."

Carl and Elaine passed knowing glances. This was not the time for spending money. However, Bonnie, hardly more than a child, didn't detect the furrowed brows on her parents' faces.

Two weeks later, the Stock Market crashed, taking all Carl's money, as well as his dreams, with it. Before long, when Bonnie pushed the button on the floor in the dining room, no one answered the call. Then, boarders began living in the empty rooms to bring in more money. Eventually, Carl, whose Vice Presidency at Durant disappeared when the company folded, found a job at the

Hoover Company in Canton, Ohio. They packed up some of their most important belongings and moved into a small, inconspicuous house several hundred miles away.

No longer wealthy, Carl was unable to lavish his daughter with gifts and jewelry, which worked out well, because Bonnie had no time to work on being a lady. Instead, she learned to mend and wash clothes, two chores she never performed prior to their great fall. Four years after the crash, Bonnie, now 17, went to secretarial school before she began working at Timken Roller Bearing.

While enrolled in school, Bonnie's father took another position in Connecticut, but Bonnie elected to stay in Canton with her newfound friend, June. They worked together and roomed together in a small flat above a five and dime. Although she was happy, she longed for the days when she could design rather than type and yearned for an escape from the poverty that defined her life.

Chapter 5

WILLIAM: November 2016

William breathed "Amen" and opened his eyes. Tears sat on the rim of his eyelids, waiting for a reason to drop. He swiped them with the back of his hand before they escaped and ran down his cheek. The older he got, the more he cried. He supposed these were the tears he didn't shed as a child trying to be the soldier his daddy wanted him to be.

He remembered clearly the days leading up to his father leaving for the war. His mother insisted he was too young to remember. However, despite being a young child, it had been quite traumatic.

William retained no memory of Pearl Harbor. He was not quite two years old when it happened. To William, those years after Pearl Harbor and before his father left were simply spent in the world of childhood, unbothered by adult concerns. But he did fully remember the train as it pulled away from the station, leaving him with nothing but memories for two long years.

William shook his head to clear his thoughts. The past did not matter now. He needed to set about the task at hand.

He hauled the large wreath over to the gravestone. The view here was lovely, with dozens of shades of green as far as the eye could see. William chose the spot specifically because of how much his father loved natural beauty. William did not want his father to be buried somewhere that faded and died away at the end of every year. Jakob witnessed enough death in his lifetime. There was no need to experience more of it once his life here ended.

Next, he hauled out the metal stand he stashed in the pickup's bed the night before. It was a skimpy three-legged thing with appendages barely thicker than a wire coat hanger, causing him to grab some twine and the utility knife out of the toolbox he always carried.

Like his grandfather Carl before him, William had been blessed with the creative gene. His father would often say, "William, you can make something out of nothing." Whether William puffed himself out in pride or bristled with indignation depended on the tone of voice. Creativity led to either compliments or derision.

William let out a long, slow breath. It had been like that once his father returned home from the war. He remembered being ever so careful to always say and do the right thing. Something as simple as knocking over his tower of blocks might end in a spanking. Or not. The uncertainty had been the most challenging.

William thought back to the father he remembered before the war. He was brave and strong. He was gentle and kind. And although that man occasionally materialized, in reality, the prewar Jacob never fully returned from the war. Upon arriving home, Jacob's carefree laughter was rationed like wartime coffee, and his spontaneous hugs were as rare as sugar. Everything in William's world changed once again in response to the new man he called Vati.

After years of tiptoeing around in hopes of encountering the happy, easy-going memory of a man, only to find, more often than not, the hard unyielding one, William's resentment burgeoned. He found himself throwing ugly accusations like hand grenades. "You don't love me. You've never loved me. I can't wait to leave here and never come back."

The words would barely leave his lips before his stomach clamped tight and his skin grew clammy with shame. After all his father did for him, for his mother, and for their country...He vowed to try harder, to be the man his father needed him to be, just as he had once been the brave soldier as his father left for war. But no matter what he did, it was never enough.

Take school, for instance. William had been a poor student, struggling with even the basics of reading and math. However, he soon learned that if given the chance to use his hands or use what he learned in the real world, he excelled. So, in high school, driven by an infatuation with the invention of the diesel electric train a few years earlier, William enrolled in a mechanical drafting class. Despite making an A and receiving an honorable mention in a regional competition for a modification to a hoverboard, his father dismissed the idea of pursuing his passion.

Spitting out the word creativity, his father said, "Why don't you use this creativity of yours and do something worthwhile? Hoverboards, of all things. You lack focus, William. You're always dreaming. Why don't you put what you've learned to good use and draft house plans? I spent months after the war helping soldiers learn that skill. Floor plans are useful. Hoverboards?" He walked away, shaking his head.

So, William spent his senior year focusing on the kind of drafting that would make his father proud, joining his business immediately after graduation. But William wasn't given the opportunity to draft. Instead, his father gave him grunt work. "Haul those bricks to the other side of the house" and "Go to the truck and fetch the ladder" were standard commands. If it weren't for his new love interest, Marie, he would have struck out on his own, but she was enough to keep him grounded.

Marie was tall and beautiful, his opposite in almost every way. Where he was dark, with brown hair and eyes and skin that tanned to a deep bronze, she was blonde, blue-eyed, and had a milky white complexion. He was a city boy. She lived her whole life on a farm. He was a dreamer. She was no-nonsense. William couldn't imagine life without her.

However, after a particularly grueling day with his father, one that left him panting from exertion and exhausted from the mental strain of controlling his temper, he decided to join the Air Force. He wanted to serve his country as his father had, but more importantly, he needed to escape from him. Maybe being a Veteran would span the chasm that existed between the two men.

Immediately after boot camp, Marie joined him in Biloxi, Mississippi, as his bride. Barely a year later, his daughter arrived, and three years later, a son. William was finally his own man.

He left military life before the Vietnam War heated up in earnest and settled his family back in Canton, hoping to parlay his communications knowledge into a steady job. A little-known company, IBM, offered him a position on the ground floor. He couldn't have been happier.

William gathered his parents, two sisters, Marie, and his children for a surprise celebration. Marie, the only one who knew the secret, beamed at William, so proud of the man she married. He pulled the bottle of wine out of the ice with a flourish and poured everyone a glass. His sisters, Lynn and Ann, still too young to drink, filled their glasses with ginger ale.

William turned to his guests and said, "You are now looking at the newest member of the IBM team. I will begin training in four weeks!" Then he raised his glass in the air and clinked it with his wife's and sister's. As he turned toward his father to continue the celebratory toast, he noted his father's glass remained clutched tightly to his mid-section, his face screwed up in confusion.

"What? IBM? I thought you came home to work with me. I changed the name of the company to Miller & Son Construction. It was my surprise to you." He turned to William's mother saying, "I don't know what we are going to do. I can't manage the business on my own."

Initially, William seethed, angry thoughts swirling through his head. He wanted to excel on his own, using the skills he learned in the Air Force. There was no way he was going to sling a hammer the rest of his life as the 'and Son' portion of his father's business.

However, once the initial rage wore off, he began to relent. Despite the uneasiness existing between them, William loved and respected his father and continually hoped for a better relationship. Growing up hadn't done it – nor had joining the military. Perhaps this would be the answer. In the end, William said no to IBM and began working with his father, trying not to bristle whenever he confronted 'and Son' on the side of the truck.

William shook his head as if to erase his thoughts. No, rather than linger on the what-ifs of times past, William determined to focus on the positive aspects of working with his father. He gained the ability to fix whatever was broken and create solutions to life's problems. Today, the wind was the problem, but he wasn't going to let something as trivial as Mother Nature keep him from honoring his father.

Chapter 6

JAKOB: Fall 1938

Jakob Mueller was born in the little town of New Berlin to parents of entirely German descent. Though both sides of his family moved to America to find a better life, they embraced their German heritage.

His name was the perfect example. He was Jakob, spelled the Germanic way, named after his father who was named after another ancestor several generations back. His middle name, Wendel, was after his grandfather who brought his father's side of the family to this country – Mattias Wendel Mueller in 1898. The German surname of Mueller indicated the profession of his ancestors before coming to the states. Somewhere in the past, his family milled grains into flour, soon being distinguished as muellers, or millers. His name was a walking representation of his Germanic heritage.

Then there was the food. His mother was a fabulous cook whenever the financial conditions allowed for the proper ingredients. On those good nights, the house had the fragrance of sausages, onions, and peppers, or pork with sour kraut or pickled fish with homemade bread.

However, Elisabet's desserts made her famous. Her pflaumenkudhen was known throughout the county. She often used her leftover shortcrust dough, spreading it evenly onto a baking sheet and covering it with plums. Jakob was always happy to come home from school on days with extra dough. However, Jakob also loved bratapfel, a simple dish of baked apples. These were abundant throughout the fall and winter months, as Elisabet had access to an orchard not far from their home.

Of course, no confections would be complete without marzipan. Her stollen, bethmännchen, and muskazine recipes were those from the homeland, generational gifts that stood between her and hunger.

Christmas traditions came to the New World, as well. Elisabet used a gingerbread recipe she claimed came from the original gingerbread trade guild back in the 1600s. "There is nothing more German in all New Berlin than this recipe for gingerbread," she would proclaim. In the evenings, when she finished her work, Elisabet would sit with Jakob in front of their old piano and hammer out some Christmas carols. Neither were great singers, but both loved the music and delighted in singing together.

By the time Jakob turned three, he sang Silent Night in both German and English, as well as O Tannenbaum. Although Jakob learned little of the German language despite the fluency of his mother, he memorized many carols in the German language, as was the tradition of the entire community.

Finally, on Christmas Eve, Elisabet would take Jakob out to the edge of the town to find the perfect tree. Jakob remembered these excursions. His mother lugged the hand saw from tree to tree until he found the one he wanted to take home. Then, she would spread a small shawl on the ground, lower herself down, and begin to cut at the trunk with steady strokes. Eventually, Jakob was old enough to help, and finally old enough that his tiny mother didn't have to do the work at all.

Jakob nearly danced with anticipation as they hauled the tree home on the sled used to haul wood for their stove in the winter. Once they maneuvered the tree inside, Jakob and his mother would decorate it with candy, apples, nuts, cookies, tinsel, and a few candles to make it sparkle and shine. To a child, the idea of bringing in a tree from the woods and decorating it with treats was pure magic.

Although Elisabet and Jakob rarely attended church, they were Lutherans, following the break from the Catholic Church established by Martin Luther. Often, Christmas Eve would find them at church singing hymns and lighting candles as they listened to the Christmas story of Christ's birth.

Despite this strong German heritage, Elisabet considered herself entirely American, with a fine American son. Once, during a parade honoring Civil War Veterans, Elisabet, all of five foot two and weighing less than 100 pounds, knocked a hat off a full-grown man when he didn't remove it as the US flag went by.

It was for this reason, she was so disturbed when

New Berlin changed its name to North Canton after the First World War. Anti-German sentiment was high, so the trend was to change Germanic sounding names. Hospitals, schools, streets, and, yes, the town of New Berlin. On January 30th, 1918, without changing their address or their way of life, Elisabet and Hyrum, along with their baby boy, became residents of North Canton.

Eventually, as Jakob grew and anti-German sentiment reached a fever pitch when Hitler and the Nazi Party began their cruel reign, he did more to disguise his heritage. Despite his mother's protests, he changed his name to Jacob Miller. He wanted no one to suspect him of Nazi harboring, Nazi views, or assuming he associated with Nazi sympathizers.

Unlike his mother, who assumed living in the United States was all she needed to prove her allegiance, Jacob was more politically astute. He understood how the Alien Enemy Act caused problems for German Americans, giving the government the ability to arrest or deport those not born in the United States, as well as imprisoning anyone who disagreed with the government.

"But, Jakob," his mother would say in her thick accent, "You were born right here in America. No one is more American than you." Except there were many people more American. People who didn't say *vindow* or *Vashington, DC*. People who had never eaten wienerschnitzel. People who, in no way, had a connection to Adolf Hitler. For those Americans, Jacob, with or without the k, was German to his very core.

Shortly after Americanizing his name, he started working at a local grocery store beyond the borders of his highly Germanic neighborhood, into the broader community with distant German ancestors, but no connection to their home country. During the day, he was an American, but each night he returned home to the guttural intonations of his neighbors.

Then, on one fateful day, he met Bonnie, a girl he loved from the moment he first set her groceries on her kitchen table. He wanted her to feel the same way but instinctively knew the truth. Why would she? He was a lowly grocery delivery boy with a German background in a world that found him suspect.

Chapter 7

BONNIE: Fall 1938

Despite the many years between losing everything and now, Bonnie did not adjust well to her new life. She hated being poor. She hated worrying about the cost of her silk stockings or the fear of creating a run. She hated the mundane work at Timken. She hated having to do all the chores herself.

So, though it cost more, she indulged in one service that made her feel wealthy – she had her groceries delivered rather than go to the market with the "common folk." Her roommate, June, was amazed Bonnie would rather skimp on a few groceries and have them delivered than make the trek to the store herself. "Bonnie, grocery shopping is no more unsophisticated than cleaning the apartment or humping it to work each morning." Demonstrating with a swish of her hips, she said, "Sashay through the aisles, choose the foods you want to eat, pay the friendly cashier, and bring it home. Why waste your paycheck paying some boy to deliver your food?" Having never lived in a mansion, she couldn't understand what the fuss was about.

For Bonnie, who appreciated intimately what she was missing, the luxury of delivery was worth every cent. On a Saturday afternoon in September, someone trudged up the stairs to the flat. Despite knowing how steep the stairs were and that anyone waiting at the door would be precariously balancing on the top step, she waited for the knock. No lady, and she was a lady, would open the door to a delivery person before they asked to enter.

Within moments, a heavy hand rapped on the door, and Bonnie took her time answering. When she did, a very tall boy with dark hair smiled broadly. He said, "Hi! I'm Jacob from Flory's Grocery. May I set this box on the table?"

Bonnie couldn't help but notice the enamored look on the boy's face. She thought of him as a boy, but as she studied him, she realized he must be nearing 20. She was accustomed to men's stares. With her natural beauty coupled with her early training on how to dress, stand, and speak properly, she stood out – predominately to boys, or men, who were not familiar with such things.

She looked him over, frankly, determining he could be quite the looker, if only... But the 'if onlys' – his too short pants, his too thin shirt, his unkempt hair – were enough to spoil the effect. Plus, no one had ever taught him not to stare.

She thanked him abruptly, handed him a nickel for his troubles, and motioned towards the door. Jacob mumbled a quick thank you, and with a backward glance over his shoulder, disappeared from the kitchen and back through the door and down the stairs that led to the street below. When he hit the pavement outside, a whistled tune she didn't recognize floated from below.

When June came home a few hours later, Bonnie made no mention of the grocery delivery or the boy who brought them. He had completely faded from her memory, as did most of the people who served her in some capacity. It wasn't that she was mean or cruel. She fondly recalled past butlers and maids in Detroit. However, she had been taught that classes didn't mix, so letting them into and out of her life easily was the only way to make the idea work.

The following Saturday was bitterly cold despite being only October. "No doubt, there will be snow before the end of the month," she thought as she pulled the crimson scarf closer around her face. It was at times like these her newfound status stung. Instead of being at home, contemplating which material to buy for a new dress and responding to an invitation for a weekend gala, was battling against the wind and cold after taking her once monthly weekend shift. By the time she arrived home, the tip of her nose was numb. Once inside, she did not plan to set foot outdoors again until Monday morning.

As she took off her scarf and matching hat, she shook her head at June's things stuffed carelessly into the closet. Blue wool coat, a cast-off men's red and black plaid scarf, and a pair of pink mittens. Bonnie could not understand why her friend was willing to be seen in public in such inappropriate attire. Bonnie would never leave the house wearing mismatched outerwear, especially without a hat, and always purchased stylish clothes that fit her body like a glove.

Despite the Depression's cruel tyranny, Bonnie believed she would eventually regain her status. She saw no need to pretend she was something other than who she was simply because the financial market took a swift downturn. Thankfully, her designing experience came in quite handy as she walked the fine line between poverty and being a lady. "I'd rather have one sophisticated skirt than a closet full that make me look like I'm wearing a flour sack," she would say when June would say something about the cost of her clothes. Although she owned few pieces of clothing, each was timeless and interchangeable. Bonnie was, if nothing else, quite fashionable despite her impoverished state.

Before she fully closed the closet, a faint step sounded in the stairwell. Then, more loudly, a distinct rap of knuckles on the thick, wooden door. Quickly patting her hair into place, she tried to appear as if she had been lounging at home all afternoon.

It was the delivery boy from Flory's. What was his name? John? James? Jacob. Yes, it was Jacob. She gestured once again to the table, and he loped into the kitchen with the box. This time, however, he was a bit more talkative, apparently not wishing to leave. She never considered he was merely cold and hoping to warm up before departing again.

His flirtations, though endearing, were terribly misguided. Certainly, he understood she was not his type. She had no intention of being the girlfriend of a grocery delivery boy. She was merely waiting out this infernal depression to begin living life as it was supposed to be – Bonnie on the arm of a handsome, wealthy man – Bonnie wearing diamonds and furs – Bonnie laughing gaily at a soiree celebrating her engagement.

She contemplated his boldness. Few men she met possessed the nerve to flirt with her so openly. Most would stare and then look away, not daring to approach her. She found this aspect of him to be a bit intriguing, but after a few minutes of banter, handed him a nickel for his troubles and turned away, with a 'you are dismissed' wave at the door.

This time, after Jacob lumbered down the stairs, Bonnie imagined a whistled tune that stayed in her head for the next several days.

Chapter 8

JACOB: Winter 1938-1939

Jacob's breath caught in his throat, and the blood pulsated near his Adam's apple. He blinked rapidly before fixing his gaze on the slender girl with shimmering hair as she beckoned him to set the groceries on the table. Pulling his mouth closed, he forced his eyes to follow the delicate hand gesturing to a compact wooden dinette with two mismatched chairs.

He blanched as his left foot knocked carelessly into the door frame, overly conscious now of his awkward frame and oafish disposition. The ten-foot trek to the kitchen was endless as he willed his blundering feet to move forward and his clumsy arms to do their job as he pled silently, "Do not trip. Do not spill the groceries on the floor. Do not make a fool of yourself." Though he recognized a pretty girl when he saw one, never before had he been in the presence of one who he simultaneously wanted to cling to and escape from.

His work buddies would mock him mercilessly if they realized he was 20 years old and had never held a girl's hand, let alone kissed one. His mother sheltered him as a young boy, and the farm with its laborers and animals had not lent itself to much in the ways of romance. The thought made him blush, causing him to fumble the cabbage, which rolled precariously to the edge, threatening to dive unceremoniously to the floor below. "Oh, I'm sorry," he grunted as he grabbed at the escapee.

Before he found the courage to do anything more than stare, she dismissed him without a backward glance. Jacob recognized he should feel rejected, yet he couldn't help but whistle a tune as he headed down the street. Without any doubt, this girl, this woman, was going to be his wife someday.

She hadn't introduced herself, but the delivery slip indicated her name – Ms. Phillips. He wondered how he missed her existence during his first months at Flory's. Was she new to the area? Was she a new customer who recently started using the grocer? Had the other delivery boys been keeping Ms. Phillips all to themselves? Whatever the case, he now knew of her existence and was going to be sure to become part of the rotation.

Over the next several weeks, Jacob would be elsewhere when her call came in, realizing, too late, that her box was being prepared by another delivery boy. Once the others realized his interest, they made sure to grab the delivery quickly, purely to poke some fun at him.

Undaunted, Jacob began trading chores with the

others to land Ms. Phillip's deliveries. He was willing to throw out the rotten fruit, sweep the storage room filled with mice, and take deliveries in the most unbearable weather. Before long, he was going to her door each time she called in an order.

On his fourth visit, he boldly asked her name. She stared at him, shock opening her eyes wide. For once, he was not the one left open-mouthed and stammering. "B...B...Bonnie." Composing herself quickly, she finished in a clipped voice, "My name is Bonnie Phillips." He thought of the song, "My Bonnie lies over the ocean, my Bonnie lies over the sea, My Bonnie lies over the ocean. Oh, bring back my Bonnie to me." He began whistling that tune on the way to her house, wondering if she would recognize the tune.

As Jacob studied her food orders carefully, making sure there were no errors in her delivery, he noted her fondness for oranges. Each week, she paid for two or three over something more substantial like oatmeal. That's when he devised a plan. Bonnie ordered her groceries for delivery every Saturday afternoon. On Friday, he offered to go through the bins of fruit and throw out anything rotting. His boss loved his gumption, and Jacob loved his Bonnie. He made sure to save any oranges that were too tainted for the store shelf but were still good enough to eat. Then, when he delivered her food, he would present her with the extra oranges.

This exchange of extra fruit and quick dismissals went on for weeks, but Jacob began to perceive a trend. Each week, Bonnie spoke to him a bit longer before sending him on his way, and each week, her smile was a bit broader.

Jacob was no fool. Bonnie obviously had breeding and class beyond his own. Her attentions would surely be toward a man who provided her with the luxuries of life, something he was unable to do. Nonetheless, he couldn't help loving her and prayed mightily that she would find a way to love him, too.

Winter turned to spring, with Jacob bringing his sacrifice of oranges to Bonnie's door each Saturday. The time came to make his move. He could continue to worship her from afar, grabbing measly minutes with her once a week, or he could be bold and ask her on a date.

"This is what men do," he said to himself as he freshened up after work on Friday. He couldn't ask her out while working, or he'd risk losing his job. So, he buoyed himself up throughout the day, getting up the nerve to walk boldly to her front door.

He was careful not to let his mother know of his plans. She continually fretted about him leaving her, and there was no need to cause any contention at this point in the process. Bonnie could just as easily slam the door in his face as say yes. Why create a stir with his mother for a rejection? So, he told her a harmless lie about getting an extra shift at the store. Then he sneaked out the door, yelling "Goodbye, Mother" once he reached the yard, so she wouldn't recognize he was dressed in his best white shirt, his hair had been combed and plastered down with a dab of Brylcreem he scrounged from one of the boys at work, and his face was freshly shaven leaving behind the scent of her homemade soap.

Jacob strode purposefully along the edge of town, picking an assortment of yellow spring flowers to present as tonight's offering. As he walked the last half mile to her flat, he ruefully acknowledged that the flowers, already beginning to wilt, were not likely to make if he didn't quit taking out his nerves on their delicate stems.

He rehearsed his arrival, each time with disastrous results. She laughed in his face. She insisted he never deliver groceries to her again. She called his boss and had him fired. With each imagined outcome, his steps slowed and his grip on the flowers tightened until he was standing feet from the five and dime store that housed her flat.

"This is my destiny," he whispered to himself. "How will I ever convince Bonnie to be my bride if I don't have the courage to ask her on a date?" Then, nerves, half-broken flowers, and all, Jacob took the steps two at a time, breathlessly knocking on the door. Bonnie's lilting voice in conversation with her roommate ceased as footsteps advanced toward the door.

Her roommate's "Who is it?" sounded cautious. They had not expected company and wouldn't open the door without knowing who stood on the other side.

Jacob cleared his throat, stating, "It is Jacob Miller. I've come to talk to Bonnie," in a voice he hoped didn't reveal his inner turmoil.

His proclamation was met with silence. He couldn't see the frantic look on Bonnie's face through the door or read her the thoughts bouncing around in her head. "I'm not dressed for visitors. My hair is a mess. Doesn't this stupid, stupid boy know anything about calling on a lady?" He didn't know that Bonnie waved her hands, trying to get her roommate to tell Jacob she wasn't home. He was not privy to the look of utter horror when these instructions were misinterpreted.

Finally, when he assumed she had simply stopped communicating with him and would not open the door, the voice said, "Please wait just a moment. She'll be there shortly."

Inside, Bonnie cast June a glowering look and ran to the bedroom where she jerked on a beautiful light pink skirt and a gray jacket with a matching gray and pink hat. Her stockings were still damp, but she slipped them on anyway, along with a pair of gray pumps. She pinched her cheeks for a bit of blush and ran her lipstick across her lips, blotting them on a bit of tissue. There. That would have to do.

When Bonnie finally opened the door, Jacob's ability to appear calm and in charge dissolved in a puddle on the floor. Bonnie looked stunning, and he stood on the threshold, mouth gaping open, the flowers and his manners all but forgotten.

Finally, tiring of waiting for him to state his business, she said, with a trace of humor in her voice, "Good evening, Jacob. Are those for me?" as she pointed to the damaged flowers in his hand.

"Uh...yes...yes, they are...here." He thrust them unceremoniously at her, realizing he was making a mess of the whole thing. He took a deep breath and tried again. "You look beautiful." Then, without knowing where the words came from, he said, "You look too beautiful to stay at home tonight. Would you like to join me at the movies?"

He had no idea when he learned to turn a compliment into a proposition but looked at Bonnie to determine if it worked.

She hesitated briefly. He sensed what she was thinking. Should she go out with a lowly delivery boy? But he couldn't know that no one had asked her out in months or that she couldn't remember the last time she had gone out on a Friday evening for fun.

Finally, she uttered the words he hadn't dared to consider. "Yes, Jacob, that would be lovely." She handed the sad flowers to June with instructions to put them in water, and the two headed out, Jacob barely breathing, fearing he'd wake from the dream.

The movie playing was *Let Freedom Ring* with Nelson Eddy and Virginia Bruce, but the movie didn't matter. Had the movie stopped midway, showing nothing but a white screen, it wouldn't have registered. His attention was fully trained on the most beautiful girl in North Canton. However, Jacob loved music, so when the actors began singing, "My Country Tis of Thee," he hummed along.

After the show, he took Bonnie to the drugstore for a soda, then walked her home. He kept wanting to put his arm around her or hold her hand, but he couldn't bring himself to do it. At her door, he thanked her for a wonderful evening and left without even a peck on her cheek. As he floated home, he relived every word, every accidental touch. He hoped to find his mother asleep in her room because he wouldn't be able to hide his grin, one that wouldn't be attributable to a few extra hours at Flory's.

Come Monday, he went to work, happy to learn he still had a job. When his shift finally ended, he nearly sprinted to Bonnie's door with no thought of his disheveled appearance or pungent odor. He knocked, and this time, she opened the door without asking. Once again, Bonnie looked stunning, but he had his words ready. "I had a great time, Bonnie. I'd like to take you dancing on Friday. Will you go dancing with me?"

This time, without the same hesitation she displayed when he asked her to the movies, she nodded her agreement. Their whirlwind romance had begun.

Chapter 9

BONNIE: Spring 1939

Bonnie leaned up against the door. As Jacob made his way down the stairs, she wondered if he would ask her out again. She wondered if she wanted him to.

The evening had been fun, though a bit awkward. She could tell he was trying to impress her with his carefully combed hair and a bouquet of flowers. She obviously impressed him – he rarely looked away from her all night. Yet, everything about the date felt unpolished, as if he had never taken a girl to the movies before. On several occasions, she caught him silently moving his lips rehearsing his next line. He hadn't tried to hold her hand and forget a good night kiss. Yet, despite his inept attempts, there was something about Jacob that sparked her interest.

"What do I see in this boy-man?" she wondered. "Is it that I haven't had a date in so long that anyone, even a clumsy German delivery boy would make me feel this way?"

"Yes," she assured herself, "It must be the lack of others' interest. I'm not the type to fall in love on a whim." She pulled upright at the words 'fall in love.' What brought that phrase to her mind? She had been on one date with a mere inkling of a man.

Shaking her head to clear her thoughts, she began again to assess what about Jacob scattered her thoughts. "One. He is good-looking." She came to realize that although he didn't have the money to be a sharp dresser, he bore a natural look that was picture-show worthy. When he flashed his flirtatious smile, he reminded her a bit of George Brent in his role in *Special Agent*.

It was that smile and those eyes. "I wonder if Bette Davis has as much trouble looking at George as I do looking at Jacob." Then she scoffed at herself. Comparing herself to Bette Davis in any way was laughable, as was the comparison of Jacob to George Brent. Other than an incredible smile and dreamy eyes, the two had nothing in common. George Brent had a career that would take him places.

There didn't seem to be a second reason for her quick infatuation. Jacob had good looks, but there must be more. She was Bonnie Phillips, a lady who expected life's luxuries after growing up with butlers, maids, and a yacht. The Depression stole that life from her, but she did not plan to give up that life without a fight.

And Jacob was not likely to provide her the means to live that kind of life. While they sipped soda, she learned he was of German descent, though he recently changed his name to Miller. His father died when he was a baby, and before working as a grocery delivery boy, he worked as a hired hand on a farm in exchange for food and shelter. What would a boy like that have to offer her?

"This is absurd," she thought. "This cannot go any further. I had a pleasant time, nothing more. Next week, I'll switch grocers. Surely, he'll get the hint." With that, she took off her stockings, gave them the second washing of the day, and headed to bed.

Despite her resolve to put Jacob firmly out of her mind, she was surprised at how often thoughts of his smile or snippets of a conversation would float into her head when she least expected it. She never had trouble dismissing anyone before. She couldn't wait to head back to her boring job to give her mind something else to focus on.

On Sunday, she devised a plan to put Jacob into her past and someone new into her future. Although she did secretarial work, she interacted with several executives at Timken. What if she tried to be more outgoing and friendly? The looks and quickly averted eyes proved that several noticed her, but no one ever went beyond sneaking a look.

"Perhaps I need to be more friendly and engaging," she surmised. "If I want to live the life of a lady, then I need to look in the right places for a husband instead of carousing with a delivery boy."

On Monday morning, she woke with a purpose, choosing her clothes with care. "I need to be professional, but feminine," she thought as she looked through her clothes. She added the one strand of pearls that had been spared from the creditors before they left Detroit. The off-white strand caressed her throat in a provocative manner, one that caused men to gape and rub sweaty palms against their trousers.

Throughout the day, she made a concerted effort to be friendly and outgoing. Not too friendly, of course, but friendly enough to invite an offer for lunch or coffee. She made a point of looking the men she worked for in the eye and using their first name. Now, instead of merely working for a paycheck, her goal would be to find a husband. It definitely made the hours go by more swiftly than usual, because before she knew it, the day was over.

Bonnie barely closed the door to her apartment and had yet to remove her pearls, when an emphatic pounding sounded on her door. "Who in the world would be pounding like that?" she thought with disgust. Without thinking, she threw open the door, intending to teach the offender a thing or two about manners. Instead, she came face to face with Jacob.

He was out of breath, smelled mildly of perspiration and rotten fruit, and had hair going in a thousand different directions. But unlike his Friday night visit, he began speaking as soon as the door opened. "I had a great time, Bonnie. I'd like to take you dancing on Friday. Will you go dancing with me?"

Her heart began singing a song that reminded her of the tune he whistled each time he delivered groceries to her door. Her mind reeled, happiness and love exploding like fireworks on the Fourth of July. Without realizing she was going to speak, the word 'yes' tumbled out of her mouth. Before she gathered her wits and changed her mind, he said, "I'll pick you up at eight," and was gone.

Once again, Bonnie found herself leaning against the door as Jacob descended the stairs. This time, she had no intentions of trying to forget him.

Chapter 10

JACOB: Spring 1939

Jacob was in love. He had yet to tell his mother, but he was most definitely in love with the most beautiful girl in the world. He was certain his mother noted the difference in him. He smiled more. He was always singing. And he spent more and more time away from home. Surely, she realized something had changed, but she didn't ask, and he didn't tell.

That had been the way with his mother since he was a small boy. He never told her things that could hurt her. She worried about his health. She worried he would do something stupid and die young. She worried something or someone would take him away from her. So, rather than see her upset, he didn't talk. And rather than be upset, she didn't ask. It had been an arrangement that worked for years.

He thought about some of the things he had done in his life that were "secret-worthy" when it came to his mother. Typically, those secret-worthy items were of the "do something stupid and die young" variety. For example, there was the time he and his buddy, Dieter, decided they could make a lot of money by retrieving things from the bottom of Lake Cable. They fashioned a diving helmet out of an old water heater and used a hand pump and a hose to supply it with air. Dieter would sit in the rowboat pumping air to Jacob who walked on the bottom of the lake.

He fully realized it was not a very smart thing to do. Not only could the air system quit working, but Jacob didn't know how to swim. Despite these small issues, they made quite a bit of money scavenging items and, once, the police called them in to help with a search for a missing child. No, there was no need to ever tell mother about those adventures or the many others like it he had while growing up. What his mother didn't know couldn't hurt her.

He felt the same way about telling her about Bonnie. Bonnie was the best thing that ever happened to him, but his mother wouldn't see it that way. Bonnie would be that "someone" who finally took Jacob away from her. She would view Bonnie as the enemy. So, rather than share his love, he hid it. And, as with any secret Jacob hid, his mother did her part by asking no questions.

Despite going out several nights a week and no longer hiding the fact he was combing his hair or wearing his best shirts, his mother never questioned the fact that he said he was working an extra shift at work. She also didn't question the lack of extra money coming home from these extra shifts or the abundance of money being spent on "nothing in particular." There is no doubt Elisabet knew Jacob had a girl, but she likely hoped it was a passing fancy. If she didn't ask, then Bonnie couldn't exist. Living with her head in the sand simply made life easier to bear.

Jacob took Bonnie all over the city to places she had never seen. She sometimes rode in the boat while he walked the lake. He would often take her with him as he made deliveries to houses further from town so they could talk on the way. She never entered the homes but waited outside before accompanying him back to the store. He showed her the neighborhoods full of immigrants where strange words were spoken across fences. She discovered tiny churches with cemeteries containing simple wooden crosses or small stones marking the grave site. There were many homes with chickens wandering in the yard or small goats eating grass. This was the part of North Canton she had never seen. She wondered if Detroit had its share of these forgotten nooks and crannies and began to realize how sheltered her life had been.

But Bonnie also showed Jacob parts of the city that were new to him. She took him to an art museum and introduced him to the wonders of van Gogh, Seurat, and Monet. She taught him about design and architecture. She began to teach him about culture. He was a fast learner and soaked up new information as fast as she gave it to him. Once again, she realized the difference between Jacob and her wasn't anything more than money. Those without worked too hard to make ends meet to worry about Monet.

However, the thing they enjoyed the most was dancing. Jacob, despite his lack of formal training, loved to dance. He had a real ear for music and found the beat in any song. There was nothing that made his eyes shine more than swirling Bonnie around on the dance floor to the sound of big band music with a style known as swing. Nights under the stars or in cramped halls listening to Benny Goodman and the like, energetically dancing until Bonnie couldn't dance another step. Those were the nights Jacob loved the most.

Although their first date didn't happen until March, and it was only now the middle of May, Jacob believed with all his heart that he wanted to spend the rest of his life with his dear Bonnie. So, on May 19th, 1939, after a lovely night of dancing, he got down on one knee and proposed. He gave her no ring but simply a promise to love her every day and until his dying breath. She said yes without a moment's hesitation and three weeks later, they eloped to West Virginia.

Still, Jacob didn't tell his mother.

Chapter 11

BONNIE: Summer 1939

Jacob was not the only one keeping secrets. Bonnie had to keep a few of her own. Married women were not allowed to work at Timken in the secretarial pool. Neither she nor Jacob wanted her to lose her income, so they came up with a plan that worked well for a time. They pretended to the world that they were not married, but merely two young people in love.

Keeping secrets was not easy for Bonnie. June sensed something was going on and kept asking questions, but Bonnie skirted around the answers, hoping June would let her meager responses be enough. It caused a little rift in their friendship, but it was important to keep her marriage to Jacob hidden.

Bonnie Marie Miller. She couldn't believe she had

gotten married to the grocery delivery boy. What would her parents think when they met him? What would his mother think when she met her? What would June think? But then, as with most young and blushing brides, Bonnie didn't really care what anyone thought.

She was madly in love with Jacob. They would make a beautiful life together. In fact, if their lovemaking was any indication of their upcoming life, it was going to be idyllic. She had heard stories from older women about the obligations of being a wife. These stories were usually said with a bit of disgust mingled with disdain, but the appropriate amount of duty.

Because of these stories, she always assumed sex was a chore that a woman had to do to keep her husband satisfied. She never expected to enjoy the experience. How wrong those women had been.

Lovemaking was not some burdensome task to check off her to-do list. It was new and magical, filling her with joy and light. During the day, she longed for his strong, calloused hands to touch her delicate skin. When they were together, her fantasies turned to realities as they discovered the art of pleasing one another.

She had thought she was sophisticated when it came to men, but the physical side of love was new to both of them. She was often surprised at her body's response or her strong desires. How she molded her body to fit his, how her fingers discerned where to go and what they'd find, how her lips wanted to taste every inch of this man she married.

She not only enjoyed but looked forward to her times spent with Jacob. True, the conditions weren't quite what she would have hoped. They weren't lying in a four-poster bed with silk sheets and a fan circling lazily overhead. Except for the one night in a hotel while in West Virginia, which was almost impossible to explain away to June, their love making took place in some very unusual places.

There was the neighbor's barn loft behind Jacob's house, what they called their "secret garden," a spot in the woods surrounded by large holly bushes, and the mice-ridden storeroom at the grocery store. However, no matter where they made love, Jacob was kind and gentle and always made sure she enjoyed the experience.

Though he had been slow to kiss her the first time, and she soon learned she was the first girl he had ever kissed, he caught on quickly and became an arduous lover. They could easily spend hours in each other's arms, and she began to long for a time when they could be together all night every night, for the rest of their lives. For now, however, before the night turned to dawn, Jacob would creep back to his mother's house, and Bonnie would sneak back to the flat she shared with June.

By the middle of August, after two months of marriage, Bonnie's energy lagged. While her body moved in slow motion, her emotions moved in the opposite direction. Tears stood ready to fall and anger erupted over trivial matters. She assumed it was due to the stress of hiding the marriage until the day she had trouble zipping up the back of her skirt.

Since passing through adolescence, Bonnie's weight never varied. She ate anything she wanted or nothing at all, and her figure remained the same. June hated her for it. She was always dieting and trying to keep trim, but Bonnie never gave it a single thought. Until the morning the skirt didn't fit.

Quickly, she jumped on the scales to discover she hadn't gained any weight at all. That made absolutely no sense, but no matter how hard she tried, the skirt would not snap in the back. Had something happened to it in the wash? She pulled another skirt out of the closet to discover it, too, was tight. Mystified, she got down a third skirt only to find the same problem. And then, the answer caused her breath to catch in her throat.

When was her last cycle? She counted on her fingers, remembering she had one two weeks before they got married and...she hadn't had one since. Ten weeks. With all the excitement and time spent with Jacob, she hadn't realized she was late. She sat down on the ceramic-tiled bathroom floor and put her head on her knees. She was pregnant. Bonnie, the girl who hadn't yet met her mother-in-law or told her boss or her parents she was married, was pregnant.

A mixture of excitement and nerves rolled across her stomach. This was going to change everything, and she needed to tell Jacob right away.

She ticked a list off on her fingers. They would have to find a place to live. She would need to find a doctor. She would have to resign from her job. He would have to obtain a better job, since she would no longer be allowed to work. And the biggest one of all, she was finally going to have to meet Jacob's mom.

She sent word with June that she was feeling ill and would not be at work that day. Bonnie never missed work, so June was quite concerned. "Here, let me take your temperature," she said as she slipped the glass thermometer into her mouth. When the mercury rested on 98.6, she said, "Well, you don't have a fever. I'll check in on you at lunch."

Bonnie thanked her, but said, "Oh, June. Don't do that. I'm fine. Really. It's probably just something I ate. I'm sure I'll feel better if I sleep a bit. I'll see you when you come home tonight."

As soon as June left, Bonnie dressed in one of the skirts that still buttoned and walked to Flory's to find Jacob. His eyes lit up momentarily, until he realized she should be at work. "What's wrong, Bonnie? Why aren't you at work?" The horrible thought crossed his mind that she decided marrying him was a colossal mistake, and she was here to break the news in person.

Instead, she pulled him to the side, in front of the display of oranges, and whispered in his ear, "Jacob, I'm going to have a baby."

Jacob's eyes opened wide, his lower jaw falling away from his face before quickly switching to the biggest lopsided grin she had ever seen. Then, without realizing it coming, he swept her off her feet, twirled her around the fruit bins, and yelled to all who were inside the store, "I'm going to be a father!"

Since no one knew of their marriage, the looks from the other employees ranged from shocked to scandalized. "SHHHH, Jacob! No one knows we are married!! You are making me out to be...well, you know...SHHHHH!"

Only slightly contrite, Jacob continued his dance until he came before his boss and announced, "Bonnie and I got married in June. We are going to have a baby. I was hoping you would give me a raise." And then, turning to the others with a bow and a flourish of his hand, he said, "I'd like to introduce you to Mrs. Jacob Miller."

Although the shocked expressions remained, everyone began offering congratulations all around. Before long, Mr. Flory brought out some apple cider for a toast. Then, he sent Jacob on his way home saying today was a day for celebration and to arrive back at the store in the morning.

Jacob's reaction thrilled Bonnie. Becoming pregnant so quickly after marriage could have been difficult for him to handle, but he seemed to be very happy. Very happy indeed.

As they left the grocery store, Bonnie looked up at Jacob and said, "We need to find someplace to live. I'm going to have to quit my job now. I don't know how we are going to survive. And Jacob...I think it is time I met your mother."

Chapter 12

JACOB: Summer 1939

Jacob's mother was not going to take the news well. He couldn't decide if he should break it to her and then bring Bonnie or tell her with Bonnie present. Both had their advantages and disadvantages. She often spoke without thinking, so keeping Bonnie away from the initial reaction might be the kindest thing he could do. On the other hand, having someone new in the home often tempered her a bit. In the end, they decided to face the dragon together.

That was how Bonnie put it, but Jacob didn't actually imagine his mother as a dragon. He viewed her as a protective mother who loved her son, and he said as much to Bonnie. "She has been through so much, you know. My father died when I was a baby. She's had to work hard her whole life to keep me fed and then spent many lonely years while I lived on the farm. Sending me away was an enormous sacrifice for her. Even now, her life is tough. I can understand how my leaving could be interpreted as abandonment. Can't you?" He looked pleadingly at his wife. If he could help her to understand his mother, half the battle was won.

Bonnie nodded. "Yes, Jacob. I do understand. But you've been so reticent to tell your mother about me that I've come to think of her as an enemy to battle. I promise," she said, placing her hand on his forearm, "I will be kind and considerate of her past experiences."

He squeezed her hand. Now that he was assured of his wife's attitude, he hoped he could persuade his mother to feel the same way, to view Bonnie as an addition to their family rather than the enemy. He sent a silent prayer up to heaven as they approached the picket fence now badly in need of white paint. "Please, please help mother see how much Bonnie and I love one another. Please help mother want to see me happy."

They walked to the front door hand in hand and looked at each other during a brief pause. Jacob mouthed "I love you" to Bonnie who smiled in reply. Jacob took a deep breath to steady his racing pulse, pushed open the door to what had been his home for the last 20 years, and yelled, "Mother, are you here? I have something I want to tell you and someone I want you to meet."

Elisabet had been in the kitchen making a batch of her famous chocolates. A special order came in that morning from the wealthier side of town. She came into the front room wiping her hands on her tattered apron, expecting to meet one of Jacob's co-workers. She was startled to see a beautiful young woman at her son's side instead. She slowly let her hands drop to her sides and waited for the news.

"Mother, this is Bonnie. Bonnie, this is my mother, Elisabet."

Bonnie, always the lady, moved forward as if to shake hands, but Elisabet didn't move or offer her own hand in return. She stared wordlessly at her son and back again to Bonnie, her face becoming more pinched with each passing second.

Bonnie's hand slowly dropped back to her side, her own smile fading, her own face taking on the same pinched quality. Bonnie's breath quickened, and Jacob detected a bit of lightning in her eyes. The two most important women in his life squared off. They had each taken a stance and were poised for the next move, like pieces on a chessboard.

Realizing there was no delicate way to ease the tension and having no solid plan of action, Jacob did what he always did when faced with a difficult task. He ran headlong into the fray, blurting out, "Mother, Bonnie is my wife. We got married in June. We are going to have a baby." Although he said this with as much enthusiasm and excitement as he could muster, the emotion was completely lost on his mother.

Elisabet's face grew pale except for spots of red high on her cheekbones. Her mouth turned into an angry snarl as she spat out, "You...you...you whore...what have you done to my son? Gone and got pregnant and forced him to marry you!"

Bonnie's mouth gaped open having never been spoken to in that manner in her entire life. Jacob's mouth gaped open even wider, and before his mother said another horrible word to his beautiful bride, he shook himself into action and quickly said, "No, Mother. No. Listen to me. You have it all wrong. We got married in June. Two months ago. Bonnie got pregnant afterward. We found out today. We didn't get married because of a baby. We didn't tell anyone we got married because we wanted her to keep her job at Timken." He couldn't tell her the rest of the truth. He couldn't tell her he hadn't told her because he feared her reaction, and, it appeared, rightfully so.

He looked at his mother with pleading eyes. The eyes of a boy caught on the precipice of manhood with his wife on one side and his mother on the other, both beckoning him to leave his ledge and make the leap. His mother wanted him to stay a boy. His wife needed him to be a man. He wanted to be with Bonnie and wanted his mother to let him go.

He watched in agony as the anger slowly drained from Elisabet's face to be replaced by complete sadness. Her clenching jaw give way to a trembling one as she finally crumpled into tears. Sinking onto the threadbare sofa in the front room, she cried without consolation – deep throaty sobs interrupted only by long gasps for air too thin to be of much use.

He realized there would be no apology for calling Bonnie a whore and no congratulations on their wedding or impending parenthood. He realized she was not going to be happy about her new status as a grandmother or the idea she was gaining a daughter rather than losing a son. Instead, she would focus on the loss of her son and the sure knowledge that the day she dreaded had finally arrived.

After a few more tense moments of Jacob trying to console his mother while staying true to his wife, they left Elisabet crying on the sofa, the chocolates in the kitchen quite forgotten. They walked in total silence for several blocks, each lost in their own thoughts and concerns.

Jacob kept shaking his head. That had gone far worse than he expected. He had known his mother would be unhappy but to accuse Bonnie of ...he couldn't say it. His mother's accusations were distasteful and unseemly. But then, he reasoned she was shocked. Certainly, his mother would come around and love Bonnie the way he did. Certainly, she would realize the joy that was coming into her life as well as his own?

Bonnie, lost in her own thoughts, was certain of no such thing. Her certainty was this was the beginning of a perfectly dreadful relationship. No one had ever used such coarse words in her presence, let alone meant exclusively for her. To be called a whore by one's own family...how would she ever forgive the woman who had given birth to the man she loved more than the world itself? She understood Jacob's desire was that his mother would grow to love Bonnie, but she believed in her heart no such reconciliation would happen. Elisabet had drawn a line in the sand and was not likely to call a truce.

Eventually, Jacob broke the tense silence but chose to avoid talking about the horrid scene with his mother. Instead, he focused on the next task at hand. He learned from his days on the farm when circumstances prevent you from taking care of one aspect of your life, you simply move on to the next thing on the list.

With as much confidence as he could muster, he put a

smile on his face, turned to Bonnie, and stated matter-of-factly, "We need to find a place to live. I have a little bit of money saved up. I know of a little flat not far from the grocery. I saw it was for rent when I made a delivery last week. Would you like to see if it is still available?"

Bonnie nodded and Jacob took the lead. He loved Bonnie. He needed nothing more than that love and a determination to make it work. He would create a beautiful home with her. They would have a son...he was sure it was a boy...and his mother would come to love Bonnie as a daughter, as it should be. It simply had to work this way because he could not conceive of any other outcome. So, as he always did with his mother, he buried the truth underneath the fancies of his mind and heart and focused his attention on Bonnie.

Despite the dreadful encounter with his mother, luck appeared to be with them. The apartment was still empty. Though tiny and a bit dingy, it became palatial as they imagined their life together. The two lovebirds moved in that very afternoon. Of course, it didn't take much in the way of moving. Neither one had much of anything to move.

Jacob's mother refused to speak to him when he came home for his things. He dared not take anything she believed belonged to her, so he simply took his clothes. As he walked from his room, he looked wistfully at the furniture that would sit empty in a room he would no longer use. They could have used the dressing table and small chair, but it was prudent to give his mother more time before he asked. In the meantime, they would do without.

Then Jacob took Bonnie back to her little flat and

helped collect her things. Her belongings, though substantially more than Jacob's, still did not amount to much. June came home, confused by the piles and disarray. All Bonnie's clothes were in piles, and her small twin bed was now missing from the tiny bedroom they shared. She looked at Bonnie, then at Jacob, and back to Bonnie, unasked questions in her eyes.

With Jacob standing valiantly by Bonnie's side, she broke the news to June. Unlike Jacob's mother, who could not grasp the wonderment of the news, June immediately grabbed Bonnie in a hug, then grabbed Jacob. Jacob was slightly uncomfortable with all the affection, but June didn't appear to notice. She babbled on about how she knew something was going on and how relieved she was to finally know what it was. Oh, sure, she was not happy she'd have to find another roommate, but she couldn't think of a happier reason for it to happen. She prattled on joyfully while they finished the packing.

The juxtaposition of the two reactions to their news hit Jacob hard. His mother's reaction had been abysmal, and no amount of rationalization would change that. Here, a perfect stranger to him, and a friend of less than a few years to Bonnie, was showering them with love and congratulations. She was happy and helpful. She was everything his mother was not. "Perhaps," he thought wryly, "my mother is a dragon, after all."

Chapter 13

BONNIE: Winter 1939

The next several weeks were rocky for Bonnie. In addition to quickly outgrowing all her clothes and being forced into dresses that were neither form-fitting nor stylish, she began to experience morning sickness. Food, something she had always enjoyed with abandon, now made her queasy. To her surprise, the mere thought of food caused bile to rise in her throat, leaving an acidic aftertaste that became a permanent fixture in her mouth.

Jacob, during this time of unpredictable nausea and vomiting, was her hero. He brought her glasses of room temperature water – cold water hung heavy and formidable, making her gag. No matter what the concoction or how bizarre the request, Jacob immediately set about picking her weird cravings from the store or whipping them up in the kitchen. She was constantly amazed at his patience, even when she refused to eat what he had so carefully prepared because her stomach had lurched again, making the desired treat no longer desirable.

She wrote to her parents in Connecticut the day after moving in with Jacob, telling them she had gotten married and was expecting their first grandchild. Although their response was better than Elisabet's, totally devoid of words like whore, it was still rather frosty. They stated they were happy for her and would come to Ohio when her father took vacation time to visit with her and meet Jacob. But the tone of the letter was a far cry from June's overwhelming acceptance.

She tried not to blame them. They hadn't met Jacob and couldn't know how perfect he was or how happy he made her. They didn't witness him up at all hours of the night fixing her something to eat because it was the only time she could force the food down. They didn't know how hard he worked. All they knew was what she had told them, and she was acutely aware he didn't make a great first impression on paper: *"Dear Mother and Father, I ran away and secretly got married to the German grocery delivery boy. We are living in a tiny two-room flat in the middle of town, sleeping in a narrow twin bed, and expecting our first child. Doesn't he sound dreamy?"*

This, of course, wasn't the letter she wrote, but it was the truth she assumed they gleaned from her words. She imagined the shock her parents must have experienced as they realized their precious Bonnie had gotten married, was pregnant, and was not living the life of ease they always envisioned for her. Despite finding the man that would make her happy for life, her parents couldn't be expected to be ecstatic over a first-generation American with no obvious means of moving up the social ladder.

Despite these thoughts, Bonnie missed her mother terribly. She longed for her mother's wisdom, knowing if she were here, she would quickly embrace Jacob. She would also provide all the nurturing a newly pregnant daughter desired.

When she thought of her own mother far away, her thoughts automatically turned to her mother-in-law. Elisabet lived right here in town and could easily talk to her about pregnancy, birth, marriage, and her son. But she had still not spoken one word to Bonnie after that first terrible encounter. It was as if she simply did not exist.

The lack of a mother figure in her life was one of the most excruciating parts of her new life. Coupled with the fact she was no longer going to work or meeting up with friends, loneliness settled in quickly. Thankfully, Bonnie chose not to feel sorry for herself for long. She determined to make the best of the difficult circumstances, working hard to turn the tiny apartment into a home.

It was much harder than in the days of her youth when she snapped her fingers and magically made new furniture appear. But Bonnie loved a challenge and pressed on to achieve what she could, given the restrictions of their current financial situation. She turned to the one place that had potential materials for free, despite the dismay doing so would have caused her mother had she known – the trash. On days when the nausea was absent, she scavenged through trash piles, finding a staggering assortment of odds and ends.

In a matter of weeks, she had put together enough kitchen items to cook almost anything they desired. Once he realized what she was up to, Jacob joined in the adventure, procuring an old wooden spool from the freight house. Bonnie covered it with a piece of pink cloth given to her by the neighbor in exchange for one of her old skirts, transforming the spool into a kitchen table. Little by little, the tiny rundown flat took on a less dreary personality.

Nonetheless, no amount of clever decorating fixed the issue with the bed. With Jacob's 6-foot 4-inch frame and her ever-expanding belly, trying to fit on the narrow bunk was not going to be possible for much longer. She considered making a pallet on the floor but hated the idea due to her inordinate fear of insects. The thought of a roach running across her hand or foot in the night while she slept immobilized her. Wings and wiggly antennae kept her in the tiny bed for weeks beyond what others would have endured.

One afternoon close to Thanksgiving, after another restless night in the "growing tinier every day" bed, she strolled through town while Jacob worked. She tried getting out of the house on any day with warm enough weather. Stretching her legs and breathing fresh air always made her pregnancy symptoms dissipate, particularly on the queasy days.

She stopped at the window of Livingston Furniture Company and looked longingly at the lovely beds for sale. Oh, how she would love to have a bed devoid of lumps and divots that fit her growing size. While admiring the bed, she became aware of the window display, a haphazard mess of this and that with no real purpose. In fact, the whole thing was rather ugly. If it weren't for the fact she wanted a bed so badly, she would have never been enticed to stop and stare. She mentally rearranged the window, thinking, "If I were putting this window together...."

Her mind whirled. What would she do if the opportunity presented itself to put together a window display? And why shouldn't she be given the opportunity? Before she lost her nerve, she marched into the store to speak to the owner. She boldly introduced herself and told him about her extensive design experience, conveniently leaving out the fact that most of it occurred during her childhood. Then she offered him her services to improve his window displays.

The color rose to her cheeks as he looked pointedly at her belly. Although she tried to hide her girth with her clothes, soon she would not be able to go in public without embarrassing herself or her husband. She was pushing convention by being seen, but she didn't want to be trapped in the house.

She straightened up to her full height and looked him in the eye, answering his unasked question. "I can come in to work through the back door and work after store hours. All I would need is a helper willing to move furniture. If you'd like, I could ask my husband to do that for me. I know he would be willing to do so."

Though bemused by her proposition, he did not interrupt her with his own thoughts on the matter. She gratefully continued. "In terms of payment, I would like my hours to be put towards the purchase of that bed." She pointed to a beautiful four-poster that would dwarf their minuscule room. However, she didn't plan to live in a tiny flat forever, and if she was going to work, she may as well get something that reminded her of the beauty she once experienced.

Once she began explaining her proposition, she couldn't stop. "I propose that I do the first window to show you my capabilities. Then, each month, I will come and create a new window display until the bed is paid off. I also propose that once you determine I am capable, you allow me to take the bed home while continuing to make payments."

She knew she was pushing her luck. However, the twin bed would not grow any larger. With the baby coming soon, she hoped to acquire the bed sooner rather than later, and it would take months to own the bed from her meager earnings.

He hesitated, and she couldn't decide if he was leaning toward hiring her or kicking her out of the store. Before her courage flagged, she finished speaking. "I will sign any type of contract you'd like. You can count on me to complete the job. I will be able to continue after," she looked down and whispered, "the baby comes." Looking up, she went on, "I can bring him to work with me while I supervise my husband on what I want to have done. You won't be sorry."

Mr. Livingston considered the proposal. His wife passed over a year earlier. Mabel had always been the marketing mind behind the business. Since her death, his furniture sales plummeted despite the uptick in the economy. He didn't have anyone working in the store who knew or cared about the display windows, plus he immediately liked this cheeky girl. She reminded him of Mabel in her earlier years, when she was young and spry and wouldn't let anything keep her down. He decided to give this young woman a shot.

"I'll tell you what. You bring your husband here tonight and fix up that window. If I have more than five customers comment on it tomorrow, you're hired, and you can take the bed home with you when you sign the contract."

Without thinking about her actions, she threw her arms around his neck and thanked him, promising to bring Jacob in. They would come by at 7 o'clock. He wouldn't be sorry.

Chapter 14

JACOB AND BONNIE: Winter 1939

Jacob was torn by his wife's announcement. On the one hand, he was proud of her for her pluck and determination to get what they needed for their home despite her ever-growing belly. On the other hand, he was supposed to be the provider for his home and wasn't sure how he felt about her taking that role.

In the end, her excitement and the reality of their financial situation won out. His boss gave him a raise, but it in no way made up for the lack of Bonnie's job at Timken. He provided the basic necessities, but he couldn't figure out how they were going to afford a bed on his salary. So, he embraced Bonnie's plan as if it had been his own and gladly accepted the position of chief hired hand and furniture mover.

After a quick supper of vegetable stew – meat was still hard to come by on his salary – Jacob and Bonnie headed to Livingston Furniture. Mr. Livingston greeted them both warmly, insisting they call him 'Johnny' within minutes of their introductions.

Johnny, they learned, lived above the store. "I'll be upstairs tending to the accounting if you need anything. Feel free to help yourselves to anything in the store to make the window look good for the Thanksgiving season. Let me know when you are through, so I can come down and lock up." With that, Johnny headed upstairs, the wood steps creaking under the weight of his feet.

Bonnie set to work immediately, first taking an inventory of the store while considering the many different items on display. As with most furniture stores, Johnny's store also sold accessories such as lamps, vases, and other items to make the furnishings look more like they would in a home. As Bonnie walked purposefully through the store, Jacob studied her with pride. His wife, he decided, could do anything she put her mind to, and this was one of the things he loved best about her. He also came to realize that with her by his side, he could do anything as well. Once again, he sincerely hoped his mother would be able to realize this someday and embrace Bonnie as a daughter.

However, today was not a day to dwell on his mother. Instead, he was here to support his wife in her desire to get them the solid oak four-poster bed that was well beyond their means financially and almost too large physically. Nonetheless, the thought of making love in that bed kept him from laughing at her dreams.

Bonnie moved at a dizzying pace, considering she was

now almost five months pregnant, touching things and collecting small items in her arms as she mumbled. At first, Jacob thought he was supposed to understand her mumblings and kept asking her to repeat herself. Finally, he realized she was thinking out loud and left her to it. After about an hour of wandering around the store, she got a delighted look on her face and turned to him with excitement. "I know exactly what I'm going to do. Here, take this table to the window. You can haul it there, can't you?"

Jacob grinned. He was many things, but weak was not one of them. With the ease of a machine, he moved the dining table to the front window.

Over the next several hours, they created a flawless display. Bonnie decided to create a spectacular Thanksgiving feast with China and flowers and the "faux food" currently on display in the kitchen table section.

By the time she was done, Jacob had a strong desire to sit down and enjoy the feast despite knowing the scene contained nothing more than wooden food. He figured if Bonnie's display moved him that way, it would surely move Mr. Livingston's customers.

Jacob walked up the flight of stairs, rapping on Johnny's door. "We're going now. Bonnie is done. I think you'll like what she's created. She told me to tell you she'll be by tomorrow at 6 o'clock to sign the papers." Jacob grinned at Johnny. "She's certain you'll have your five comments."

Bonnie's muscles ached and her feet swelled above her shoes. Despite doing no lifting, she had been on her feet for hours. It felt good to arrive home and sit on the small sofa she had purchased from a passing gypsy wagon while Jacob rubbed her swollen feet.

"I know the bed is too bulky, Jacob. But I just had to have it. I could see it in my mind's eye in a bigger home. Our next home. Eventually, we'll move from here and that bed will be the centerpiece of our bedroom. The dark wood is masculine enough to suit you but can be made feminine with the right linens to suit me."

She looked at Jacob to determine if he agreed. Little did she know he would have slept on pink ruffles and lacy eyelets if she asked.

The next day was a long one for Bonnie. By noon, she had paced the floor until she was sure there would be a permanent trench around the living room. Rather than go crazy, she determined to walk downtown and pass by the furniture store to see what the window looked like in the daylight.

To her amazement, people lined up around the window, exclaiming about the beauty. "Who did Johnny hire to do that window? You know he didn't do it himself!" and "That table makes my mouth water." and "I've never seen anything quite so beautiful, have you?" Bonnie stood stunned and speechless.

However, Mr. Livingston was not. He spotted Bonnie through the glass and came directly out of the store to her side. "Bonnie, you are hired. Right here and right now. I've never had so much traffic." With that, despite her size and obvious belly, he marched her through the front door, handed her a pen to sign the contract, and ordered the delivery men to take the bed to her house before dark.

That day, Bonnie got more than a new bed. She began a career that would be an asset to her growing family. She was proud of herself and wished her parents and Elisabet could understand what she and Jacob would accomplish together.

Chapter 15

WILLIAM: November 2016

William stood back to admire his handiwork, his father's voice in his ears, "If you are going to do something, do it right." He squinted his eyes, tilted his head, and then nodded in satisfaction. He completed the task to honor his father and began putting the tools away, stuffing the fishing line he used to secure the wreath to the bottom of the box.

Had this been his father's toolbox, the fishing line would have been much nearer to the top. Jacob, unlike William, loved to fish. William hated sitting still for hours, hoping a fish would magically decide to bite on the line. He mused about his own son's love of fishing, a love that created a bond between grandfather and grandson that didn't exist between father and son. He wondered if such bonds skipped generations and if he, too, would become closer to his grandsons as they grew.

It wasn't as if he didn't love his son, it was that he and Christopher were so different, neither able to understand the other. Christopher hated cars and loved to fish. Christopher was clumsy with a hammer, cried easily, and would rather spend hours talking with the elderly neighbor next door than play baseball with the boys.

Despite both being creative, they still couldn't find a way to connect. William loved to paint in oils while Christopher preferred learning to play the banjo, focusing his energies on North Carolina bluegrass music instead of something more palatable like The Beatles.

As Christopher grew, William began to hear his father's voice coming out of his own mouth. He uttered criticisms. He became demanding and pushy. In fact, he became everything he hated about the way his father treated him. Yet, he didn't know another way. How else was he supposed to do his job as a parent and instill the values of hard work, patriotism, and honesty? How could he both emulate his father and be someone else entirely?

William would start each day with a hope that today would be the day he would connect with his son. Unfortunately, they would either have no interactions at all, or the interactions would be riddled with contempt – father to son and back again. William understood the desired outcome – how he wanted to be – but simply didn't know how to move from point A to point B. Father-son relationships remained as incomprehensible as high school math.

He found relationships easier with his daughter, Emily. He didn't feel as responsible for her development, believing Marie had that well in hand. Plus, there was something about Emily that seemed to be missing in Christopher. She was willing to...try? Yes, try to be part of his life, asking about carburetors and brake lines despite not really caring. Holding tools for him as he worked. Asking for help – and accepting it – on her science fair projects. She was... easier.

He wondered, not for the first time, if his father felt the same way about him. Had William been stubborn? Unyielding? Unwilling to try? Or had it been his father exhibiting these characteristics? And what of his relationship with Christopher?

He thought back to the stories of his grandmother – how she'd been unable to let Jacob grow up and move on. Then his father did the same. Then he, too, followed along, like another train car on a track. The names changed, but the situation remained the same. Would Christopher be the one to break the mold or would his great-grandsons one day be having these same thoughts as they tended to their father's grave on a cold, windy November day?

William glanced up toward the sky. Despite the constant wind, the sun's upward progress gave the impression of warmth. The golden rays were synonymous with his mother and her sunshine hair, just as the tall pines signified his father's strength. Here, at the cemetery, with his mother's sunshine blazing and his father's tall trees bending slightly in the wind, he imagined his parents together again.

He remembered them as happy and in love. They often danced in the living room to the Big Band sounds, and his father would sing, "Beautiful, beautiful brown eyes," much to his mother's delight. Everything appeared as it had always been between them.

Then, with a clarity that belied the years, a memory bounded into his head. It was nighttime. He was asleep in his room in the pink house. His father had been home long enough that William began attending school. He was startled awake by screaming. His father's screams. Not the screaming he did when William made too much noise but something worse – something that frightened the small boy into complete stillness, huddled beneath his covers. Then, his mother *sssshhhhing ssssshhhhing*, soothing noises until his father's screams turned to moans, then whimpers, and finally, nothing at all. Only a gentle *sssshhhhing* for hours into the night.

That poignant memory combined with a simple fact like an exclamation point. He was almost twelve, six years after the war, before there was another child. Then another sister a year later. With two sisters so close in age, he doubted his parents spent six years trying to conceive to no avail.

How was it that he was a grown man with grown children before he realized his father had come home not only a different father, but a different husband – a different man altogether?

His mother understood and made allowances. She smoothed over the rough edges and ignored the prickly spines. She treated him as her Jacob, and in time, he became her Jacob, the man who sang and danced and loved. As he stooped to remove the errant weeds growing around the tombstone, he wished he had been able to do the same.

Chapter 16

JACOB: Late Winter 1940

March 8, 1940. An unrecognizable sound slowly roused Jacob. He rolled to his side, reaching his hand toward Bonnie only to discover she had already gotten out of bed. It was not yet daylight, and Bonnie was not in the habit of rising early, more notably since earning the oversized bed. He often left for work after bringing her a cup of tea while she lulled in the bed.

Swinging his legs to the side of the bed, he rubbed his eyes, struggling to find her small frame in the dark. "Bonnie, honey. What are you doing up so early?"

Bonnie didn't answer him immediately, which he found slightly unnerving. She eventually answered in a strained voice. "I couldn't sleep. Don't worry. Get some more rest."

Jacob walked toward the sound of her voice. "Bonnie, honey, come on back to bed." Before he said anything else, her face contorted, tiny beads of perspiration breaking out on her forehead and across the bridge of her nose. Within moments the pain passed, and she gaped at him with wide, searching eyes.

"Jacob...I think the baby is coming."

Now Jacob was wide awake. The baby. It was here. Bonnie was in labor. He needed to boil water. Fetch the doctor. Put on pants. He was a mess. How could she stand there looking so small when the whole world was tilting sideways?

Bonnie laughed, realizing how ridiculous they were acting. Women gave birth to babies every day, and here the two of them stood acting like childbirth had never been accomplished before. She calmly suggested to him that he get dressed and go find the doctor. She would put the water on to boil. It was bound to take a long time. That was something her mother told her in a letter.

By the time Jacob returned, the pains were coming close together, and Bonnie could barely catch her breath before the next one started. Instead of pains across her abdomen, she also experienced shooting pains in her back, across her hips, and down to her knees. At times, she imagined her legs were being ripped out of their sockets only to be put back, so they could be ripped out once more. She had been told that childbirth was painful, but no one prepared her for the experience.

She wanted to be brave, but the truth was she was terrified. What if something was wrong? What if she died in childbirth? Who would take care of the baby? Worse yet, what if the baby died? She couldn't bear to think about it.

As Bonnie, covered in sweat, steeled herself against the next pain, he took a step forward, ran a hand through his hair, and then backtracked a step, not knowing what to do. He glanced wildly around the room until he spotted some bathroom towels stacked in a corner. Striding toward them, he spoke over his shoulder in a tight, slightly higher pitched voice than normal. "The doctor said he would be here soon. He said you should walk around some. That will help. And towels." He grabbed the towels and held them outstretched in his hands. "He told me to put towels in the bed."

Just then, a contraction began, and Bonnie clutched at her middle. Jacob dropped the towels in a heap, ran to her side, and stroked her hair while she panted. When the pain passed, she smiled weakly at him. "Jacob, darling, you dropped the towels."

He stared at her, uncomprehending for a moment. "Towels? Oh, yes, towels." He smoothed the hair out of her face, wiped her brow, and leaned to pick up the towels. However, another pain hit, and he abandoned his task to be at her side once again.

He hated seeing Bonnie in pain. He wanted to help her but didn't know what to do, and standing idly by while she suffered made him feel useless, and not much of a man. His job was to keep her safe, but the terror in her eyes suggested he wasn't doing a very good job. As he held her hand, he murmured, "I'd trade places with you if I could. In an instant." She only groaned in response.

Then, during a particularly intense pain, water gushed down Bonnie's legs and onto the floor. She threw one hand over her mouth and clutched her belly with her other. With tears streaming down her face, she sobbed,

"What happened? Is everything okay with the baby? What if I hurt the baby? I don't know what I'm doing, but I think must be doing it all wrong."

Jacob stared at the liquid on the floor, trying to remember this happening when he helped with the calving on the farm. But that had been in a barn with four-legged animals that didn't sleep in his bed at night and kiss him goodnight. This was nothing like helping cows.

Thankfully, the doctor arrived shortly thereafter and calmed everyone's fears. "Your water broke, Bonnie. It happens. Jacob, put some of those towels on the bed and help Bonnie get comfortable. Then clean up the fluid while I check her progress." Jacob followed the doctor's instructions, lifting Bonnie gently to the mattress as another contraction hit. When it passed, he left her side to swipe at the puddle with a towel, a flush rising to his cheeks when he realized what the doctor meant by checking Bonnie's progress. "Well now, Bonnie. I think you must be a natural. The baby is already crowning." As her eyebrows knit in confusion, he clarified. "I can see the top of the baby's head. It won't be long now, and this fine young baby will make his or her entrance."

Bonnie sucked in her breath. She had only been laboring for two hours, and she wasn't ready to have the baby yet. Her mother said labor would take hours, even days. She was prepared for that, but not this. This was happening too fast, so she made a determined decision to stop having the baby.

She swung her legs over the bed, walked to the middle of the room, and announced, "I'm done now. I'm no longer going to have labor. I'm not ready for the baby to come yet, so you both may as well go about your day. There is nothing to see or do here."

Jacob looked at the doctor with wild eyes full of fear. What was Bonnie saying? She couldn't go for a walk. She was having a baby! Was she crazy? Had she lost her mind? "But...Bonnie...you...I, mean...it's..."

The doctor, having dealt with a good many women in this stage of labor, ignored Jacob's stuttering and gently led Bonnie to the side of the bed where she dealt with another major contraction. Before she could think about leaving again another one hit hard. The doctor convinced her to lie down and before she could get comfortable, another contraction hit, this one looking like ocean waves rolling down the length of her stomach. Her body, on its own accord, began to push.

At the doctor's urging, Bonnie began to push in earnest with each contraction. Jacob would have ordinarily been pushed to another room or taken outside, but everything happened so fast and there were no women here to help. Instead, Jacob began following the doctor's orders, gathering the needed medical tools all the while murmuring to his beloved sweetheart.

Within a matter of minutes, the baby's head and then shoulders and then body emerged. The tiny little child, covered in blood and mucus, was the most beautiful thing Jacob had ever seen. When the doctor lifted it up by the feet and gave it a smack on the butt, the baby burst into a loud wail. Both Jacob and Bonnie began to cry as well, but theirs were cries of joy.

The doctor bundled up the baby and said, "You have a beautiful, healthy baby boy." Jacob couldn't have been prouder. They had discussed names before the birth. If

they had a boy, he would take on the name of the 25th
President of the United States, as well as the name of
Jacob's own father. He looked down at his new son and
said, "William Hyrum Miller, welcome to the world."

Chapter 17

BONNIE: Spring 1940

Bonnie secretly feared she would have no idea what to do as a mother. Her childhood training taught her to be a lady, and ladies gave most of the duties of child-rearing to wet nurses and nannies. She wasn't even sure she could change a diaper.

She clung to the knowledge that Jacob was at her side. Though he had no experience with babies, he also had no fear. Within minutes of William's birth, Jacob scooped him up, washed him clean, and swaddled him in a warm blanket. His easy acceptance of the baby and the new tasks surrounding him calmed her racing heart, giving her the courage to be as fearless as her husband. The two of them together were so much more than either one of them separately.

William, too, seemed to know exactly what to do and begun suckling at her breast as soon as he was laid in her arms. She smiled down at the tiny mouth, head of brown hair, and long eyelashes. William. Her son. No, she shook her head almost imperceptibly, their son. The son she and Jacob made, a sign they would go on to make many more beautiful things together, babies and otherwise.

Although the first weeks were uneventful, having a baby in the home was a major adjustment. William's two-hour feeding schedule, one that ran without fail through the night, left her foggy and forgetful. Bonnie also had to adapt to being attached to another human a dozen times each day, her body no longer her own. Everything she did, from personal hygiene to household chores to sleep revolved around her new baby bottle role.

Thankfully, William was an easy child and content to follow her with his eyes as she went about her daily work. So, despite heavy eyelids and intermittent interruptions, Bonnie became adept at keeping supper on the table and the most necessary chores accomplished.

When William turned three weeks old, she packed him up on a Tuesday evening so she and Jacob could create her next window display. When they arrived, Johnny momentarily started without comprehension. "Bonnie? What are you doing here? You just had a baby!" He stepped forward, pinching the corner of the blanket swaddling William to peek at the boy. "He's beautiful," he said, directing his words to Bonnie. Then, looking at Jacob, "And strong. But, what? Three weeks? I didn't expect you."

Bonnie stepped between the men, making sure they both remembered she was the employee. "I signed a contract, Johnny. I signed it knowing I was going to have a baby. And now that he is here, I have no intention of reneging on the deal."

"Oh, no, Bonnie, I didn't ever think that. I knew you'd come back. I mean...I hadn't thought...well, never mind what I thought. You are here, and I'm grateful to have you. I've had far more business since hiring you. Plus, I'm rather fond of little ones. It will be nice to see William – you did name him William?" Bonnie nodded, "It will be nice to see William. I miss having the noise of children in my life. May I hold him?"

Bonnie carefully passed the bundle to her older boss. "I fed him before we left the apartment. He should be happy for a little while, at least."

Johnny gazed at the boy, tickling his chin with the tip of his finger. "Your initial contract is almost over. One more window display and that grand bed is truly yours. I hoped you might consent to more work, another contract? If you still want the work, that is?" He looked up from the baby, eyes full of hope.

Bonnie was delighted. Her long-range plans included working after William arrived, but she hadn't officially broached the subject with Johnny. She wasn't entirely sure what he thought about having a baby tag along during the design process. His words settled everything. "Absolutely, Johnny. I'd love to continue as your employee, but I'd better start now while the baby is still content. We'll settle on the details before we leave tonight, okay?" At his nod, she quickly went to work.

As she busied herself with the evening's tasks, Bonnie thought about the long list of other things they could use in their home. She had been over this list a million times in her head but never tired of the activity. A kitchen table with matching chairs, a sofa large enough to fit Bonnie, Jacob, and William at the same time, a dresser to keep their clothes since Elisabet had yet to hand over Jacob's old one from childhood. A bed and dresser for William once he no longer slept in the small wooden cradle at the side of her bed.

Of course, the fantasies always ended with a dose of reality. They lived in a tiny flat, and the four-poster bed greedily swallowed up any extra space. If they found a way to push everything on her wish list in the front door, there would be no room left for living.

At the evening's conclusion, Johnny sat Bonnie and Jacob at his kitchen table and began the process of renewing her work contract. She determined to be frank with him about their need for furniture but their inability to put it anywhere. She hoped she might collect credits for her work for now and then use those credits when the timing made more sense. She and Jacob had already discussed the lack of space and believed this was a good way to save for the future.

"Have you thought of moving?" asked Johnny. She nodded. "Yes, but we have to be realistic. Jacob has a stable income with the grocery, which is far better than many have. But that job isn't meant to support a wife and child." Jacob cut in quickly. "I've been looking for work. When that happens, we'll find something bigger, but it is out of the question for now."

At this statement, Johnny banged his fist onto the table. Bonnie jumped violently at the noise, which startled the baby into a ragged cry.

Johnny's face grew soft as he lifted his shoulders

apologetically. "I'm sorry. Shhh. Shhh. William. It's okay."
He reached over to pat and shush the baby until William's cries turned to whimpers and finally disappeared.
"I didn't mean to startle you, little man. It's just that I've
had a grand idea."

With that, he explained, "There's another flat across
the hall from me. It is almost the size of my home here.
My eldest daughter used to live there with her husband,
but they moved away two years ago to find work. They
now live in Upstate New York. I'd been saving it for their
return, but in her last letter, she told me they loved it
there and planned to stay. I haven't had the heart to try
to rent it out. I couldn't imagine who I would want living
across the hall. But if you want it, I think that would be a
perfect match."

Bonnie looked at Jacob, knowing they were thinking
the same thing. How much could they afford? How much
more would a home over Livingston Furniture Company
be compared to their tiny flat in a less desirable part of
town?

Bonnie looked pointedly at Jacob. That was a man's
question. Women in her world pretended money did not
exist and never discussed it.

Jacob didn't take the hint, so she nodded her head
toward the hall door and looked pointedly at him again.
This time, Jacob looked toward the door, back at Bonnie,
and shrugged his shoulders, bewildered by her subtle
gestures.

Sighing loudly, exasperated Jacob couldn't grasp
something that simple, she stood up and declared, "Well,
that sounds like a wonderful offer. I'll leave it to you two
gentlemen to work out the details." With that, she

flounced out of the room with a baby on her hip.

Had she been looking toward her husband instead of the door, she would have seen Jacob's eyes light up as he finally figured out what all her earlier gesticulations meant. Of course, now that she had excused herself from Johnny's home, she had nowhere to go. It was dark and a lady with a baby couldn't wander down the streets of North Canton without asking for trouble. So, she sat down on the bottom step, waiting quietly for her husband to appear.

When the door finally opened, Jacob's smile stretched across his face. Johnny waved at her from the doorway as they headed out into the dark. Sitting on the uncomfortable stairs had done nothing more than add to her irritation. If Jacob hadn't been so daft, he and Johnny would have stepped out leaving her to sit in the comfort of the house. She planned to let him know exactly how she felt about it. However, as he whistled a jaunty tune, she realized she couldn't stay irritated with him. He didn't always understand the ways things should be, but he was a good man and worked hard to provide for her and the baby. Plus, whenever he flashed his smile, her stomach did flops and turns, and she wanted to hold him against her and never let go. She wondered how long they would be married before she didn't feel like a young girl in love.

As they walked back to their tiny flat, Jacob regaled her with all the details. "Bonnie, you will continue to create window displays. Johnny will determine how many windows you need to complete for each piece of furniture you choose. To pay for the rent, I will help deliver furniture when I do not have a shift at Flory's.

You will also be given the duty of sweeping and dusting the store in the evenings after it has closed."

He stopped, then, to determine what she thought of that, but Bonnie urged him on with her smile. "Our rent will be covered by those two duties. Do you know what that means, Bonnie? It means we can start saving money from my job at Flory's to purchase a house. A real house! With a yard for William, and a dog, and a garden. You'd like a garden, wouldn't you?"

His excitement was contagious, so she exclaimed, "Yes! A house. That sounds divine. It will have many bedrooms to fill up with children." She looked shyly at him from under her eyelashes, and he playfully swatted at her rear end. "And I'll decorate it with the beautiful furniture from Livingston's. Oh, Jacob, I love you so."

That night, despite having a baby sleeping quietly in a bassinet only feet away, they made love for the first time since the birth. Jacob feared he would hurt her, but Bonnie urged him forward and delighted in their intimacy.

Afterward, as she lay snuggled in his big arms in the four-poster bed, she thought about their fortune. Johnny was being more than generous, and that generosity would help them get started in their life together.

Chapter 18

WILLIAM: November 2016

Without conscious thought, William traced his fingers along the letters of his parents' tombstone. Jacob Wendel Miller. September 16, 1917 to August 7, 2011. Bonnie Marie Miller. November 13, 1918 to July 11, 2000. How he missed them.

He thought back to what he usually referred to as 'the difficult years.' Shortly before turning 40, he began bristling under his father's tutelage. The constant advice was smothering and over-critical, and as far as William could determine, meant to keep him as 'and Son' and nothing more. He was not to grow up. He was not to become the head of his family. He was not to become Miller Construction or even Miller and Miller. It was like being stuck in a Monopoly game unable to pass Go.

The tension between him and his father grew palpable. William desired for his father to retire, so he could take over their two-man construction business. It was time for him to be the boss. His father, though often hinting of retirement, never made it happen.

The breaking point, however, was his father's infuriating way of giving William a bit of independence and then pulling it back without warning. William convinced his father to let him begin bidding new jobs, so when a new customer called in, William prepared to meet with them later that evening.

He completed his day's work, showered, and changed out of his dingy jeans and sweaty t-shirt, exchanging them for khakis and a button-down shirt and tie. As he readied to leave the house, his father called.

"William, there is no need to head over to the Andovers'. I discussed the project with Mack earlier today. I have what I need to bid out the job and promised him an estimate in the morning."

William could think of nothing to say. His father had, yet again, shown William his true place in their relationship. He respected his father enough not to yell, so he simply hung up the phone.

After a night of tossing and turning, he determined his only option was to move. Far away. He uprooted his family and landed over 500 miles away in North Carolina.

Looking back, he wasn't sorry he moved, though he wished it had been under better circumstances. North Carolina offered his young family opportunities and experiences they would not have encountered in Ohio, but the distance created considerable tension between him and his parents. Simple statements such as "We sure miss the children" by his parents or "I absolutely love my job" by William created hard feelings. Of course, they never stopped loving him, or he them, but those were troublesome years he would never want to repeat.

Now, as an old man himself, one finally committed to retirement, he understood his father's own unwillingness to stop working. As a young man, he viewed retirement as something to work toward, as a goal he couldn't wait to achieve. The closer he got to the end of his career, the more retirement signaled the end of his usefulness.

He wished his father had been here when he finally figured that out. "No," he thought, "I wish I had understood before leaving Ohio in anger."

Forgiveness on both sides came in fits and starts, with feeble attempts at apology and togetherness intermixed with hurtful digs and broken communication. When his father did finally retire, his parents spent several years traveling about the United States in their little silver bullet of a camper. They would pull into North Carolina a couple of times a year, sparking family gatherings full of stories and laughter, the last shreds of angst fading away.

Each time the silver bullet would pull away heading to some natural wonder, an emptiness overcame William. He missed his parents with a fierceness he hadn't considered when he rashly left them years ago. So, when they announced they wanted to sell their home in Ohio because of the extensive upkeep, particularly in the cold, snowy winter months, William immediately asked them to move to North Carolina. Just as quickly as he asked, they agreed. The last years of his parents' lives had been spent together again.

Once his mother died, William learned more about his father, what he believed, and why he did the things he did. During his final years, he finally opened up about the war, occasionally recalling the times of grief and pain. "I watched friends die, always wondering if I would be next, always wondering if you and your mother would get a letter and a flag back from the war instead of a father and a husband." William began to truly understand what it meant to be an American without reservation and the cost of doing so.

With a shake of his head, William let his hand drop from the stone. His shoulders sagged at the weight of unnecessary anger and wasted years. His father was absent during the war. Then William shut him out as a teen and ran away as an adult. Those were years he could never get back.

It was time to head home. He had done his duty as his father did his duty so many decades before.

Chapter 19

JACOB: December 1941

Life was idyllic for Jacob and his small family. The move to the apartment above Livingston's changed their days from ones of hardship and 'making-do' to ones of comfort and ease. With two full bedrooms, a larger living room, and a kitchen substantial enough to hold a full-sized table, they more than doubled the space of their newlywed abode. Not to mention, the landlord was friendlier, and the money they saved grew very substantial.

Jacob reflected on the last twelve months. He watched his wife grow heavy with child, participated in the birth, and now William, at nine months old, neared toddlerhood. Despite being so young, he was on the brink of walking. He often stood at the couch with a quizzical look, as if to say, "How can I get from here to there on my own steam." In no time, William would be running from place to place with breathless parents trailing behind.

Understanding how quickly his son would grow and run is what compelled him to begin looking at houses over near Orchard Park. Jacob spent his childhood in very small quarters with little space to play. It wasn't his mother's fault, of course. She did the best she could. But Jacob wanted more for William. He dreamed of a yard ample enough for hide-and-seek, a dog to be his son's best friend, and flowers for his beloved Bonnie.

Before long, they found something perfect for their family. If everything went as planned, they would move in shortly after Christmas. He and Bonnie would miss Johnny terribly. He had become another father figure for Jacob and a surrogate grandfather for William. However, the idea of a home of their own lured them like a siren's song.

Jacob let out a sigh halfway between contentment and exasperation. Except for the tension between his mother and his wife, he couldn't imagine life being any better. He still held out hope that his mother would come around, but she sure was taking her time. Even a baby hadn't softened his mother's stance, and although Jacob took William by to visit his mother regularly, the chasm between the women remained impenetrable.

Shaking off the exasperation, he headed down the stairs to do a little extra work for Johnny. It was Sunday, but Johnny had a few small projects in the showroom that needed attention, and Jacob had the time to help. When he arrived, Johnny was already working and whistling along with Metropolitan Opera Auditions of the Air. Jacob didn't much care for opera, much preferring the orchestra's big band sounds, but Johnny listened to this broadcast weekly as an avid fan.

At 5:14 pm, a news bulletin interrupted the show – a news bulletin that would change the course of Jacob's life forever. Japan had bombed Pearl Harbor, a US base in the Hawaiian Islands, and declared war on the United States and Great Britain. It was December 7th, 1941.

The workroom, where Jacob had been repairing a broken leg of a small table, became deathly still. Jacob slowly sank to the ground, a roaring sound, that of blood rushing through his veins, filled his ears. A war. The country he loved was at war.

The war brewing in Europe was not news. Those issues had been ongoing for years. However, he had maintained a strong conviction that the United States would not become involved in another war. The World War over two decades before had been too devastating. American politicians did not seem inclined to put the country at risk again, and Jacob agreed wholeheartedly.

Except, now Japan had bombed his country and declared war. Every conviction he held the moment before the announcement, those of neutrality and isolationism, were no longer valid.

Jacob stood and glanced at Johnny, who no longer focused on his work. "Go," he said. "Go to your wife and son." Jacob turned and raced up the stairs. He wanted to hold his family close and protect them. From what, he was not yet sure.

When he pushed open the door, he found Bonnie sitting on the floor with her hair down around her shoulders, playing with little cars with William. They both looked up happily as he entered the room, and William crawled to his father for his "I'm back from work" kiss. Jacob dutifully kissed his son as he sought out Bonnie's eyes.

His fear must have been evident, because she stood slowly, smoothed down her skirt, and said, "What is it, Jacob? You look like you've seen a ghost. Is it your mother? Is everything okay?"

"Bonnie...we...the United States...Japan..." He couldn't say it. He caught her eyes again.

"What, Jacob? The United States and Japan, what? I don't know what you are talking about."

Wordlessly, turned on the radio in time for Bonnie to hear the repeated news that Japan had declared war. Somehow, the proclamation within the walls of his cozy home, a home filled with love and laughter, made it more real and more terrifying. He scooped William up off the floor, moved quickly to Bonnie's side, and held his family close.

That evening, Jacob and Bonnie kept the radio on continuously, hoping to glean a little more news, or an explanation that would stop their world from rocking so violently from mundane to surreal. One minute, soft music emanated from the brown box. The next, breaking news filled the air. Then, with little fanfare, the scheduled programming would resume again, leaving the listeners wondering if they actually heard it right. Before going to bed, both Canada and the Netherlands declared war against Japan. And President Roosevelt announced he would address a joint session of Congress the following day.

As Monday dawned, Jacob was thankful his shift at

Flory's didn't start until noon. His sleep came in small bursts, interrupted by racing thoughts of what he could do...what he should do. War meant soldiers, and he was the right age to be a soldier. He loved this country and felt drawn to defend it. On the other hand, he had a wife and child he loved even more strongly. "Certainly," he thought, "I should be here with them." Then, he would counter his argument with, "What good would it do to love Bonnie and William if the Japanese take over the United States?" This reasoning led him directly back to being a soldier, an endless loop.

He noted his son playing on the kitchen floor at Bonnie's feet, unbothered by the bombing the night before. For William, today was the same as yesterday. He slept in his bed. He ate food provided by his loving mother. He woke to the sound of his parent's voices. He played in the kitchen while his mother went about her morning chores. For him, at this moment, the Japanese bombing of Pearl Harbor changed nothing.

Then Jacob studied Bonnie. The difference for her was striking. Despite having a child playing on the floor at her feet like every morning for the past nine months, and despite going about her morning routine, her world had changed. She looked haggard from lack of sleep and her eyes, bright with unshed tears, kept darting nervously from his face to the radio. He had said nothing about signing up for the war, but Bonnie intuitively surmised what he was considering.

Around 9 o'clock, a report from London interrupted *The Breakfast Club*, letting the world know Britain declared war against Japan.

"To bring you up to date, if you've just now turned on

your radios, Great Britain is at war with Japan. Prime Minister Neville Chamberlain announced this fact in a broadcast at 6:15 New York Time. 6:15 Eastern Daylight Time. A brief broadcast of about five minutes duration which was carried over this CBS network."

Jacob looked at Bonnie with a dawning of understanding. It wouldn't be long before the United States made a decision, and they both agreed they knew what that decision would be. The only question remaining was what decision Jacob would make.

As Jacob got ready to go to work, a news flash substantially changed the casualty figures from the Pearl Harbor bombing. Now they estimated 1,500 dead, and a battleship destroyed. Then, despite so many dead and the declarations of war across the world, the soap opera, *Mary Marlin,* continued as if nothing had happened.

That was the hardest part for him to grasp as he laced up his boots. Here he was, going to deliver groceries, while his wife cooked, and his son played. The sun was still shining. Christmas was still coming. They still planned to buy a home. People were still shopping. But the world crashed down around them. He was having trouble reconciling all of it in his head. He contemplated staying home, but for what? To listen to soap operas while waiting for the news he knew would eventually come? That made no more sense than delivering groceries.

After a quick kiss to his son and wife, Jacob made his way to Flory's, where, of course, the radio was on and surrounded by employees and customers alike. Although the grocery store opened for business, very little shopping occurred. Instead, everyone waited with anxious fear for President Roosevelt's message. At 12:15, he began: "*Mr. Vice President, and Mr. Speaker, and Members of the Senate and House of Representatives...*

Yesterday, December 7, 1941 – a date which will live in infamy – the United States of America was suddenly and deliberately attacked by naval and air forces of the Empire of Japan."

He went on to say that US leaders spoke with the Japanese ambassador hours before the attack. Although this man had given no hint of what was to come, it was now obvious this attack had been deliberately planned. "*The attack yesterday on the Hawaiian Islands has caused severe damage to American naval and military forces. I regret to tell you that very many American lives have been lost. In addition, American ships have been reported torpedoed on the high seas between San Francisco and Honolulu.*"

He listed the number of other areas attacked by the Japanese on the same day as the attack on Pearl Harbor. Malaya. Hong Kong. Guam. The Philippine Islands. Then, into the night and this morning, they continued by bombing both Wake and Midway Islands.

Jacob's stomach lurched. Despite a weakness in his knees that made him want to sit down, a strong sensation welled up inside – a cross between patriotism and hatred. The Japanese were trying to destroy his country and many others as well. They intended to take over the world. The desire to be part of the forces that stopped this barrage overwhelmed him.

He stopped ruminating just in time to catch the last of the broadcast: "*No matter how long it may take us to overcome this premeditated invasion, the American people in their righteous might will win through to absolute victory. I believe that I interpret the will of the Congress and of the people when I assert that we will not only defend ourselves to the uttermost but will make it very certain that this form of treachery shall never again endanger us. Hostilities exist. There is no blinking at the fact that our people, our territory, and our interests are in grave danger. With confidence in our armed forces – with the unbounding determination of our people – we will gain the inevitable triumph – so help us God. I ask that the Congress declare that since the unprovoked and dastardly attack by Japan on Sunday, December 7, 1941, a state of war has existed between the United States and the Japanese Empire."*

It was time for Congress to debate the pros and cons of going to war. One hour after the President's announcement began, NBC broke the regularly scheduled program to cover the Senate and House votes on the war resolutions. America formally declared war.

Chapter 20

BONNIE: 1941

After Jacob left for work, Bonnie kept the radio playing. She didn't want to hear the terrible news that was sure to come. On the other hand, she couldn't tear herself away from it. She prayed mightily that the United States would remain neutral, but she knew in her heart they would go to war. They had been attacked. There was really no other course of action to take.

War. The desire to fight for the country he loved so completely glowed in Jacob's eyes. She loved this about him. Their first movie date with him humming a patriotic song. The way he would stare at any flag blowing in the breeze. His pride at being an American – born here in this country. He had a strong sense of duty and patriotism that would make anyone proud. But it also frightened her.

"What would I do as a single mother with a small child? How could I make ends meet? Who would be the man in William's life? Who would hold me in the night when I needed to feel safe and secure?" And of course, the unthinkable thought, "What if Jacob didn't come home? How could I learn to live without him, the man that holds my heart?" The idea that he might leave and never return took the air out of her lungs, forcing her to sit down. William, oblivious to his mother's musings, crawled over to her feet with a smile and a gurgle.

She began to cry softly, tears rolling down her face and falling onto her tiny son. Even if the worst didn't happen, and he was able to find his way home to her again, what would come of their dreams for a house? For more children? For a dog and a garden? She realized how petty it sounded to be worried about something as mundane as a dog, but she couldn't help but cry at the thought her simple dreams were disintegrating one news flash at a time. "I wonder if the Japanese considered me, and the many women like me, when they declared war? Had they considered the spoiled gardens, the tearing apart of families, the devastating loneliness?"

War. It was such an ugly word. Small but powerful. These three letters pitted nation against nation, men against men. But from her vantage point, war did something far worse. It trapped men between the love of their country and the love of their family, their wives, and their children. How was a good man, a man with strong values, supposed to choose between the freedom of his country and the love of his family, in particular, when it appeared one couldn't exist without the other?

She thought about Jacob and the decision that would

certainly come to their door as she put William down for his afternoon nap. The thoughts continued as Roosevelt made his fiery speech. *"...with the unbounding determination of our people – we will gain the inevitable triumph – so help us God."* Roosevelt, like many in the country, wanted war.

"No," she thought vehemently, "they didn't want it. They would have happily stayed out of the fray. No, Roosevelt and the others pushed for war because there seemed to be no other way. We had been attacked. Japan had made the first bold, audacious move. The United States would have to make them pay or be subject to their rule."

She couldn't fault Roosevelt. Nonetheless, his proclamation to the Congress added more tears to her day and, she assumed, to the day of women across the country. Mothers for their sons. Wives for their husbands. Girlfriends for their lovers. Sisters for their brothers. Daughters for their fathers. The tears of women mourning what they understood about war – that it would tear apart their lives in a way that would likely never be repaired.

After the vote, only one lone woman said no to war, Jeannette Rankin. Bonnie didn't pay much attention to politics, but she had always admired Jeannette. To hold office as the first woman in the US House of Representatives was an amazing accomplishment. Although Bonnie had not been aware of her as a child, she had first been elected by the state of Montana prior to the First World War. She was one of 56 who refused to vote yes to send our nation to the Great War in 1917.

Wasn't it ironic that Jeannette had been elected to office again on the eve of another war? So, when the vote came back, it did not surprise Bonnie this woman remained true to her convictions and refused to vote for war. What did surprise her was not one other person stood with her.

According to one report, Representative Everett Dirksen begged her to change her vote so the resolution would be unanimous. Jeannette refused. He then asked her to abstain from the vote, but she refused again. Eventually, Jeannette's full answer came out, *"As a woman, I can't go to war, and I refuse to send anyone else."*

Bonnie wondered what she would have done in that situation. Would she have said no to war, thinking about all the men who would be thrust into violence and death, away from their families. Or would she have gone with the others understanding that without declaring war, our entire way of life would be jeopardized? She shook her head. No, she was glad she didn't have to make that decision, and despite the disparaging remarks of her peers, she had to think Jeannette was courageous for standing up for her beliefs despite the great opposition.

She turned her thoughts back to Jacob. How torn he must be as he faced the same dilemma. What would he do? What did she want him to do?

She looked in on William, sleeping soundly in the tiny bed, dreaming the innocent dreams of a small child. As she did so, she thought about Jacob at that age, growing up with no father, having no man in his life to provide love and support. She determined, in that moment, what Jacob's answer must be.

"I will ask him not to go," she concluded. "The US government won't ask him to go because he is married with a child. Plus, there are things he can do here at home to support the war. Our son doesn't need to grow up without a father, and I'll make him understand that. I have to make him understand that." She refused to acknowledge that by staying, she also benefited. She was not a selfish woman. No, this was about William.

With that settled in her mind, she went to work in the kitchen to fix a delightful evening meal. She wanted to have everything in order as she worked her magic and kept her husband home.

Chapter 21

JACOB: December 1941

The next few hours went by in a foggy haze that permeated Jacob's mind and heart and billowed out to everything he saw or touched. He filled boxes and ran deliveries as though it were an ordinary Monday, despite the fact the war, which was once a lurking shadow, had become a looming monster. But to say his mind was not on his work was an understatement.

He had just turned 21. On the one hand, he was the perfect age for soldiering. On the other, he had a beautiful wife and son. On the other, the country he loved was at war. On the other, he didn't want his son growing up without a father. On the other, Japan had made the first move and must be stopped. On the other, why should it be a father of a small son who did the stopping? On the other...He had no idea what he should do.

His own father did not join the last Great War despite being young and able. Instead, he stayed home with his wife and child. Jacob never thought to wonder why. Oh, how he wished his father were alive to ask him. "Why, Vater? What was the reasoning you used to stay home rather than fight? Was it the right decision?" If he were alive today, what would he advise?

Of course, this war, the one thrust upon Jacob's life, was already different. When his own father made the decision, no one had bombed a United States military base. No one had declared war on the US after a sneaky Sunday morning raid. But even with the differences, his father had been faced with a choice and could have left him and his mother to fight a war. He chose to stay.

Jacob longed to know why. He wanted so desperately to talk with him about his own feelings and how a tug of war raged in his heart and mind. He briefly considered telegramming his father-in-law, Carl, but calculated what he would hear in return. Carl would most certainly urge him to stay home, not because it was the right thing to do but because he would want his daughter to be happy. Jacob wouldn't blame him for that. He realized how protective he already felt about William. It would be difficult to advise someone to do something that had the potential to devastate his son.

Perhaps mother? But as quickly as the thought came into his mind, it left again. No, Elisabet would not hear of him going to war. She had lost her husband. She would not lose her son. She would never be able to think rationally about the issue. She couldn't accept his marriage and a move to the other side of town. She'd be more likely to tell him to leave his wife and child and move home than to suggest he consider becoming a soldier.

As he agonized over his decision, he realized there was only one person with whom he could talk. A man who had taken on a father role when he was a hungry teen with a hollow leg. He would go and speak with Axel Hersch. Although they didn't see each other very often now that Jacob was married and living in town, Axel had been the one person who helped him to understand what he needed to do to be a man. Axel would be impartial and listen to both sides. Jacob respected him and trusted him. He needed his wisdom today like he needed food back then. Yes, he would go speak to Axel.

Although he had only been at work for two hours, he asked his boss for the rest of the day. The store was slow except for those listening to the radio, and his boss absently waved him away. Jacob began walking the eight miles to the farm. He strode quickly along, a man with a purpose, and arrived at the farm barely an hour later.

He found Axel fixing the fencing in the back pasture. Axel looked up as he approached but didn't act the least bit surprised to see him. Jacob wondered how he knew.

Without saying a word, Jacob picked up the waiting tools and fell into rhythm with Axel, as if no time had separated the two men. For a full ten minutes, neither spoke, both working in comfortable silence, focusing on the job. It felt good to be working with his hands again, and Jacob realized he missed working side by side with Axel more than he had let himself believe.

Eventually, Axel cleared his throat, a sure sign he was going to speak. That was something Jacob observed about Axel soon after arriving on the farm. He always cleared his throat before speaking, as if he stayed silent so long his throat became a nesting ground for small bugs and animals that needed to leave for the words to come forth. "Jacob, I'm more than happy for the help and the company, but I suspect something more than an itch to fix a fence has brought you out this way." Then he waited.

This was something else about Axel. He waited. He was a patient man who didn't waste his words. He understood when to talk and when to listen. Now was a time for listening, so he waited.

Jacob didn't know where to begin. He opened his mouth to speak, then closed it again. After a few more unsuccessful tries, he hung his head and let the tears that had been pressing against his eyes all day slide slowly down his cheeks.

Axel wasn't a man of grandiose emotions. Jacob couldn't remember seeing him cry, and only recalled a few bursts of laughter in all those years. Nonetheless, Axel was a compassionate man, and Jacob's distress moved him. He pulled Jacob to his shoulder, gave him a slap or two on the back, and then straightened up again. He turned back to his fencing and began to talk, issuing more words than Jacob had ever heard come out of Axel's mouth at any one time.

"I was too old to go to war back in 1917. Already had five kids and the farm. My daddy didn't have no war to consider, though his daddy did. War between the states, that one. He fought for the Union 'course, like most everybody in the area. Granddaddy talked about the war some, but not much. Says it changed 'im. Saw things no man should have to see.

"I 'spect my daddy was glad he didn't have to go to no

war. Easier to not have to make the choice, don't ya reckon. And me, well, the choice was done made by the timing of the thing. Oh, sure, in my granddaddy's war they took 'em 'til they was old, but not during the Great War. They wanted ya young and preferred ya to be single.

"Sincin' I was neither, I didn't have to make no choice. Figure it was a good thing, too. War changes people, least says my granddaddy."

Then he stopped talking and went on fixing the fence, almost as if his words had been an aberration.

Finally, all the thoughts and feelings that wouldn't come before began flowing out of Jacob's mouth like a river that had been undammed upstream. He talked about his daddy and how difficult it had been to grow up without a father. He talked about how his own father was young enough but hadn't joined up in the war because of his family. Jacob also talked a lot about after the war. All the anti-German sentiment. How it was no better now. How with the US going to war, certainly we would take on Hitler, too. "I don't want to be seen as a German sympathizer, Axel. I mean, you know I'm not, and I know I'm not, but what will others think?"

Axel said nothing. Jacob stopped talking and began working again. The words that were no longer coming out of his mouth swirled around in his head. He wanted to fight the Japs if he fought. No need getting mixed up with the whole German thing. He was German, and he was American. He didn't quite know how to reconcile that. Lots of people in Canton now hated the Germans. They hated him despite him having never laid a foot on German soil.

Even more difficult was that sometimes he hated the Germans, too. But he was German and proud of his heritage, so that got all tangled up inside. He mostly didn't think about it. He changed his name at 18 to be more American, but that didn't mean he didn't love his roots. He did. He hoped to instill in William all that he was – American and German. But this war might change everything.

No, if he fought, he wanted to fight the Japs. They were an enemy he could get behind with no quandary at all. They had attacked our soil and now they should pay. He said as much to Axel. Axel merely grunted, then quietly said, "Is it you that has to get it done?" Jacob said nothing in return. He had considered the same thing himself.

That is where Axel stood. The war needed to be fought, but it should be fought by someone else, someone young and single. Someone who, when they came back changed, wouldn't be forcing that change onto a wife and child. Someone who wasn't Jacob.

It was with these thoughts that Jacob perceived what he had to do. He was cognizant that no answer would fully satisfy him, but he resigned himself to the idea that he needed to be a husband and father first and an American second. Jacob finished a last swing with the hammer, thanked Axel for the chat, and walked back to his apartment and his family.

It was late by the time he got home. The day had worn Jacob out, and the walk back to town took him hours as he slowly put one dusty shoe in front of the other. By the time he opened his front door, Bonnie's face was puffy, and her eyes were bloodshot. William was already in bed. The table had been set for dinner, but the food had grown cold and unappetizing.

She secretly suspected he signed up with a recruiter before she had a chance to convince him to do otherwise. Men began queuing up in lines city blocks long within minutes of the announcement. When he didn't come home from work, she imagined the worst.

Jacob held out his arms to Bonnie as moved toward her, held her close, and nuzzled his lips in her hair. Axel was right, and Jacob's decision was right. He couldn't come back changed. Bonnie and William needed him more than the country did. He pulled her away from him, looked her in the eyes, and solemnly promised, "I will not sign up for the war. I'm not going to be a soldier."

She crumpled in his arms and cried until there were simply no more tears to cry. Jacob chose her and their son. Both relief and guilt flooded her senses, but the relief won out in the end.

Chapter 22

WILLIAM: November 2016

After leaving the cemetery, William pondered what to do next. He could go home and work on his cars, spending hours taking apart a manifold or reupholstering a trunk. Most people didn't understand his fascination. However, he had loved cars from the time he was a small boy, exactly like his Grandpa Carl.

As a child, he would design futuristic cars with fins and angles unfamiliar to the bulky, wide rounded shapes that would go by on the street. He remembered the day a car with a fin, similar to what he envisioned, sped by on the street. He was often amazed when a new model would come out with some of the features he enthusiastically drew many years before.

But today didn't feel like a car day. His father never

cared much for cars beyond their utility. He enjoyed having a decent one to drive around town but spent little time doing much more than keeping it clean. If something were amiss, he called the mechanic. If it had been a fishing pole, he would have taken care of it himself, but cars...no, it was not his thing. Since this was his dad's day, William considered other options.

Thinking of fishing gave him a thought. He could call his son and ask if they might go fishing. He was certain that would make his father smile no matter where he was now. William wasn't quite sure what he believed about the afterlife, but believed his dad participated in this world in some manner. He often felt his father's presence but didn't discuss that with others for fear of sounding crazy.

Despite how much his father loved fishing, it was not something William enjoyed, and fishing in the cold was too much to consider. He shook his head slightly at the thought.

It was then he thought of the art gallery. Smudge was a small studio and gallery off Pennsylvania Avenue. His dad loved this place and spent hours talking with the owner and the patrons. Over time, Jacob had been asked to set up a little space. The owner enjoyed having live artists work to entice those walking by on foot to come into the shop. Jacob spent many happy hours there painting beautiful oil canvases. Before long, he became a household word among the locals and a legend among the tourists.

When Bonnie died, Jacob quit going to the studio. He quit doing much of anything he once enjoyed. When she died, his life crashed to a stop. Eventually, his friends and his son encouraged him to go back and dabble with his brushes. In those final years, the gallery was one of the few places that brought Jacob joy.

As William pushed open the door, the familiar tinkle of bells tied to the handle rang out their greeting. Joseph, the owner, looked up and immediately stood with a wide grin consuming his face. He was a broad, burly man and resembled a lumberjack more than an artist with his beefy hands and ruddy complexion. "William! It has been ages since I saw you last. How have you been? What have you been up to?"

William smiled in return and gave Joseph a few details about the past months. Yes, he was still working on the old cars. Yes, he had seen his children recently. Yes, all the grandchildren were doing well.

As William spoke, he looked around, happy to note that a few of his father's paintings still hung in the gallery. Joseph saw his satisfaction, stating, "That one there, of the Native American princess on slate? I won't sell it. I have had several offers, but it reminds me too much of your dad and the good times we had here in the shop. I'll keep it here for now, but when I retire, I want to be sure it goes back to you and your family."

Without warning, a lump rose in William's throat. He didn't want Joseph to see his tears, so he turned to look at the princess. It was one of dad's best because he modeled it after his one true love – his dearly departed wife. No, Bonnie did not claim a Native American heritage, and she didn't have dark hair, but anyone who had known her in real life would realize the delicately painted features were entirely hers. In fact, as William gazed at the painting, his mother's gaze caught his eye as though she were not gone but merely an arm's length away. His father had done a spectacular job capturing her countenance. William figured it must be easy to do when you loved someone as long as Jacob had loved his Bonnie.

William was glad Joseph would not sell this painting. He was also very pleased that, one day, one of his children would have the painting patterned so patiently after their grandmother. When the lump finally disappeared, allowing William to trust his voice once more, he turned back to Joseph and continued chatting about the family, the weather, the coming election, and the shop.

He absently picked up a paint brush left out by another of Joseph's "live artists" and began dabbling at a blank canvas. Although not as accomplished as his father, he, too, loved to paint with oils. He had several paintings in his home and a few that he'd given as gifts over the years. He often wondered if he had spent more time painting rather than tinkering with cars if he could have been an artist.

Joseph perked up at the site of William dabbling in the paints, and, as he had done many times before, suggested he take up the spot his father had occupied before his death. "Everyone loved your father, William, and they would love you, too." William smiled and put down the paintbrush. "Thank you, but no. I'm not the artist, nor as personable as my father." He laughed wryly. "But thank you, again, for all you did for him. I owe you a lot."

With that, William intended to head back to his truck and back home, having done what he could to honor his father. But before he took more than a half-dozen steps, his gaze rested on a painting he had never seen before, though he felt certain it was one of his father's. The angle of the strokes, the use of color, and the intensity of the eyes all screamed Jacob Miller.

The painting was of a young boy, someone terribly familiar, like an unknown word on the tip of the tongue. In fact, the face drew him closer and closer until he almost touched the canvas. There in the corner sat his father's tiny signature. He stared once again until he comprehended why the face looked so familiar. He, William, was the subject of the painting.

The painted child couldn't have been more than four, the same age as William when his father went to the war. With shocking clarity, he realized his father remembered him this way throughout the two years he was gone. Those incredibly lonely, difficult two years when William's grandmother raised him while his mother took on a job to keep food on the table.

He couldn't tear his eyes away from the child's eyes. What did he see? Fear? Sadness? Longing? Hope?

Quietly, William turned to face Joseph again. "When? When did he paint this?"

Joseph said, "Shortly after your mother died. It was the first time he came back to the studio. He picked up his brush without saying a word and began to paint. The eyes of the child held all the emotions he held in his heart. It was like therapy for him."

William only nodded because the lump had formed again in his throat. As he continued to stare at the painting, he realized he received a gift – a glimpse of the past in a way words would never portray. He came to understand that Bonnie's death hit his father in the same way going to war and leaving his son hit him so many years before.

For Jacob, Bonnie's death had been like going to war all over again.

Chapter 23

BONNIE: 1943

Jacob never talked much about his decision to stay home from the war. "I went out to visit Axel, and he helped me figure it out," was about all he said, and Bonnie did not push to know more. Once the decision had been made, she let the issue drop. Why remind him of a difficult choice?

The flurry of enlistments opened up jobs all over North Canton, so right after the holidays, and as they prepared to move into their new home, Jacob began working in the lumberyard. The work was harder, and the hours were longer, but the wages were better. Jacob came home from work tired, but happy. "I missed the work on the farm more than I thought," he once said. "It feels good to be using my hands again."

Their home was a little pink house on Cypress Street. When Bonnie first toured the house, she clasped her hands to her chest like a small child on Christmas morning. "Oh, Jacob! Look at this color. Pink is the perfect color for a home." She wasn't sure what made pink perfect except that perhaps it reminded her of her childhood bedroom and all the wonderful memories. Jacob, being far more practical, focused on more substantial issues.

He studied the construction of the home, crawled around the foundation, and determined if it would be possible to add a room if needed in the future. Though the color pink had nothing to do with his decision, he too, became enamored with the house saying, "It has good bones."

Not quite sure what bones had to do with houses, Bonnie simply agreed. She wanted to live here because she envisioned her family happy and thriving in this little spot. She also had extensive plans for turning the house into a home. If Jacob needed bones, then he could have them, as long as she got her house.

For William's birthday, they brought home a dog, making their dream complete. For reasons only a child understood, William immediately began calling the dog Vonk. Bonnie reasoned Vonk was a childish attempt at the word dog. Regardless of the why, the yellow-coated mutt determined immediately that little William was his master and rarely left his side.

The first order of business was to build a doghouse for Vonk. Though loved by everyone, including Bonnie, Vonk would be an outdoor dog. "I am happy to live somewhere that William can have a pet. But animals and people do not live in the same quarters. Period." This was an argument she prepared to stand firm on but found no need to do so. Jacob didn't have strong opinions on the matter and capitulated without any contention.

Though not far away, the move meant they didn't see as much of Johnny as they did when living across the hall. When they moved, Johnny agreed it would no longer be practical for Bonnie to clean the store each evening. However, he still wanted her as his designer, and she was happy to oblige. With a new home, her furniture wish list nearly tripled in length.

Jacob saw less of Johnny, too. His hours at the lumberyard were long, often lasting well past nightfall. When he had free time, he spent it with his family and doing little projects around the house. However, occasionally, when Johnny needed a bit of extra help, Jacob leant a hand. They both understood this man who had become like family was instrumental in pushing them toward their dream.

Life flowed this way from day to day for several months. Bonnie cooked, cleaned, and cared for William. She made sure supper was on the table when Jacob arrived home after his shift. In the evenings, they played with William, put him to bed, and spent some time together discussing the day. Bonnie, for the most part, was content. She did wish she would conceive again, but for some reason, no babies came.

It wasn't that they weren't trying. Jacob remained quite enamored with Bonnie's body, as evidenced by their frequent lovemaking. She still marveled that other women called sex a chore when she found it so appealing. But despite their many encounters, Bonnie's womb remained barren.

"Don't worry, Bonnie. We will have more children. You got pregnant with William so quickly and easily. It is bound to happen sooner or later." Then, with a sly grin, he would add, "I don't mind practicing until then." This would set her to giggling, and often to the bedroom, but a nagging fear still roamed around Bonnie's mind that William might be their only child.

The only other dent in an otherwise blissful life was her mother-in-law. Despite being married now for over four years and producing a grandchild whom Elisabet adored, she still insisted Bonnie call her Mrs. Mueller. Bonnie tried to be kind and patient – at first. However, Elisabet's attitude tainted Bonnie's until neither was willing to budge.

Everything Elisabet didn't like about her son's current life was Bonnie's fault. For instance, when Jacob took the job at the lumberyard, Elisabet threw a fit. "My dear Hyrum was killed at the lumberyard. That very same lumberyard," she would say as crocodile tears filled her eyes. "My Jacob would have never taken a job there knowing how difficult it would be for me to remember that horrible, horrible time." Then she turned to Bonnie and said, "You must have convinced him to take this job. It's the only explanation for my dear, precious boy to make such a horrible decision." However, the culminating experience happened not long after moving into the pink house, almost two years earlier.

Despite Bonnie's misgivings, the pair invited Elisabet to their new home for a visit. At that time, Bonnie still hoped to find a way to ingratiate herself with Elisabet. Plus, she loved her husband, and this was his mother.

As they had done since marrying, they hid their

liquor from sight before her visit. From the moment of Hyrum's death, she became a vocal teetotaler. "Hyrum and I caused his death. If we had not been so overcome with pride and levity over his promotion, he would still be here. The accident was God's way of dealing with us."

No spirits of any kind ever crossed Elisabet's threshold. In fact, she hated alcohol so much that she wouldn't allow glass containers in her home if they resembled those that held alcoholic beverages. During his entire childhood, Jacob didn't know other people's ketchup came in bottles because his mother emptied theirs into saucers, throwing the bottle away in the trash.

Until he met Bonnie, Jacob had never tasted alcohol. Bonnie, though not one to become inebriated, enjoyed a dry Manhattan and loved the taste of fine wine. Once they married, they always stored a few basics for cocktails and guests – whiskey, gin, vermouth, and wine. Despite being a grown man, Jacob didn't want to cause more problems with his mother, so they hid their bottles to keep the peace. "She wouldn't understand, Bonnie," Jacob said in a pleading tone. Bonnie agreed it was a small price to pay for a bit of peace.

Elisabet came to their home for dinner a few short weeks after they moved in. She seemed more relaxed than usual, even offering a few compliments, though they were directed at her son. "I'm so proud of you, Jacob. This is a fine house. Very fine." By the time supper was over, Elisabet had managed a quick smile in Bonnie's direction.

Bonnie took the dishes to the kitchen after supper, feeling better about her mother-in-law. "She is beginning to realize that Jacob and I make a good team. I need to be patient, that's all." But when she walked back into the living room, she realized she had been wrong.

When Jacob left the room to change William's diaper, Elisabet took the opportunity to look around. She ran her hand along furniture, pulled back the curtains, and stooped to open cupboards and drawers. She discovered their small cache of alcohol behind the door of a small cabinet in their living room as both she and Jacob reentered the room.

Elisabet, with a red, pinched face, turned viciously on Bonnie. "You are exactly what I have always known. Not only are you a whore who stole my son out from under my nose, you are also a two-penny drunk, doing everything in your power to make my son a miserable failure. No matter what you do, you will always be nothing more than a whoring drunk to me. You will never be my daughter."

With that, she walked out the door, demanding Jacob take her home.

Jacob's mouth hung open and chills ran the length of his arms. How could his mother say such things to his wife? But he had no choice. He drove her home. Once the shock wore off, Bonnie was not aghast but furious. When Jacob got home, shoulders hung in defeat, she blurted, "I have had more than enough of that woman. She may be William's grandmother, but she will never be my family. That woman who calls herself your mother is no longer welcome in my home until she apologizes to me. And Jacob, if I die before you, don't you consider burying me next to that harpy. I don't want to spend eternity in her company." Then she turned on her heel and went to bed.

Chapter 24

JACOB: December 1943

Although Jacob agreed to stay home from the war, he had not agreed to ignore it was happening. He followed the news very closely, but rarely spoke of it to Bonnie. Whenever he mentioned the war, her eyes would cloud over with worry, and she became sad and clingy. Sometimes, several days would pass before she was happy and carefree again. So, he handled her much like he handled his mother, letting his beloved wife bury her head in the sand firm in the belief the war couldn't touch her or her loved ones.

As a rule, he focused his interest on the Pacific front. The war with the Japanese was easier for him to understand than the war with Germany. Many Americans recognized no separation between being a Nazi and being a German. As a first generation American, he had seen the results. Many in the community avoided meeting his gaze, and he'd even had someone spit in his general direction. He became aware of a petition going around North Canton for anyone of German descent, no matter how many generations past, to be put on a Nazi watch list.

Although anti-German incidents were becoming more frequent, he kept them from Bonnie. Sitting at home in their little pink house, she didn't witness what he witnessed. She didn't have to stand by helplessly as German-born Americans were interviewed or had their movements monitored. She didn't have to worry about the number of Germans, even American-born Germans, being rounded up and sent to internment camps.

Although he comprehended that his neighbors were afraid, he couldn't comprehend the actions that accompanied the fear. His friends and neighbors had done nothing wrong – they simply had a German heritage. The logic that anyone of German descent would still be loyal to Germany was decidedly flawed. Most of the German community in North Canton knew no one in Germany and hated the atrocities committed by Hitler and his party. But these vigilantes were not looking for truth. They simply wanted to assuage their fears, so they pointed at men like Jacob, proud Americans, homeowners, husbands, and fathers, and determined they were Nazi-sympathizers.

Bonnie was not completely blind to the difficulties of some German Americans. However, she didn't understand the extent of the trouble. She assumed those experiencing trouble were likely bringing it on themselves. He was partly to blame for her myopic views. He kept things from her, so she wouldn't worry. However, she was partly to blame, too. She chose not to see.

He had no idea how someone like himself was supposed to prove he was not a spy and prove his loyalty to the United States government. Stating the truth was not enough because spies and loyalists would certainly lie. The surest way was to become a soldier in the US Army, but that option was out of the question for him. On most days, he was grateful that Axel helped him understand his duty as a husband and father. Occasionally, he wished he received a different answer.

Because he couldn't express his concerns at home, he began chatting with a buddy from work, Hanz Schaeffer. They often found themselves paired together, and before long, they were inseparable friends. Many early evenings found them having 'just one' ale at the local pub before heading home, during which time they would discuss the latest war news.

The two young men had similar views about the war and about the anti-German sentiment. "How can we help the community realize that simply being German is not something to fear?" Hanz would muse in his thick accent. Hanz was "more German" than Jacob. Not only was his name still very Germanized, but he came to America as a teenager during the Great Depression, about the same time Jacob began working for Axel. Because of this, he still had active connections with relatives in Germany, bringing letters from 'home' in his pocket to read out loud during their lunch break. Jacob surmised that he must have living relatives in Massenbach, his father's hometown. They never corresponded and wouldn't know them if they showed up at his door.

Nearly two years after Jacob began working at the lumberyard, he and Hanz went on a delivery together. They parked the truck along a side street to deliver a sizable load to the back of a city lot. They returned to the truck to find a brochure under the windshield. Amerikadeutscher Volksbund. The German American pro-Nazi organization. Both men looked quickly around. "Who left this here? Do you think someone is trying to trap us?" Jacob whispered. Hanz quickly folded up the paper and stuffed it into his pants pocket.

Neither man talked about what they found. The Amerikadeutscher Volksbund was well known and widely hated among those in North Canton. German Americans feared its presence because the organization tried to create a favorable impression of Nazi Germany. Non-German Americans feared its presence because it proved the Germans in their backyard were dangerous and a threat to their way of life. Although the Amerikadeutscher Volksbund was no longer allowed in the US after a declaration by the House Committee on Un-American Activities, it lived on in secret meetings.

For several days after the discovery, both Hanz and Jacob paid close attention to their surroundings. They stiffened whenever someone approached, relaxing again when that someone passed them by. However, after a time, when neither man heard anything more, and no one contacted them, they began to relax. Perhaps it had been someone's idea of a sick joke. Since neither man expressed interest in the Bund, there was nothing to fear, right? So, they went on living their lives, going to work, enjoying their friendship, and stopping by the local pub after work.

As Thanksgiving approached, the news from the Battle of Tarawa was grim. Prior to the war, few in the US would have known the location of Tarawa Atoll. However, after the battle that killed 6,400 Japanese, Koreans, and Americans, everyone following the news from the Pacific Theater knew the atoll made up part of the Gilbert Islands southwest of Hawaii.

Jacob listened carefully to the news, learning that, for the first time, the US faced Japanese opposition as they tried to land their units. Well-armed Japanese soldiers refused to let the island fall to the Americans. In three days, the US suffered more casualties than they had for the entire campaign.

Americans were horrified that so many Americans died trying to take a tiny island. He spoke to Hanz about it at work. "I wonder why we are fighting so hard for that island. It doesn't make logistical sense to me." Hanz agreed. "Apparently, some general said we were going to have to become accustomed to high casualties if we want to win the war. I can't imagine too many people want news like that as we reach the two-year mark on the war."

It was this battle and the discussion he had with Hanz that began to turn Jacob's thoughts once again to being a soldier. With so many men dying and more men to come, he could be of value. He wanted to fight for the freedom of his nation. Despite Axel's warning that everything would change, and Bonnie's strong desire to stay with her and their precious son, he was having a harder and harder time remaining satisfied with his decision to stay out of the fray.

"I'll broach the subject with Hanz," he decided.

"Maybe saying what I'm feeling out loud will help me untangle all these thoughts and emotions." However, when he arrived at work the following day, Hanz was no longer employed. Someone came for him in the night and took him to an internment camp after finding an Amerikadeutscher Volksbund pamphlet in his possession while ransacking his home.

Jacob gulped, knowing where the pamphlet came from. Why hadn't Hanz thrown it away? Surely, he knew the danger of having such a thing in his possession. Hanz had been followed, interviewed, and harassed ever since Jacob first began working at the lumberyard. He had to register as an "alien enemy," because of his adult male born outside the US status. Certainly, Hanz understood the risks.

Although Jacob was furious and believed Hanz was not an enemy, he said nothing. Any defense of Hanz would make him guilty by association.

Anxiety, however, overshadowed his anger. They could come for him next. No, he had never been to Germany. No, he had no known living relatives in Germany. No, they didn't speak German in their home. No, he had never attended a Nazi meeting. However, he and Hanz worked together and socialized together. It was not uncommon to find them at the local bar, and Hanz had been to their home for dinner. Without realizing the implications, Jacob brought danger to his door, while Bonnie remained blissfully unaware.

Jacob began looking over his shoulder as he walked to and from work, believing someone was following him. He was certain they, whoever they were, were coming to snatch him. With the war heating up and the safety of his family at stake, his earlier decision and promise were moot. He no longer had the luxury of neutrality.

Three days after Christmas, Jacob sat down with Bonnie. He was joining the Army.

Chapter 25

JACOB: April 1944

As he said the words to his beloved Bonnie, she sat silent and unmoving. She looked at him blankly, as if the words he spoke had no meaning or were in a foreign language. When seconds ticked by with no response, Jacob repeated himself. "Bonnie, I am going to the recruiting station at the first of the year, right after the end of the holidays. I am going to sign up to go to war. The Army needs me. I can't sit on the sidelines any longer. I need to prove I'm a real man – strong and capable. My country needs me. Our country needs me."

He didn't tell her about Hanz. Or his fears that men were following him. He didn't want to frighten her. He wanted her to be safe, and she was safer if she knew nothing.

When Bonnie finally found her voice, she tried using sugar and honey. "Jacob, darling...I understand. Of course, I do," she crooned. "You want to stand up for this great nation. I love that you are so patriotic. I still remember you singing all the words to 'My Country 'Tis of Thee' on our first date."

She looked up at him, hoping to get a smile or a nod or some sort of confirmation that her words made sense to him. When he said nothing, she pushed on. "But Jacob, you have me and William. He needs you to be here. Let's find a way for you to be more involved in the Civil Defense. Maybe you could be a spotter or work..."

Before she went any further, Jacob interrupted with more force than he intended. "NO. Bonnie, no. I can't stay here while I know what is happening out there. I listen to the radio. I read the reports. I know where I should be and why I should be there. I simply can't stay here any longer." He pleaded with his eyes for her to understand, but she couldn't. His words shattered the illusion of tranquility she had been so carefully creating.

Bonnie's voice rose, too. Gone was the honey as she rapidly spouted reason after reason for him to stay. "Do you want William to grow up without a father the way you did? Is that what you want for your child? Is that how you show love?" Although Jacob flinched at the last sentence, his actions came from a place of love. He remained immovable.

When that didn't work, she forgot about her son and held herself out to Jacob. "And me? What of me? I'm the woman you say is the love of your life, but you are willing to cast me aside to prove you are a man? I already know it. Everyone already knows it." He wanted to sob and explain everything, but that would be dangerous. He was making the right choice. The wise choice. He simply turned his head away and said nothing.

Now Bonnie's anger melted away, replaced entirely by fear. She began to plead, "Jacob, you cannot leave us. What will I do without you? How will I live if you don't come home?" Despite talking long into the night, despite the rapid changes from anger to fear and back again, Jacob would not, could not listen. He had made up his mind.

The scene repeated night after night, each time ending with Jacob sitting stony-faced and Bonnie weeping. Although she never did understand, she finally gave in. She didn't agree with his decision, and his logic made no sense to her. That was not entirely her own fault. His unwillingness to share all the facts left her with only part of the story. Even he had to agree that needing to be a patriot and prove his manhood sounded weak when held up to his responsibilities as husband and father.

Despite this, she had grown weary of fighting. Weary of pleading. Weary of crying. He won, but at a great price.

When he told William he was going to war, his dear, sweet child of almost four years cried, leading William to cry as well. However, he assured himself that William didn't really understand – he simply reacted to the emotions in the room and the silent tears of his mother. Jacob couldn't have borne the anguish any other way. No, William would be fine.

As he regarded his son playing in the evenings leading up to his departure, he convinced himself that William was unaffected and understood nothing of what was going on. He told himself that William would barely know his daddy had gone. Though that thought haunted him, the thought allowed him to leave with a clearer conscience.

And Bonnie. Dear, sweet Bonnie. As soon as she gave in and begrudgingly accepted the fact that he was going no matter what she thought or said, she began to plan as though making the best plan in the world could somehow make everything right again.

Going to war meant a multitude of changes for his little family. One of the biggest, besides losing him to the Army, was moving. Bonnie and William would move to Connecticut to live with her parents. His father-in-law had a steady job there and could find work for Bonnie. He was beyond thankful to her parents for taking them in. He would worry less knowing she would be cared for by her father and that William would have a man in the house. His in-laws were kind and good hearted. They tried to understand the situation but were as perplexed as Bonnie. Nonetheless, they did what they could to help.

His mother, on the other hand, persisted in being as unhelpful as she had been since the day he introduced her to Bonnie. Rather than becoming more agreeable with age, she continued to become more difficult with each passing year. He had gone to her home alone to tell her the news. He steeled himself for crying, assuming she would throw herself at him and beg him not to go. Which is why he was so surprised by her reaction. Elisabet was furious, and not with Jacob and his decision to join the fray, but with Bonnie.

"That...that...whore," she spat with a viciousness that pushed Jacob back on his heels. "How did she do it? Get pregnant. Marry you. Move you into some fancy house. Ply you with liquor. And then, when she grew tired of you, send you off to war, so she could trounce around with men too smart to take up arms? Was that her plan?"

If his mother's words hadn't been so venomous and said with such hatred, her reasoning would have been laughable. No woman, especially Bonnie who loved him so completely, would send their husband off to war to get a change of scenery. However, nothing he said convinced her it was not somehow Bonnie's fault. Couldn't she see that Bonnie and Elisabet were on the same side? That neither wanted him to go? Shouldn't his decision to defy them both bring them closer?

But no. His mother remained determined to make an enemy of his wife, and he left his childhood home more despondent than when he came. He would never tell Bonnie of the newest affront to her character. There was already enough between his wife and his mother to add more to a fire already raging beyond control.

Christmas came and went. Both he and Bonnie plastered fake smiles onto their faces while William opened a few toys, and they ate a wonderful meal together. The days following Christmas both dragged by as if bags of sand hung on the clock's hands and flew by in a whirl, hurtling Jacob closer and closer to abandoning his family for a cause he felt he must join. How time could be both fast and slow simultaneously continued to be an incomprehensible mystery.

The day before he left, he memorized Bonnie and William's every move. How Bonnie swayed when she walked from sink to stove. How she hummed a little tune without evening knowing she made a sound. How her mouth would turn up in a smile when William would say something to her about his cars or his dog or anything at all. How William zoomed around the kitchen on his knees, pushing his cars over and under and through anything in their way. How his smile, a bit crooked and dotted with a dimple in his right check, lit up his whole face, making his intense brown eyes dance.

These memories were the only things he could take with him when he left the following morning. They would be the images that kept him moving forward on the path he felt forced to take. Axel's words, that war changed men, kept running through his mind. He didn't want to come home changed. He wanted to come home and take up where he left off, as if the bloody war had not happened. As if being German in the United States was not a crime. As if he had never left home at all.

He wondered how old William would be when he got back. If he were lucky, the war would be over in a matter of months. It was April. He might be back for Christmas, not even missing a birthday. That thought gave him hope. He realized, deep in his heart, he was simply burying his head in the sand, but he couldn't face the idea that he might miss more than a few holidays or that he could easily never see his son again. Each time that thought pushed through his platitudes, he shoved it deep inside again, locking the box on those thoughts and refusing to give them any credence.

That night, Bonnie wanted to make love. Jacob feared she would finally become pregnant. He didn't want to add the burden of another child now. The nagging thought that he would die in war came raging out of the locked box to shout, "You could be the father of a child who you never meet. Your little baby would be nothing more than a war orphan." With excruciating effort, he shoved that thought down deep, but agreed it would be no good for her to have a baby while he fought in a war.

But Bonnie needed Jacob's hands running over her skin. She needed her body to meld into his and feel him move inside her one more time. She, too, battled the demons that he would never return. She wanted to abandon herself to his caresses one last time. Eventually, her desires beat out his fears. They made love and memories they hoped would last throughout the war.

When he awoke the next morning, groggily reaching out for Bonnie, she was already up and in the kitchen. He sniffed the air, recognizing her famous sweet bread baking in the oven. He shook the sleep out of his eyes and came to stand in the doorway as she cooked, gliding from counter to oven, smoothing rose-water scented hair, frowning at a recipe. She turned to see him standing there. Walking to him with quick steps, she gently held him in a way that held forgiveness. It was as though she wanted him to know she was trying to understand and that even though she couldn't, she was willing to forgive him, anyway.

The warmth of her body pressed up against his, the smell of her hair, the gentle rising and falling of her chest. It was a moment in time that seemed endless, and he wanted to hold her that way for the rest of his life, but that was not to be. Carl, Elaine, and Otto arrived, followed swiftly by his own mother. He was amazed she had the audacity to show her face but was proud of his wife for being a gracious host and helping her to the table.

The noise woke William who came bounding through the doorway straight into his Uncle Otto's waiting arms. While retrieving a piece of stick candy from his uncle's pocket, a treat his uncle always had waiting for him, William warily eyed the rest of the family. He became shy and unsure of himself, looking down at the floor with no trace of the smile that had been so ample as he entered the room.

This strange reaction confused Jacob. William loved his grandparents and Oma. Why would he look so frightened? It took a gentle push from his mother to encourage him to say good morning. After a few awkward moments, William became himself again, and Jacob relaxed. His son was fine, simply startled by the number of people in the kitchen so early in the morning. He repeated the mantra he said several times each day, "He will be fine. Yes, he will be just fine."

Bonnie created a wonderful breakfast of eggs, bacon, and the sweet bread that wafted through the bedroom as he woke. But when he tried to swallow his first bite of eggs, they stuck in his throat like a cork on a wine bottle. He nearly choked as he forcefully moved the eggs along with some juice. After that, he pushed his food around on his plate with his fork. He was happy to note both William and Bonnie were able to eat.

After breakfast, Jacob stood apart and watched his family, as though from a faraway dream. Otto leaned down and spoke to William, who nodded with solemn eyes. Whatever Otto said made an impression on his young son. Bonnie spoke softly to her parents, gesturing toward first Jacob and then William. His mother sat alone, saying nothing, and showing no expression.

Then everyone in the kitchen began bustling around, all talking at the same time. Jacob took the car keys from the counter, but Otto took them out of his hands and insisted he sit in the back with his wife and child while he played chauffeur. Carl and Elaine would ride up front and his mother would ride in the back.

Jacob looked blankly at his mother. He still couldn't figure out what she was doing here. She was not supportive of his decision, she had not supported him in any of his decisions over the last several years, and she certainly was not supportive of his family. She was an enigma.

He wanted to understand her and was glad she wanted to be here to see him off, but he wasn't going to let his mother to intrude on his last minutes with his family. So, when he got into the back of the vehicle, he purposely sat against the window, leaving only one side free, which Bonnie rightfully took while clutching his arm. William jumped into his lap, excited to see the trains. His mother, with a pitiful expression starred morosely out her own little window.

Before he got comfortable, the train station came into view. The platform was crowded with others like him, who had decided to join the Army. Several were familiar families, acquaintances over the years. Good German families. Some had been here for generations. Others had not. He understood why they were here. They understood back. It was like a secret they all shared without having to say a single word.

He wished his parting was more private. He had things he wanted to say to his family, but the combination of English, German, and sobbing made speaking difficult and listening nearly impossible. Nonetheless, it was time to say his final goodbyes. He squared his shoulders, drew in a deep shuddering breath, and turned to his mother.

Despite her behavior over the last several years, he loved her. He would not be the man he was without all she had done for him. However, when she began to wail, begging him to stay, and talking about the death of his father, he also realized she was no longer the woman of his childhood. She was no longer able to give him what he needed as a man leaving for war. He hugged her circumspectly and turned to Carl and Elaine.

"Please, keep Bonnie and William safe for me while I'm gone. Please do for them what I would do if I could be here." He hoped they came to understand that he had no other choice. Elaine gave him a hug and said she would take care of William, not to worry. Carl pounded him on the back, saying gruffly in his ear, "I'm proud to call you my son."

Next came Otto. They grasped each other by the shoulders, trying to act manly. However, the tears slid down their cheeks, making a mockery of their bravado.

Then Bonnie. Dear, sweet Bonnie. The woman who made him the man he was. The woman who was willing to believe in a German delivery boy. The woman who was willing to send him off to war and wait for his return. He gathered her into his arms and murmured words of love. "I love you, darling. I'll come home again. I promise. I promise with all my soul. I have to go. But I'll be home. I love you, my darling." He hung to her like a drowning man clinging to a life raft, but eventually disentangled her arms to kneel toward William.

His big, brave boy. Jacob was certain he had no idea what was going on. How could a four-year-old boy have any clue? Jacob scooped him up into his arms, letting his tears mix into the dark brown hair on his child's head. "I love you, William. I'll be home soon. Please take care of your mommy. I need you to be my big, brave solider."

Suddenly, the whistle blew, causing the last of the well-wishers to grab at their loved ones in hopes of one more goodbye, one more kiss, one more tender word. Jacob couldn't stand it a moment longer. On the verge of emotional collapse, he needed to be strong for all that awaited him. So, instead of grabbing for his family, he reached down and snatched up his duffle, slung it over his shoulder, and handed his ticket to the uniformed conductor.

As he pushed forward into the car, it gave a lurch, and a belch of smoke surrounded his family. He pressed his hand against the glass that separated him from everything he had ever loved. Bonnie held her hand up to match his, as if she could touch him despite the distance. The rest of the family began waving frantically. He stared at them until they were nothing but dots on the horizon. It was then that he finally realized he was really going to war.

Chapter 26

BONNIE: April 1944

Jacob's pronouncement that he was going to war stunned her. She worried about it in the early months following Pearl Harbor, but when he settled into his job at the lumberyard, and they began making a home of their little pink house, she detected no telltale signs of a man hankering for war. So, his declaration that he was signing up for the Army, a full two years after the US entry into the war, flummoxed her.

His insistence that he needed to prove his manhood was nonsensical, but no amount of pleading changed his mind. In fact, the more she talked, the more determined he became. He was going to leave her and his son to fight the Japanese.

When she finally came to that conclusion, she did

what she always did when life spun out of control – she began making plans. A solid plan and long lists took any mess and turned it into something manageable, though in this case, not completely tamed.

She loved her pink home at the start of a small dirt lane but realized immediately she wouldn't be able to stay. Not without Jacob.

Although Jacob's mother lived close by, the rift between them remained. Bonnie maintained that Elisabet was totally to blame. She had never apologized for her outburst at the house. She had stuck to her narrative that Bonnie trapped William and was a no-good woman out to harm her gullible son. Though Bonnie believed she was a forgiving woman, she firmly believed an apology was in order. Until that happened, a real mother-daughter relationship remained out of the question. So, turning to Elisabet while Jacob fought in the war wasn't a viable option.

In terms of work, she recognized her window designs at Livingston's would come to a halt without Jacob to do the heavy lifting. When she and Jacob worked together, the deal she had with Johnny made sense. With Jacob at war, there was no sense to anything. Plus, her little job would not pay the bills even if she managed to move the furniture alone. She was more than willing to find a job doing something else, but there would be no one to tend to William. She refused to put him into Elisabet's care and have the shrew turn her child against her.

No matter how she tried to rearrange her life, North Canton simply did not have the support she needed while her husband fought in the war. So, she did what any child would do and turned to her parents. After much back and forth and a surprise visit from her mother who always found traveling by train with all the dirt and noise quite dreadful, they devised a plan.

She would take William to Connecticut to live. She and her father would work, and her mother would stay home and take care of William. It seemed like the best possible plan, given the circumstances. Sure, Bonnie would miss their little house, but she would come back when Jacob came home from war. She always avoided the word "if."

That is why her parents came all the way from Connecticut on the day Jacob left for boot camp. After seeing him off at the train station, they would stay a few days to help her pack the things that would go with her and store the things that would stay. She would shut up her little pink home, the home she dreamed would be the start of great things. Then, her parents would drive their daughter and grandson to their new home.

Jacob worked at the lumberyard right up until the Friday before he left. As he left the lumberyard where he had worked the last two years, they told him he would have his job when he returned. No one at the lumberyard was willing to say "if," any more than Bonnie. But sometimes at night, when she was too tired to keep the scary thoughts stuffed at the bottom of her heart, the "ifs" came out. "If he came home alive. If he came home whole. If he came home still the Jacob she loved."

Bonnie tried to make the final full day a festive one, spending time talking with Jacob, making sure they ate together as a family for every meal. She made a special supper, his favorite, baked lemon chicken. It cost her more money than she was normally willing to spend on a meal to find a decent chicken, but she wanted to send Jacob off with a full stomach and good memories.

That night, after putting William to bed, she and Jacob made love. She wanted to leave him with a reason to come home again to her. Long after he began snoring, she lay watching him sleep, trying to memorize every inch of him.

Jacob, the grocery delivery boy. Jacob, her husband. Jacob, the soldier going off to war. Tears, her constant companion, lulled her to sleep.

The following morning rushed by, filled with chatter and food, everyone doing their best to pretend this day was a simple period at the end of a sentence rather than a question mark. No one said a word about war, but it sat in the room with them, nonetheless.

Soon, they piled into the car and before she could blink, the train station came into view. The spacious green building bustled with activity. Jacob was not the only soldier to head to basic training that morning. Bonnie was surprised at the number of men obviously heading to war. She would have thought, at this stage in the game, there would be few men left.

As she glanced around, she realized how many men were like Jacob – of German descent. She had been aware that more and more men were being asked to prove their loyalty to the US and the main way to do so was to join the Army. She gazed at her husband, a new understanding dawning. He said he was joining due to the conditions in the Pacific. Due to that battle on some God-forsaken island in the middle of nowhere. But that never made any sense.

She contemplated their nightly arguments. He yammered about their freedom and their safety. In the heat of the moment, she assumed he meant the Japanese and the German forces. Maybe his fears centered on the American government. Jacob was a first generation American, born on American soil. Shouldn't that be enough? But now she knew the answer – no. She looked up at Jacob, her eyes asking a thousand questions. He just inclined his head without uttering a word. What could he say that she couldn't see for herself?

She studied him now. The haggard expression. The glistening eyes. The tense cords in his neck. Despite his decision to go, he was torn. He had so much to prove. His American-ness. His manliness. His patriotism. To do what he must, he had to give up so much. His wife. His son. His mother. His safety. She loved him with her eyes, letting him know she was grateful. She still firmly believed there had to be a better way, but she finally understood.

As Jacob turned to her, his tears flowed freely down his face. Until now, she had remained dry-eyed, but his tears were too much. She fell into his arms as he murmured into her ear. He promised to come home, but the promise rang hollow, like the promise he once made not to go to war at all. Jacob couldn't promise to come home. She just had to pray he would.

She clung to him, growing smaller with each passing moment, knowing that the time was coming to send him to war. She couldn't let go. Her arms refused to obey. Eventually, Jacob gently removed her fingers from his arm.

Then, the whistle blew, and Jacob, without another look in her direction, slung his duffle over his shoulder and presented his ticket as the train started to move.

Black smoke nearly obscured her view, but she made out Jacob at a window, pressing his hand against the glass. She raised her hand as if to touch his. She stayed that way until the train was out of sight, nothing more than a dot on the horizon. Her Jacob was gone to war.

Chapter 27

WILLIAM: April 1944

In the days that followed, William discovered more changes underfoot than just his father's absence. He tried finding one of his books, but everything on the shelf had been moved. As he looked around his room, he discovered many of his toys were gone as well.

Quickly, he went running to his mother. "Mommy, Mommy! Someone took my books. And my train. They are gone! Does daddy need them in the war? Is that why they are gone?"

Stooping quickly to her frantic son, Bonnie said, "Oh, William. Honey. No. Come here." She took him onto her lap. "We are going to live with Grandma and Grandpa. So Mommy has packed up all your toys to take with us. You would want to take them with us, right?"

William nodded solemnly. Yes, he wanted his toys. But he wasn't sure he wanted to live with Grandma and Grandpa. It was far, far away. So far that they couldn't visit very often. His mother was still talking with him, trying to soothe his anxiety.

"So, they are not gone. They are in a big box we will unpack when we arrive at our new house."

William sat thoughtfully, considering the move. He wondered about many things. What would his room look like? Would there be a big tree in the backyard where he could play with his cars? Would he be able to pick flowers from his grandma's garden? But he asked the question that was most pressing, "Will Daddy be able to find us when he comes home from being a soldier?"

Without warning, his mother began to cry. Her tears startled William, who began to cry as well. Maybe Daddy wouldn't be able to find them! "I don't want to live with Grandma. I want to stay where my daddy can find me," wailed William. He grew stiff in his mother's arms. He was supposed to take care of Mommy, but he wasn't going to hide from his daddy. He was going to stay right here until he came home again.

Bonnie held her stiff but struggling son close to her chest, trying hard to contain her tears. "Darling, darling boy. Yes, your daddy will find us. In fact, we will come back here to this house when this nasty war is over and live right here. All three of us." How could she tell him she was crying because she was afraid his father would never come home, at least not alive? How could she explain they may never be together again? How could she explain the innocent question of a small child unraveled her best laid plans?

Of course, he could never understand all that, so she calmed him down, dried his eyes with the corner of her blouse, and began talking about the long car trip. Then, William noticed his grandfather moving the doghouse. He hadn't thought about Vonk, and, as a child will, he asked the next most important question on his mind. "Will Vonk be able to ride in the car with us, Mommy?"

Bonnie looked away quickly, willing fresh tears to stay within their bounds and not spill out onto her cheeks. She hadn't broken the news to him. She had hoped, apparently in vain, he would not notice. William loved Vonk with as much love as a small child could muster. It was going to break his heart that Vonk would not be going to Connecticut with them, and she hadn't wanted to present him with the devastating news.

But now, with him looking at her earnestly, she had no choice but to say, "No, honey. Vonk...Vonk is staying here. Well, not here at the house, but down at Mr. Schneider's. At the farm. He said he would take care of him until we came home again."

William began to cry in earnest. The tears he had shed for his father were nothing in comparison to the tears he had for his dog. Vonk was his friend. Certainly, he didn't have to lose his daddy and his friend, too! He began to plead in his little boy voice, one that pierced his mother's soul. "Please, Mommy. Don't leave Vonk. I want to take Vonk with us. He'll be good. He'll behave."

Despite his desperation, and despite her desire to spare her son any more pain, Vonk could not go to Connecticut. Her parents were willing to take them in, but not a dog. It would be too much of a burden. Bonnie understood but wished it were not so, realizing that even

Vonk was a casualty of the war.

Grandpa Phillip finished placing the doghouse and Vonk into the back of Mr. Schneider's pickup, and they were gone before William pushed outside to say goodbye. He finally wrestled out the front door and started running down the road as fast as his little 4-year-old legs could carry him, screaming, "Vonk. Vonk. I love you, Vonk!" with dusty tears streaking down his cheeks.

Finally, he stopped, out of breath, inhaling kicked-up dust as the truck made its way down the lane. Vonk wasn't going to Connecticut. Daddy wasn't going to Connecticut. He wasn't sure what a Connecticut was, but he didn't want to go either. He sobbed until his mother gently picked him up and brought him back into the house.

That night, as the sun went down, a strange noise emanated from the yard. Something made a terrible whining sound, a cross between a baby and a wounded animal. Bonnie, not sure what she would find, went to the back door to have a look with William right on her heels.

There, in the yard, still attached to the doghouse, was Vonk. Behind him, the path he created as he dragged his house by his tether down the long dirt road back to his boy, William. That night, for the first time and despite her earlier protestations that dogs do not belong indoors, Bonnie let Vonk in the house where he slept cuddled up with William until morning. The next day, Mr. Schneider picked him up again as the little Miller family left Ohio.

Chapter 28

WILLIAM: 1944

The train ride to Fort Benjamin Harrison in Indiana was a relatively short distance by train, but the 300 miles seemed incredibly long to Jacob. With each turn of the wheels, he got farther and farther from the place he lived his entire life and the family he created there. It wasn't so much the distance by foot as it was the distance by heart that caused his chest to ache.

Had the train not been taking him from a world of love to one of enemies and hate, it would have been beautiful. Mid-April Ohio was in full blossom. Small green buds were popping out on the trees, and the apple orchards were awash in white flowers with a hint of pink. Occasionally, Jacob would spot a tree sporting bright red or purple flowers – a crab apple tree put there to lure the bees into the orchard.

The bees weren't the only ones who had been busy, however. Many freshly plowed fields with the dark soil turned over after a winter spent under feet of snow rushed past his window.

In Columbus, the train made a short stop to take on more passengers. As Jacob ate part of the sack lunch Bonnie lovingly packed for him, he observed the good-byes happening on the platform under his window. He witnessed hugs and tears and wondered if that's what a bird's eye view of his own farewell just over an hour earlier looked like. He wondered how many of these young men had wives and children. How many were joining the Army to prove their American-ness? How many feared, as he did, that they would never go home again?

Despite pushing his breakfast around the plate and eating next to nothing since the previous evening, he found he was still unable to eat. The lump in his throat threatened to choke him with each bite of chicken making swallowing impossible. He wrapped the leftover lemon chicken back into the cloth napkin, tucking it away for later.

Men began boarding as the whistle blew. Then, he witnessed a replay of the train leaving the station. Waving. Tears. Goodbyes yelled above the roar of the train moving down the track. Without thinking, Jacob put his hand up on the window as he had done for Bonnie, but this time, no one cared. He dropped his hand back into his lap, lonelier than he had ever felt in his life.

He had done the right thing. He was proving his patriotism, and his family was going to Connecticut where they would not be suspect like they had been in North Canton. Though Bonnie's parents were German, too, her father's earlier wealth and his good job now kept him out of the eye of the US Justice Department. They had been truly American and embracing the American ways rather than living in a little German town for far too long to be of any threat.

He wondered why doing the right thing was so insufferably difficult. Shouldn't it be that the right thing for the right reason would be enough? Did God have to make it hard to handle as well? Or maybe it wasn't God's doing at all. Maybe it was fate, or man's need to control life.

He thought about the fear running amok through the country. He had it easy compared to the Japanese. They were being rounded up by the thousands, and with their obvious ethnicity, a simple name change or move to a different state couldn't hide the fact that they were Asian. Japs, as people had come to call them, had become to America what Jews had become to Germany.

He was guilty of it, too. He shouldn't feel this way or act this way because he had seen it happening to his own fellow Germans. It was this attitude that had him on a train heading away from the family he adored rather than working at the lumberyard and coming home to a warm supper. However, when he crossed paths with someone obviously Asian, a cold prickling tingle creeped up his spine. The "dirty Japs" had bombed Pearl Harbor, which is what led him to be on this train. Although the final decision to join the Army had been due to the enemy status, the Japs had started the whole thing.

He figured there were others on this train looking at

him thinking the very same thing. True, Germany hadn't been so bold as to bomb the United States, but it wasn't for lack of desire. Those heading to the European Theater would be fighting the Germans. His ancestors. His people. Him?

He was glad he was going to fight in the Pacific, against the Japs. It would be easy for him to know the good guys from the bad. There, being German would not be an issue. It was American against Japanese. In that arena, he would definitely qualify as an American with his creamy white skin and mid-western accent.

He thought about Hanz again, as he did often. Was he really a traitor, a spy, as they said? Did he have ties to the Nazi party? Did he keep the pamphlet because he forgot or because he was interested in what it had to say? Sure, the Bund was a small group, but it was active and believed what the Nazis were doing was right and justified. Although he had never seen any Bund activity in North Canton other than a singular pamphlet, he heard tales. He couldn't imagine Hanz belonging, but rumors at work said he was not only a member, but very active in the demise of the US government.

Of course, Jacob was aware that rumors got larger and larger the more they were told. He made sure to never ask any real questions. Too much concern would put him in the spotlight, just like any attempt to deny the accusations leveled at Hanz. During his last months at work, he kept his head down and worked hard, no longer chatting with others during lunch or going for an ale after work. He didn't know who to trust or who might be spying on him, hoping to send him to the camp along with his buddy.

He was glad Bonnie figured out the truth before he left. She still didn't know about Hanz or the pamphlet or how close he had come to landing in a camp, but she understood he felt pressure to be American and prove he was a true patriot. He hated keeping things from her and being dishonest. On the other hand, her response would be indignation. She would have fought to prove his innocence, and by doing so, jeopardized the whole family.

He worried a bit about his mother. She still clung tightly to her Germanic ways. She spoke German almost exclusively in her home, went to a German-speaking church, and shopped at local markets where German foods were more prevalent. Despite being honored to live in America, she was a Mueller, not a Miller, and had no intention of toning down her ethnicity.

He consoled himself that she had no husband, no contact with relatives in the homeland, and a son in the Army. Certainly, she would be safe? Of course, there wasn't anything he could do about it now.

He heard the steel on steel as brakes hit at the wheels of the train. The grating sound turned to a screech that pierced through the passenger cars, making several people clutch at their ears. They were arriving at Fort Benjamin Harrison. There was no turning back now.

Chapter 29

BONNIE: April 1944

The heavily loaded car pulled onto Main Street in Hartford, Connecticut and into the drive at number 169. Her new home. Walking down the long front sidewalk, she studied her surroundings. "How different this is from the home we had in Michigan when I was a girl," she mused.

This home was a white Cape Cod brick house with a tall chimney running up the front and dormer windows on either side like sentinels. The small front porch was barely spacious enough for the front door and the small rockers, one to the left and one to the right that welcomed her parents on warm summer nights.

Altogether, the house contained three bedrooms, a living room, dining room, small study, and a kitchen. Though spacious compared to her little pink home in

North Canton, it was cramped in comparison to their mansion in Detroit. She wondered if her parents accepted being "regular folks" living on Main Street. She doubted it suited her mother at all. She looked haggard from the long car ride, and Bonnie was sure she wished a butler would stiffly march down the front steps to help unload the car.

Bonnie and William would occupy the two bedrooms upstairs. The space matched their needs, because other than some of William's toys and their clothing, everything else was covered in sheets on Cypress Drive. Her four-poster bed. Her dining room table. Her pots and pans. The artwork that hung on the walls. Everything remained in North Canton, where she also left a piece of her heart.

Not wanting anyone to recognize her sadness, she planted a bright smile on her face and began telling William of all the fun he would have in his new neighborhood. She talked of other families with little boys and playing with his cars in the yard. That is when William asked, quite innocently, "Will we get another dog? I could name him Vonk."

Bonnie's tears struggled to break past her counterfeit cheerfulness. There would be no dog. Her parents didn't approve of pets. It was their one substantial disagreement before moving to Connecticut. She wanted to bring Vonk for William, but no amount of cajoling changed their sentiment. They remained adamant that the dog must stay in North Canton.

That is why, when Vonk came home the night before they left, she let the animal in the house to sleep with William. She didn't care what her parents thought. It was her son's dog, and they were going to miss one another terribly.

"No, William, you won't be able to have a dog here. That is why Vonk stayed with the Schaeffers on their farm. We'll bring him home again when Daddy comes home from the war. But maybe a neighbor has a dog you can play with."

William's bright eyes turned murky and uninterested. Playing with someone else's dog was no compensation for losing his own.

Her aging father struggled with the trunks, brushing off her offer of help. "No daughter of mine is going to do the heavy lifting in this house." Veins bulged in his neck and arms, while heavy puffs of breath escaped through thin lips and clenched teeth. Bonnie was thankful when some jovial teenagers walked by on the way to town and offered their services.

Her father, impressed with their thoughtfulness, produced a quarter for the two boys for their efforts. Bonnie turned her head to avoid eye contact with the boys who didn't stop to help an old man but to ogle a pretty girl. She didn't want to encourage them further, nor did she want her father to realize he'd been played for a fool.

As the afternoon waned she helped her mother fix the evening meal. The kitchen was warm and friendly, painted a pale yellow with a white oven and white counters. Unlike her home in Ohio, her parents had an icebox rather than an electric refrigerator, but the kitchen was very functional, and Bonnie set about making herself useful.

Though it had been years since the start of the Depression and her meteoric drop from wealth, her mother still did not have the hang of cooking. The meals she prepared were bland and often slightly burned. In fact, her father renamed Elaine's attempt at rolls, "Black Bottomed Biscuits." Bonnie determined to take over cooking as often as possible, out of both a sense of duty and one of personal preservation.

While they ate, Bonnie watched William closely. She wondered what her child was thinking, whether he missed his daddy and his dog. But she dared not ask. There was no reason to give him things to miss if he wasn't missing them on his own. He ate a healthy supper, and like she had taught him, removed his plate to the kitchen when he was through, before going to the bathroom to wash his hands and face. From all outside appearances, he was adjusting well.

Bonnie tucked William into bed that night with his little bear, the boy looking like a tiny replica of his father. His strong Miller genes had been obvious since birth, but this evening, the resemblance was even more startling. She resisted the urge to call him Jacob. After promising she would help him unpack his toys in the morning, she kissed him on top of the head, made sure he knew her room was directly across the hall, and quietly closed his door.

She tiptoed down the stairs to spend a few minutes with her parents in the study. When she couldn't keep her eyes open any longer, she excused herself to bed. It had been a long day, actually a very long couple of months, and she was exhausted.

She studied her small room as she readied herself for bed. The furniture did not belong to her parents but came with the rental house. Other than the addition of a few personal items here and there, none of which were in the rarely used upstairs bedrooms, they had made no changes.

She ticked off furniture as she turned a slow circle: cherry wood bed with a white coverlet, small cherry dresser, and matching mirror. Though functional, neat, and clean, the room lacked warmth, making her long for her grand four-poster bed and the husband who should be sharing it with her. After brushing out her long, blonde hair and removing her lipstick, Bonnie crawled into the lonely space beneath the sheets, missing Jacob more than she thought possible. "How am I going to make it through the war if I feel this desolate after only four days?" The day's unshed tears slid onto her pillow until, spent, she fell asleep.

Chapter 30

JACOB: Late Spring 1944

Basic training was grueling, but more importantly, it was miserable. Jacob had done hard before. He worked for years on the Hersch farm in four-foot snows and in punishing heat. He spent the last two years loading lumber onto wagons, making his arms the size of tree trunks. So, it wasn't the physical difficulties that bothered him, unlike many of the recruits with him.

Some of the men in his unit were slight and looked like they had never been outdoors before. These men couldn't run in boots or carry the packs. At the end of the day, their sore muscles kept them awake, making the next day more grueling. Jacob was glad to be fit and strong, though he would trade sore muscles for a shattered heart.

He missed his family, something his sergeant rubbed in his face whenever possible. On the day of his arrival, Jacob made the fatal mistake of posting a picture of his wife and son near his bed. His sergeant, a burly man with a sour attitude, immediately began calling Jacob "the man of the house," demanding he complete chores no one else wanted to do.

Jacob didn't mind toilet duty or any other job heaped on him at the end of the day. Being busy and tired meant he had less time to miss his family. However, he hated the taunts aimed at his wife. "That woman of yours! Mmm Mmm. Golden hair and big brown eyes. What do you think, men? Did ol' Jacob here get lucky?" Such comments were met with cat calling and whistling, egging the Sarge to continue.

Jacob comprehended what was happening. The point of boot camp was to break the men down and build them up to be better soldiers. Jacob kept his temper in check until the day Sarge pushed too far. "So, Jacob, do you think you could bring that sweet woman of yours by the barracks, so we could all get a little something?"

The raucous laughter and jeers died out when Jacob whipped around and glared, first at one man and then the next. His mouth worked and the muscles in his arms twitched as he balled and unballed his fists. He didn't say a word, but the fury in his eyes conveyed his intent. One by one, the men looked down, inspecting their boots.

Jacob rounded on his sergeant. "No, no sir!" to which the man turned and walked briskly from the room, leaving everyone a bit subdued.

From that moment, Jacob stood a bit taller on the ladder than the other men. He received his ration of harassment. He still marched and grunted. But everyone knew talking about Bonnie was off-limits. No one wanted to find out what would happen if he unleashed the fury in his eyes.

Beyond mental and physical conditioning, the goal of boot camp was to prepare these men to take on the role of soldier. Jacob was not a novice when it came to guns. But the military weapon assigned to him had little in common with the shotgun he used as a youth. When it came to these guns, he was as ignorant as some of the men were weak – but only at first. Because he understood how things worked and wasn't afraid to learn new skills, he soon could field strip his rifle, an M1 Garand, and reassemble it as fast as most of the men in his unit.

"Your rifle is your new best friend. You will eat with it. Sleep with it. And eventually talk to it. Your gun is what will stand between you and the enemy. Without your gun, you will not make it home."

Jacob's desire to make it home pushed him to excel at everything he did, in particular those things that would be crucial to his survival. Though everyone there believed they would make it home, he understood many of them were wrong. He prayed he was on the right side of this particular equation.

The only good thing about boot camp was no one questioned his patriotism. No one asked him about being German or who his ancestors were. Since he didn't have a German accent and his name didn't scream Germanic heritage, the soldiers in his unit didn't see a "spy" or "traitor" when he approached. Instead, they saw Jacob, a fellow soldier who grunted with them in the field and ate with them in the mess hall. This realization made him confident he made the right choice.

At night, the men talked about the war and heading to the islands to fight the Japanese. They listened to the radio and kept up with the different battles – the Japanese Operation Ichi-Go in central China with a goal to conquer any area with an American bomber. Americans landing in Biak, Dutch New Guinea, a fierce battle which continued for months. The Japanese retreat from India after heavy losses.

Of course, the men also followed the war in the European theater. "Something huge is happening. You know it is. Every day we learn about air raids and skirmishes across Southern England."

"And France," inserted someone from the top bunk. "Don't forget the fighting in France."

Everyone played General, with an opinion of what should happen next. However, regardless of the opinions, everyone had the same goal – knock the Nazis back.

During these debates, no one singled out Jacob or any of the men in the unit with German ancestry. Nonetheless, Jacob was always glad when the focus went back to the Japs. When talk of Nazis and Krauts were bandied about by the men, his stomach clenched, waiting for someone to stand and point at him, asking if he was a traitor. The Pacific Theater was his safe haven.

On June 6th, two days before being shipped across the country to Arkansas for more detailed training, his unit had no further need to speculate. More than 160,000 Allied troops, supported by 5,000 ships and 13,000 aircraft, landed along a stretch of French coastline on the beaches of Normandy. As they listened to the news of the invasion, especially upon learning that more than 9,000

Allied soldiers were dead or wounded, the atmosphere was grim. During all their nightly debates, no one guessed this scenario or predicted the casualties of any given foray would be so high.

General Dwight D Eisenhower famously stated, "We will accept nothing less than full victory." The Normandy landing allowed the soldiers to begin the march to defeat Hitler, but the price for that victory was colossal. With sobering clarity, the soon-to-be warriors realized 'full victory' against the enemy would require the death of thousands of men just like them.

With this undeniable knowledge, Jacob boarded the train that would take him to Arkansas and one step closer to war.

Chapter 31

BONNIE: June 1944

Due to her father's connections in the area, Bonnie found a secretarial job at Pratt and Whitney, a factory making engines for airplanes. Although she hadn't been a secretary since William's birth and was a bit rusty, she got back into the groove very quickly, spending her days typing, taking dictation, and handling communications between executives.

The factory was enormous, much bigger than the Timken plant. So, unlike her Timken job in which she worked closely with two executives, she was part of a typing pool. As such, she worked each day at a desk in a room with at least 100 other women.

At first, the noise was deafening. Sounds of clunking fingers against keys and keys against paper rattled from the moment she arrived until the moment she left. She clenched her teeth against the clanking in her head and struggled to concentrate on her assignment. However, before long, she became part of the din from 9 until 4:30 with a 30-minute break for lunch.

Many of the women were war widows like Bonnie, with their husbands off to join the fight while the woman stayed home to make ends meet. However, unlike Bonnie, most did not have a child at home. Having William made her new role as wartime breadwinner both easier and harder simultaneously. Easier, because she had someone to go home to who loved her without reserve. Harder, because every time she saw her sweet William, thoughts of Jacob flooded her mind, causing her to agonize if he would make it home to them again.

The amount of typing necessary in a factory dealing with plane engines surprised her, but she soon realized a majority of her responsibilities revolved around required government paperwork. Much of what she typed made little sense to her since she didn't understand the workings of plane engines. But she could regurgitate facts that meant nothing to her. The R-2800 Double Wasp produced 2400 horsepower and 0.71 horsepower per inch cubed. Higher grade fuel and water injection increased capacity to 2800 horsepower. But she didn't rattle off these facts because only those with a proper clearance were to know.

Despite not knowing how they worked, she did know what they were used for. The R-2800 went into fighters and medium-sized bombers for the Army, Navy, and Marine Corps. The plant in Hartford provided the engines for the Navy's Vought F4U Corsair, the first US fighter plane to go faster than 400 mph.

Every secretary at the plant had to take an oath to keep secret anything they may learn about the engines during their duties. Some secretaries, typically those not of German descent, were given more classified documents to type. Bonnie, though a fifth generation American, was still considered German enough to be denied anything with secret clearance – even though she had a husband fighting in the war. Although it infuriated her, making her feel like she had a 'potential traitor' label on her forehead, she kept her mouth shut for the sake of the money. If she got fired for creating a fuss over her heritage, she would be unlikely to find a job anywhere, despite her father's pull.

One day during her lunch break, while eating some leftovers from dinner the night before, a young girl by the name of Colette approached. Bonnie had gone outside to breathe in some fresh air and remove the shoes from her feet to stretch out her toes. Though she loved the aesthetics of heels, her cramped toes suffered from the effects of wearing thinly tapered winklepickers eight hours each day. It was her guilty pleasure to run her bare feet over the soft grass during break whenever the weather permitted.

Colette asked if she could have a seat, while Bonnie tried to stuff her aching feet back into her shoes as though she had been caught selling secrets to the enemy. Colette put out her hand and said, "No, please. Leave them off. I was planning to do the same." By the end of lunch, Bonnie was sure she made her first friend. As it turned out, every day for the next two years, Bonnie and Colette ate lunch together. On warm days, they would eat outside. During the cold months, they would eat in the break room with the others. It felt good to have such a friend in times like these.

Collette was two years older but had no children. Her husband, Charles, signed up for the war the day after Pearl Harbor, along with thousands of other men who wanted to exact revenge. Based on his last letter, he was in Italy, fighting against the Nazis. She lamented the slow mail that kept her wondering about his health and safety.

Bonnie explained that Jacob was finishing Basic, and she only received one letter from him letting her know he would be leaving for Arkansas on June 8th. It was now June 3rd, and she didn't expect another letter until he had his new assignment.

Although Bonnie rarely heard from Jacob, she wrote to him every evening after work. At the end of the week, she bundled the letters together and put them in the mail. This week's bundle, however, would have to wait until she had a new address, meaning his next install-ment may look more like a novel than a letter.

In her most recent volume, she told Jacob all about her new job to the extent to which she was allowed to tell. She also told him about William and the other chil-dren who lived on the block. Her exciting news revolved around going to the Circus on July 6th. She couldn't wait for William to experience the wonder of a circus. If she were being honest, she was excited, too. It had been a long time since she had done anything other than work and worry.

Two days after they met, Bonnie and Collette ate lunch indoors despite the glorious weather outside. A radio had been set up in the break room, and the women sat in silence as news bulletins concerning the Normandy invasion, eventually known as D-Day, broke into the regular programming. Thousands of lives were lost, and Bonnie witnessed some of her co-workers fall to the floor weeping at the news, realizing their husbands were part of that operation. She grabbed Colette's hand with a questioning look, but Collette shook her head with a look of gratitude in her eyes. Whispering quietly, she said, "I'm pretty certain he's still somewhere in Italy." Bonnie was relieved to be absolutely certain that Jacob was in Indiana, not yet out of the country.

The rest of the day was somber. Though the tap-tapping continued, the rhythm took on the arrangement of a funeral dirge. Bonnie was more than ready to go home that evening. All she wanted to do was hug her child and pray her Jacob would remain safe.

Chapter 32

WILLIAM: June 1944

William was not happy with the new arrangements. His mommy left for work every day, leaving him with Grandma. It wasn't that he didn't love his grandma, but she didn't play the way Mommy did. He would pull out his cars, running them through the kitchen while she worked, and Grandma would say, "William, for heaven's sake. Why are you always under foot? Please take your toys somewhere else." He wasn't entirely sure what 'under foot' meant, but Grandma didn't smile when saying it, so he was certain she was not happy about it.

Then there was the yard. Like his home in North Canton, he had plenty of space to play, but he missed the trees. His yard back home was full of apple trees. He got to see the pretty white flowers before moving to live with

Grandma and Grandpa, but his mommy said they wouldn't be back in time to pick them. He wondered who would pick the apples and make the applesauce to eat all winter. Maybe Mr. Schaeffer was going to do that just like he was taking care of Vonk.

William missed Vonk. Before they moved, they played together every day. No matter where William went or what he did, Vonk followed along, tongue hanging out and tail wagging. There was another little boy down the block with a black dog, but Grandma didn't take him there very often. If Vonk were here, he'd keep him company. But Vonk was far away. Just like daddy.

Mostly, he missed his daddy. Mommy read him a letter the postman carried to their front porch after she stopped crying. She said she cried because she was happy, but that made no sense to William. He only cried when he was sad. Mommy tried to explain that grownups cried whenever they wanted to. He decided he would never cry when he was happy when he became old enough to make those decisions.

The letter from daddy was very short, but there was something in it just for him. "Tell William I love him and think of him every day." William wanted Mommy to write a letter telling Daddy he loved him and thought of him every day, too. Mommy promised she'd tell him that very night.

Letter writing fascinated William. He marveled that Mommy used a pen to draw squiggles on the paper and when daddy got the squiggles in the mail, he would know what they meant. Then, Daddy wrote down his own squiggles and Mommy figured out what they meant. William tried to understand the squiggles, taking the letter from Daddy and scrutinizing the page for the marks that meant Daddy loved him, but everything looked the same.

When he asked Mommy, she pointed to the squiggles that were his. She pointed out his very own name, saying, "Your name is William and starts with a W. See this?" She pointed to a pointy mark on the paper. "A W goes down, then up, then down, then up again." During the long afternoons, William drew the letter W in the dirt with a stick until it resembled those in Daddy's letters home. Now, when daddy wrote about him, he would be able to find the part all by himself.

Mommy often read William the letters she wrote. She told his daddy about the circus, which William learned consisted of a big tent with lots of animals and people that did tricks and flew in the sky. "Oh, William. You are going to have so much fun. There will be lions leaping through hoops of fire. And elephants that can stand up on their back legs. You'll even get to see funny clowns."

William saw a clown once when they went to the picture show at his old house. The clown stood outside, tossing three red balls into the air, never dropping a single one, not even once. Although William tried throwing his one ball in the air once he got back home, he dropped it every single time. He wondered if the circus clown would throw balls like the one in Ohio.

"Do we have to go to Ohio to see the circus?" he asked. After the long drive from the pink house to Grandma's house, William wasn't fond of riding in the car. "Oh, no, William! The circus is here in Hartford. It is just a hop, skip, and a jump away." Mommy was teasing because one hop, skip, and jump later, William still stood in the living room. Glancing around, he was certain elephants and lions wouldn't be allowed to sit on Grandma's sofa.

Although he would rather be at his real home, he looked forward to the circus. On that day, his mommy didn't have to go to work, so he might be able to play with his cars in the kitchen without being underfoot.

One evening after supper, having spent the better part of the day thinking about the circus, William peppered his mother with questions about elephants. "What color are elephants?"

"Gray, like Grandpa's car."

"Are they taller than Vonk?"

"Yes, William, they are very big."

"Are they taller than Daddy?"

When he learned elephants were taller than his daddy, he was amazed. "I didn't think anything could be bigger than Daddy," he breathed.

The questioning continued. What kind of noise did an elephant make? Did the elephant know more than one trick? Would he be able to touch the elephant?

His mother laughed. "William, you'll have to wait, but you don't have to wait too much longer. The circus is tomorrow."

William clapped with delight, dropping his fork on the white linen tablecloth. Grandma frowned, as she often did when he spilled things on the table. When she would sigh and say his name, he felt like he had been naughty even though he hadn't done anything on purpose. Today, however, he was too excited to care about the linen or his grandma's sighs. He was going to the circus to see elephants bigger than his daddy.

That night, it was almost impossible to sleep. He kept

thinking about the big animals and the clowns. It was sad his daddy couldn't go, too, but he'd make his mommy draw all the right squiggles so his daddy would know all about the circus. He would even draw a picture of the elephant for Daddy to hang in his room.

William was up with the sun and ready to climb in the car. His mother shooed him out of her room, mumbling, "The circus is after lunch, William. Go back to bed." William wasn't tired, but he didn't want his mommy to be angry, so he sat on his bed and thought about elephants until his grandma started bustling around in the kitchen.

Because he was up so early, he got to eat breakfast with Grandpa. He was excited about this new treat until he learned he had to be quiet while Grandpa read the newspaper. Not talking at breakfast was new to him. He intended to be quiet and keep from fidgeting, but as he was swallowing a bite of pancake, he forgot the rules and yelled, "There's my name! The newspaper has my name!"

Startled by the sudden burst of noise, grandpa jerked the upheld paper toward the table and looked over the top directly at the young boy. "William! Don't yell at the table. It isn't polite."

"I'm sorry, Grandpa, but the paper has my name!" He then pointed to the letter "W." Grandpa smiled. "William, there are many words in the English language that start with the letter W. Your name is one of them. The word that has caused all this commotion is Wall. It's part of the name of the paper I'm reading called the Wall Street Journal."

William had no idea other things beside his name

started with a W. "What else starts with a W, Grandpa? Other than William and wall? What else?"

"Wood. Whistle. Whisper. The W starts any word that has the wwwwwwwwwww sound."

William was fascinated. As soon as he was able to chew and swallow the rest of his pancakes, he asked to be excused. His grandfather, who enjoyed eating alone and actually preferred it that way, sent him on his way.

He spent the next hour touching everything in the house trying to decide if it started with a W. "SSSSSSSofa. No. TTTTTTTTable. No. IIIIIIIcebox. No. RRRRRRRRRug. No." He couldn't find anything in the house starting with a W other than himself and the Wall Street Journal. Determined, he went outside and tried some more. "GGGGGGGGGrasss. No. TTTTTTTTTTTTTree. No" He headed toward the driveway, thinking he might find something there. "Cccccccccccccar. No WWWWWWWindow. Yes! Window starts with W like William."

He was excited to finally find a W all by himself and raced into the house, letting the back door slam, so he could tell his mother the car window started with the W just like William. She had been watching him out of the kitchen window, which he now also realized began with a W, making William especially happy.

"Come along, silly boy. We are going to give you a bath and then dress for the circus." William was not fond of baths. He particularly hated washing the soap out of his hair because the water would run into his eyes and sting. However, he wanted to go to the circus, so he didn't put up too much of a fuss.

While in the tub, he tried to find other W words coming up with only one - wwwwwwater. When he was dry, he put on a pretty blue shirt his mother tucked into his khaki shorts. She told him he looked very smart, which she always said when he dressed up in nice clothes.

Once in his clean clothes, he was nearly dancing with excitement. Elephants. Clowns. People flying in the air. When would it be time to leave? Why did grownups always take so long to go?

Finally, when William thought he wouldn't be able to wait a moment longer, Mommy said it was time. William ran to the car and climbed inside before either his mother or grandmother walked out the door. He perched in the middle of the front seat, so he would be between his mother, who was driving, and his grandmother, who kept fussing over his hair, licking her finger to try to make the stray pieces to stay down.

Mommy backed down the driveway and onto their street. In his head, William thought, "MMMMMain. No." Before long, they had gotten to the busy street that Mommy said would lead them to the circus.

Chapter 33

JACOB: July 1944

Jacob did not realize a place could get so hot. Having never been outside of Ohio, he had no idea what to expect when he arrived in Arkansas in the heat of the summer. But saying Arkansas was hot was like saying his mother didn't really care for Bonnie. It simply didn't describe the situation at hand.

A month after arriving, the July temperatures were what his friend Eddy called, "hot as a Fourth of July firecracker." That was a bit more apropos, but still did not adequately describe the truth of his circumstances. Jacob woke up in the morning covered in a film of sticky, salty sweat that only got worse as the day went on. Perhaps instead of hot, he should use words such as blazing, boiling, scorching, sizzling, sweltering, blistering, fiery, or flaming. The reality was that all these words combined did not begin to epitomize the precise nature of the heat.

The breeze never seemed to blow at Camp Chaffee. It was as though the "would-be" soldiers had driven out the wind since there were no Japs to take on. Or maybe the fencing meant to keep intruders out of the camp also kept the wind at bay. No matter the reason, the air never stirred on its own accord, and Jacob wished fervently for anything to cool him down.

Some of the men had been here in Arkansas for almost a year, training and waiting for staging orders. These men were ready to move out. Jacob, on the other hand, though hot and wanting to be home with his wife and son, was not unhappy to still be in the United States. He kept hoping the war would end before being called into battle.

He only said this out loud once. The other men roared with indignation, wanting to know if he were a coward. Jacob laughed it off. "I'm just partial to my wife's home-cooked meals and am not looking forward to eating cold rations." Then, with amazing leadership ability, he quickly got others to agree the food at home was far better, and they'd all be fools to think otherwise. Being a coward was soon forgotten, and Jacob never brought up his desire to avoid battle again.

He sometimes wondered if he might, in fact, be cowardly. The idea of pointing a gun at the enemy and pulling the trigger was difficult to accept. He comprehended the "him or me" philosophy and was more than willing for death to go to the other guy, but, if he could have his druthers, he'd prefer they both have the opportunity to go home to their families.

These thoughts were curious to him because on one hand he hated the Japs and wanted them dead for ruining his idyllic life. On the other hand, he began to understand that most men in the army didn't have a personal beef with anyone. They were there to do their duty for their country. He figured many of the Japs he hated were men like him who hoped to go home before shooting a gun.

In the end, he decided he was not a coward but a pragmatist. By going home without ever going to war, he'd still be seen as a patriot, he wouldn't have changed in the way Axel said war changed men, and he'd be with his family before the holidays. It sounded like a win-win to him all the way around.

While at Fort Chaffee, Jacob discovered everyone earned a nickname in the Army. Eddy became Razor-eyes because he could spot a sniper faster than anyone else in the field. Harry became Stew because of his ability to chow down more grub than anybody else in the unit. His incredible marksmanship earned Earl the name Bullseye. Jacob became known as "Mule" because of his great strength. He could lift, pull, haul, and otherwise move more than any man and often more than two of them combined.

On Saturday morning, July 8th, Jacob was taking it easy. They had worked hard all week, and today, his entire unit had leave. He considered heading into Barling with several of the guys but decided he would rather spend the day relaxing and writing a long letter to Bonnie and William. A few other men lounged in the barracks, trying to keep cool, and someone, at the far end of the room, listened to the radio.

Bullseye called out, "Jacob. You got kin in Hartford, right? There's a news story just flashed through about some circus burning to the ground. Hundreds killed."

Jacob's mouth went dry. He grabbed at Bonnie's last packet of letters he kept in the boot locker at the foot of his bunk, scanning to find the part about the circus. Bonnie had said something about taking William to the circus, but he had paid little attention to the details.

While he scanned, he moved quickly towards the radio and listened intently as the announcer talked of the fire during the July 6th afternoon show. Today was the 8th. The fire happened on Thursday. What day was it that Bonnie had taken William? "Please, God, don't let it be Thursday. Let it be any day but Thursday."

But as he looked down at the letter, at her beautiful curly-cue writing, the words jumped off the page, "...so I got off work on Thursday to take William to the circus. Mother is going with me. I'm so excited. William can't wait to see the animals. I wish you could be here with us. I'll write to tell you all about it."

His hands began to tremble, and despite the barracks being as hot as an oven, Jacob began to shiver.

The newscaster said: *On the afternoon of July 6, 1944, more than 8,000 Hartford residents, most of them women and children, were gathered for 'the greatest show on earth'. Minutes later, a ball of flame broke out on the sidewall canvas of the big top, quickly engulfing the tent. Panic-stricken circus-goers trying to exit were blocked by iron cage chutes filled with snarling lions and panthers. In lessthan ten minutes, the big top collapsed, and this horrific tragedy claimed 168 lives. Most of thedead were found in piles several bodies deep at the exits.*

Jacob only grasped a portion of the words. Fire. Women and children. Blocked. 168 dead.

As the announcer droned on about the practice of waterproofing the canvas tents with paraffin and gasoline, and how that combination with an open flame had started a fire that couldn't be contained, Jacob's mind kept spinning faster and faster, making less and less sense of everything going on around him.

The tent caught fire right after the lions performed. As the tent burned, paraffin wax dripped from the tent top, causing horrible burns to those below. Within eight short minutes, before everyone could flee, the fiery tent collapsed, trapping people beneath. One hundred and sixty-eight people were killed and more than 700 were injured.

Bonnie. William. Circus. Fire. Dead. Dead. Dead. The newscaster continued: *The Ringling Brothers and Barnum & Bailey Circus has been experiencing shortages of personnel due to the War and had arrived late to Hartford the day before the fire. One of the trains was so late, in fact, that one of the shows scheduled for the day had to be canceled. Circus performers have stated to reporters that canceling a show is extremely bad luck and blame this catastrophe on superstition. However, fire marshals now say the flames were due to an errant cigarette butt.*

Bonnie. William. Circus. Dead. Dead. Dead.

Jacob couldn't hear Bullseye or the others talking to him, asking him questions. He stood there, trembling, with the mantra echoing through his mind and his heart.

Bonnie. William. Circus. Dead. Dead. Dead.

Bullseye, unable to get Jacob to respond, grabbed at the letter in his friend's hand, quickly scanning the pages.

As Jacob's fingers released the last words he'd ever hear from his beloved wife, his eyes focused on Bullseye and the tears began to fall. Then, for the first time, he said out loud what his mind had been internally screaming since the news story began, "Bonnie. William. Circus. Dead."

Chapter 34

BONNIE: July 1944

A loud knock came at the door. There, on the doorstep, stood two official looking men. Bonnie's father, rose from the living room sofa where he'd been listening to the news and moved to the door. "Good evening, gentlemen. What can we do for you?" He stepped onto the tiny front porch, suddenly dwarfed by the three men trying to find room.

"We are from the Red Cross. Is this the residence of Bonnie and William Miller?" the taller of the two strangers asked.

"Yes. That is my daughter and grandson. What has happened? Is everything okay with Jacob?"

At the sound of his name, colors and sounds exploded in Bonnie's ears. The room spun around, and her knees buckled under her. The last thing she remembered was thinking "Jacob. My dear, dear Jacob. Dead. Dead. Dead." All three men turned in time to see her limp body hit the floor.

Bonnie heard the commotion before she saw it. She couldn't remember what happened. She tried to gather her wits as the front door opened and closed. Footsteps tapped, strange voices shouted directions, her mother's voice crooned near her ear, her son cried. Her son! William's crying brought everything rushing back, and as her vision cleared, she realized she was on the floor, with the two men here to tell her Jacob was dead standing over her like pallbearers.

The rational side of her mind tried to take over as she took stock. Jacob was in Arkansas. Right? He hadn't left the US yet? No, no, she was sure if he had, she would have been told. But here they stood. A pair of men in some kind of uniform she didn't recognize. It didn't appear to be army. But they certainly weren't door-to-door salesmen. What fate had befallen Jacob? What fate had befallen him?

She tried to push herself into a seated position, but her mother stopped any progress with a gentle push to her shoulders. "No, Bonnie. Stay there a moment. You've had a nasty fall. Let's be sure you are okay."

But Bonnie was adamant. She needed to hear the words of these strangers. She needed to know how Jacob died. She needed to hold her son. She needed to see whatever remained of her husband. She needed the monster in her head to stop imagining the worst. The truth must be better than these thoughts swirling through her brain at machine-gun fire speed.

When she finally sat upright, the smaller of the two men bent down to eye level. "Mrs. Miller. I'm Thomas Romney from the Red Cross. I think you may have the wrong idea. We are not here to tell you anything about your husband. We are here on behalf of your husband. He received a letter from you stating you were going to the circus. The one that burned? He contacted us to find out if you were still alive. You and your boy."

Bonnie was confused. Jacob was alive? He sent these men to find her? She looked at them with eyes full of questions, unable to form any of her thoughts into words.

"Ma'am, he heard a news story about the fire yesterday. He is beside himself with worry. If you are up to it, we'd like to take you to our office in town and hook you up on a long-distance phone call to speak to him. He keeps repeating, 'Bonnie. William. Circus. Fire. Dead.'"

Bonnie's heart leaped with joy and filled with sorrow at the words. Her Jacob was not dead but was suffering his own "what ifs." He spent the last 24 hours certain his family died in the circus fire. She wanted to go with these men immediately, but her mother was firmly in charge.

"No, Bonnie. Not yet. Here. Have some water. Let's get a little more color in your face before you stand up." As Bonnie drank a few sips, her mother methodically touched each limb, bent each joint, and took stock of her daughter's health. Finally, when she deemed Bonnie was in one piece, the men from the Red Cross escorted Bonnie and William downtown and hustled them into a small room with some folding chairs, a metal desk, and a phone. The woman at the desk began dialing. After a clipped command, she handed the phone to Bonnie.

Jacob's voice rang in her ear.

"Bonnie? Oh, Bonnie!" And then she heard him cry-ing tears of relief, but also tears of fear and loneliness. He had been living the 'what if' she dreaded most. She whispered to him softly, trying to soothe his anguish until, at last, he began to laugh.

For the next 20 minutes, they stumbled over one another, trying to tell the story. Even William was al-lowed to join in for a moment, hearing his daddy's voice for the first time in months. How she longed to hold Jacob in her arms and feel his strength surrounding her. Nonetheless, she was thankful he was alive. The crisis had been averted.

"Oh, darling! I'm so sorry you were worried. I had no idea you would find about the fire all the way in Arkan-sas. Please, darling, stop crying. We are fine, perfectly fine. Let me explain."

Bonnie took a deep breath. She hated reliving every-thing again because the near miss still made her tremble. "We got ready for the circus on Thursday, just like we planned. William was so excited and would have left at sunrise if we had let him. But, once we got in the car, he got a funny feeling in his stomach. He then started complaining of something smelling funny, like dirty boots. Then he began an all-out crying, saying he didn't want to go to the circus because he smelled dirt.

"It was the strangest thing, Jacob. The strangest thing. We couldn't understand what changed. One min-ute he was ready to enjoy the elephants, and the next, he was adamant he didn't want to go. I finally pulled over to the side of the road, hoping to talk some sense into him. But no matter what I said, he cried harder, telling me over and over and over again that he smelled dirt."

At this point, William interjected. "I did smell dirt, Daddy. Yucky, old smelly dirt, like the kind in the closed-up barn near our pink house."

Bonnie began again. "He kept repeating it over and over until, exasperated, I turned the car around and headed home. There wasn't any need going to the circus if William was going to behave that way. I mean, the whole reason we were going was to have fun. Mother wasn't too happy. She felt like I was spoiling him, but honestly, going to the circus with a screaming child didn't seem like a good way to spend the day." She laughed ruefully.

"When we finally pulled into the driveway, William ran to his room, hid under the covers, and wouldn't come downstairs for supper. He said he still smelled dirt. Father was even more upset than Mother, saying he would have made William behave, but you know your son. He has a stubborn streak, and I don't think Father could have done a thing about it.

"Then, after dinner, the news reports were full of the fire. I've never been so thankful in my life."

Just then, William innocently asked, "Daddy, does fire smell like dirt?"

Chapter 35

BONNIE: July 1944

The horror of the near-miss at the circus haunted Bonnie. She didn't go to work for several days because she couldn't leave William. She needed to be near her son. "I could have lost him in the fire. I was supposed to be there with him. We could both be dead."

She had trouble grasping that idea. Dead.

She wanted to take her son to do something remarkable, but they could have wound up dead instead. A simple circus. Inevitably, this led her to Jacob and the war and death. If something as simple as a circus could kill, and had almost killed her and William, what would the war do to Jacob? She couldn't shake the thought. What she buried for months was now an angry monster let loose in her mind. Anything could happen to Jacob.

The monster, with its roaring voice and vivid imaginings, intoned the worst not only could happen, but would.

Jacob was safe for now, tucked away in some base in Arkansas. But that wasn't likely to last. Eventually, he would be shipped to the Pacific and have to fight the Japs. Then what? A bullet. A bomb. A machete. "Even something as benign as dysentery could kill him," the raging monster in her mind chanted. How would she live if he died?

She thought of her mother-in-law, Elisabet, for the first time in months. She had been a young mother with a husband with a "safe" job. She was sure Elisabet did not concern herself with the worries of losing her husband on the job. But one day, with no warning, she found herself a widow, taking care of her young son alone. Could Bonnie do what she had done? Despite their estrangement, a small twinge of respect blossomed.

Even if she could do what Elisabet had done, even if she could dig up the strength to move one foot in front of the other for the sake of William, she didn't want to have to. She didn't want to be both mother and father. She didn't want to be the main breadwinner. She didn't want to go to sleep alone every night, crying into her pillow. No, she only wanted Jacob to be by her side.

As William made car noises, racing his favorite yellow car across the rug, she wondered how William had sensed the impending disaster. She fully believed he did know, somehow, as though he had been forewarned. What had he been saying about smelling dirt? Maybe he was smelling smoke and didn't know how to tell them. Thank God she listened. What if her father had been in the car? They could have all perished in the fire because he would have insisted on taking William to the circus to prove who was in charge of the situation.

Of course, if she were honest, she hadn't listened as much as given in. She was angry. She had taken a day off work and instead of having fun at a circus, was sitting at home with a sobbing child who smelled dirt. Now, days after the catastrophe, she felt quite differently. Instead of planning a funeral, she sat in the living room with William, who drove his cars around her feet. All because he smelled dirt and wanted to go home.

As she studied William, she was amazed again at the resilience of the boy. Nothing phased him. His father was gone. His dog was gone. His home was gone. His mother went to work each morning. He nearly died at the circus. Yet, there he sat, zooming cars around her feet. She longed for the simplicity that was his life.

She looked over at her mother mending socks and her father reading the paper. They, too, seemed at ease. After supper last night, her father said the family was blessed. They survived what would have been horror at the least and potential death at the worst.

Now, as she fretted, he patted her gently, looked her in the eyes, and said, "Bonnie, let it go. It is over. It didn't happen. You can't spend the rest of the war living with what-ifs. You'll go crazy if you do. Every day there is a 'what if' that we can't control. Each day could be a catastrophe. Or it could just be a simple day. When you have the simple days, relish them." With that, he kissed her on the cheek and went to his room.

The miracle of it all boggled her mind, making her question every decision she ever made. Was there someone else in charge? Pulling the strings? Were chance events, like a child throwing a fit, the difference between fortune and disaster? Was it possible for such chance to always fall on the side of fortune in times of war?

Her father was right. Such thoughts only made her miserable. She struggled to control the monster let loose in her head, hoping to learn to live in the moment. She looked back at her son, at her parents, and vowed to follow their example and live in the day. With that resolution firmly in her mind, the monster pushed deep into a box below the love she felt for her family. She sat on the floor and played with her son, grateful for another day.

Chapter 36

JACOB: December 1944

Jacob, like Bonnie, could not shake the circus incident. He sent his family to Connecticut to be safe, but danger lurked everywhere. Bonnie and William could not be moved far enough away to be out of harm's way despite his decision to join the army. And that decision was leading him straight into a war that would change his very character if he made it home to have a character at all. Convinced that if he could become one with his gun, he would eventually make it home to Bonnie, he took his training even more seriously.

The days passed slowly. Minutes dragged by, leaden hands on the clock struggling to move forward. Tick, ticking throughout the long days of training and tick ticking into the long hours of the night.

Nonetheless, minutes passed into hours into days into weeks, until the fall settled in for a short Southern winter. During this time, he never stopped pleading with God to end the war before he deployed. His earnest prayer was, "God, please keep me safe. Please don't let me face a real battle with the Japs. Please let me go home to Bonnie without ever making it to the Pacific. Please."

As the first Christmas without his family neared, Jacob's unit finally received their orders. They would be leaving Alabama in January and shipping out on February 5.

"No. No. No," he thought. He prayed he wouldn't have to fight the Japs. He knew the day would come, but he had so hoped. However, as he looked at the orders again, his eyes screwed up in confusion. His unit was commanded to stage at Camp Shanks in Orangeburg, New York on January 28th and sail from the New York Port of Embarkation.

New York? He was supposed to leave from San Diego. The Pacific Theater always left from the West Coast.

He read his orders again. "Camp Shanks, Orangeburg, New York, 28 January 1945," and "Sail from the New York Port of Embarkation 5 February 1945."

He pulled Bullseye aside. "New York? Did you see we were going to New York? What gives?"

Bullseye shrugged. "Guess we are fighting the Germans. Japs. Germans. All the same, right?" he said with a grin. Jacob grinned back, but the smile didn't reach his eyes and the words scorched at his heart.

Bullseye had to be right. The orders only made sense if they were going to Europe. Since there were no Japs in

Europe, they were going to fight the Germans.

He thought about his silent prayers and wondered if God was having a good laugh at his expense. Certainly, an omniscient God realized when Jacob had prayed not to fight the Japs that he didn't mean he'd rather fight the Germans instead. He wanted to scream, "I didn't want to go to war at all! I just want to be back home with my family!"

The anguish in his heart blocked out the excitement to be shipping out experienced by the other men. Talk of dirty, rotten Nazis echoed through the barracks. The men were pumped up to kill some Krauts, and each man did his best to sound more ferocious than the one before.

Jacob didn't participate. Instead, he grabbed a piece of paper and began penning a letter to Bonnie. This would give him an excuse to remain aloof, while giving him time to digest the news. He had to find a way to reconcile his feelings. He joined the war to prove he was an American, not shoot at an enemy that was more like him than not.

Jacob was no Nazi sympathizer. That much was a fact. He hated what Hitler was doing to his ancestral country. He, too, wanted this madman defeated. And yet...Jacob was German. He heard the German Christmas carols echoing in his head. He tasted the pflaumen-kudhen on his tongue. He saw the German words printed in his mother's family Bible.

For the last year, whenever he held his gun to his shoulder and aimed, he always pictured a dirty Jap with his slanted eyes and a language that sounded like someone dropping metal scraps into a garbage bin. If he was forced into war, he wanted every one of them dead.

Their desire for power and their audacity at bombing his homeland warranted this anger because their actions threw the United States into the war.

But now, when he would be forced to aim his gun at a man who looked like him? Spoke in syllables that comforted him to sleep each night as a child? Came from a small town like Massenbach where Mattias Wendel Mueller had hailed? Of course, he had no choice, but this was not what he signed up to do.

He began his letter to Bonnie but couldn't tell her of his heartache. Because letters home could be censored, no one could know of his angst. Saying what was in his heart would label him as a German sympathizer. Such a label in the US Army during this second Great War could easily be a death sentence for him and a life of imprisonment for his family.

My Dearest Bonnie, My time here in Alabama is coming to a close. We got our orders today.

He sat with the tip of his pen to the paper, but no words came forth. After following the news reports religiously for months, it was apparent that the European Theater was struggling. They had to stop the advance of the Germans and quickly, or the war could end with the Nazis in charge. Yet, not once did he assume he would be part of that push. He had been so focused on the Japs he never let himself consider the possibility that he, Jacob, would fight against the Nazis.

We will be arriving in Orangeburg, New York on January 28tb and leaving for Europe on February 5th. I don't have many other details. I don't know exactly where we will be sent, but most of the action is around France and Germany. I suspect that is where we are headed.

He wondered if Bonnie would be able to read between the lines. Would she know of his ache? Would she understand his desire to fight for his country while also wanting to preserve his heritage? Would his benign sentences convey the despair in his heart?

I wish I were there with you and William getting ready for the holidays. Please give him a hug and kiss from his daddy. Tell him I love him.

Little William, now almost five, would be celebrating Christmas without his father. As he imagined his young son helping his grandfather cut down a Christmas tree, tears welled up in Jacob's eyes. It should be him. If it weren't for the war, he would be at home in his pink house with his beautiful wife, making babies and creating memories. Instead, he was here, in a barracks of men filled to the brim with mock bravado.

Out of nowhere, hate enveloped him. Hate for the Japs. Hate for the Germans. Hate for Americans who questioned his patriotism. Hate for everything and everyone who brought him to this place far away from his family. Yet, he did not write of hate, just of love.

As always, Bonnie, I send my love to you as well. The memory of your sunshine hair and imp-ish smile gets me through each lonely day. Stay strong, my love. I'll be home before you know it.
> *Love,*
> *Jacob*

He folded up the letter. It was too short, and she would want more information. More words. More comfort. But he didn't want her to glimpse the hate that bubbled up and threatened to strangle him.

There was no way he could write her a love letter with such vitriol flowing through his veins. She'd know, and she'd fret. It was kinder to make it short and keep the ugliness to himself. Let her think he was busy and had dashed off a note in a brief spare moment.

His visions of William creating memories without him was enough to push him to do what needed to be done. It was the very thing he needed to come to grips with going to the European Theater.

If it weren't for the Nazi power grab, innocent people like himself, who had been minding their own business and living their own lives, wouldn't have any problems. They'd be free to be Muellers and live in New Berlin. They wouldn't be taken off to internment camps like his friend Hanz. They wouldn't be joining the Army to prove anything at all. They would be at home, singing songs from the Old Country with their families and kissing their wives under the mistletoe.

The Nazis were also to blame for every single memory he was missing with his young child. For every single memory he was missing with his dear Bonnie. For every single lonely moment. For every ounce of his pain. Yes, he realized. He could kill the Germans. Not only could he, but he wanted to. He needed to.

The hate that engulfed his heart and soul would sustain him through the toughest times to come. But Jacob understood very clearly that the war had begun to change him just as Axel had warned, and he hadn't even left the country yet or faced his first enemy. He had yet to fire his weapon at anything other than an inanimate target. Nonetheless, his soul seethed with a blinding rage that left him empty of anything else.

He wondered if he would make it home alive. He wondered if Bonnie would recognize the man he became. He was doubtful, because as he stood in front of the mirror shaving his beard, he couldn't fathom who was staring back at him.

Chapter 37

BONNIE: December 1944

The day was December 15th. Bonnie read Jacob's letter for the umpteenth time. He was going to Germany, which she found surprising because he always wrote to her about heading to the Pacific. She always assumed he'd be on some island in the heat, and now, it appeared he'd be heading to Germany in the dead of winter.

She worried about that. Would he be warm enough? Would the Army make sure they sent him with the right boots and a warm coat? Certainly, they wouldn't send him to Germany with equipment meant for Midway.

She needn't have worried. The weeks leading up to the departure were spent readying for their landing in France. But, of course, she didn't know this. Instead, she fretted. It was her nature to worry about those she loved.

His letter also gave her another cause to worry. It was short and clipped. He said all the right things...yet, somehow, it didn't seem like he wrote the letter at all. It was almost as if someone else penned the words they thought he might say but hadn't quite got them right. That's why she kept rereading it – dissecting each phrase – looking for the clue that would help her understand the things Jacob did not say.

William was excited to see the letter as always. He now looked not only for the W but for his whole name. Ever since her father told him that W started many words, he constantly listened for the sound. When he found it, he would get excited and have her write it down to tell Daddy in the next letter. William didn't notice a problem with his father's words, nor did her mother or father. But she was certain something was bothering Jacob. She couldn't fathom what it might be.

Of course, she understood the hiding of emotions. Although she was doing her best to look forward to Christmas, she secretly wished the holiday would slip by without any fanfare. She didn't want to celebrate without Jacob. She didn't want William to have memories of a holiday without his father. She was terrified this might be the first of a lifetime of memories without Jacob by her side, making it nearly impossible to enjoy the time spent with family.

Nonetheless, she put on her happy face and pretended for William's sake. They made cookies. They sang carols. They drew Christmas pictures to send to Daddy. Someone looking in the window of their home would see a happy family celebrating the holidays despite the restraints of war. Someone looking in Bonnie's heart would have seen loneliness and heartache and worry mixed with very little Christmas spirit.

On Christmas Eve, the little family trudged out to the woods on the edge of town to let William pick out a tree, as was the family tradition. He ran from evergreen to evergreen, looking for the perfect tree, each one a bit larger than the last. Finally, he settled on a mammoth tree she was sure would never fit into their tiny living room.

But her father dutifully cut it down, and they drug it back home where the handmade decorations waited. All week, they had been making cinnamon ornaments, stringing popcorn, and creating baubles out of scraps from her mother's oversized blue sewing basket. Her father managed to scrounge up some Christmas lights with large colorful bulbs that would set the tree aglow.

Once decorated, William danced with delight around the tree, anticipating the arrival of Santa Claus. Bonnie was glad he was too young to remember trees from the past because this one was barren in comparison. She hated to think of how few presents would be under the tree the next morning. She had been able to buy him three new cars and a shiny firetruck, each wrapped separately in colorful paper and ribbons. His mother knitted him a sweater and some new mittens. Her father found a bag of marbles and was excited to teach William how to play. Bonnie knew he was too young and would likely roll the marbles around on the floor like balls, but she didn't say a word. Instead, she felt grateful her father worked so hard to give William what he no longer had – a father in the home.

The following morning, William's excitement was

contagious. His gaping mouth at the firetruck and his undying love for his grandfather as he examined each marble made her smile despite herself. She kept reminding herself this didn't have to be the beginning of something new. "Remember," she told herself, "be happy in the moment. Be happy with the simple things." William's happiness over Christmas and each of his presents was a simple thing, so she worked diligently to change her attitude.

The meal was also amazing. How her mother managed to procure the needed ingredients given their rations and the shortages of some of the most basic ingredients was beyond her. But she succeeded, and Bonnie worked her magic, putting together a feast fit for royalty with turkey, dressing, mashed potatoes, yams, cranberry sauce, and even a pumpkin pie for dessert. It was only that evening, after William had gone to bed, and she sat in the living room with her parents, that she truly missed Jacob. This is the time they would be sitting side by side, looking at the tree in the darkened room, and talking about the day, laughing over something William had said or done, kissing each other tenderly, and simply enjoying each other's companionship.

After what she hoped was a proper amount of time sitting with her parents, she excused herself to her room, stating it had been a long day. Once in the privacy of her bedroom, she pulled out Jacob's photo, the one he sent to her of him in his uniform after basic and cried herself to sleep.

Once Christmas was over, Bonnie had little to look forward to. William's fifth birthday was fast approaching, but the war didn't lend itself to lavish parties like the ones she had as a child. She hoped to take him to see a movie and buy theater popcorn as a treat, but that was still weeks away.

She fell into the boring rhythm that had become her life, with one day blending into the next. Get up in the morning. Head off to work. Eat lunch with Collette. Work some more. Come home. Cook dinner. Play with William. Go to bed. Repeat. She wondered how long she could continue living a life that was so lifeless.

On January 21ˢᵗ, she came home to find her mother waiting for her at the front door. She handed her a telegram from Jacob.

Have 24 leave in NYC on 28. Train station at 10am.

Bonnie reread the cable. Jacob, her dear sweet Jacob would be in New York City in just one week. She was going to hold him again before he left for Germany. She hadn't felt so alive in weeks. Until her father put his foot down.

No daughter of his was traveling alone on the train from Hartford to New York City. That was it, and it was final. Stating she was a grown woman with a child did nothing to appease him. Explaining she needed to be with Jacob did not move him. Begging was useless.

Sure, she could go on her own without his permission, but she needed the support of her parents now more than ever. She looked at her mother, her eyes pleading for compassion. Quietly, her mother said, "Carl, Bonnie is right. She and William need to see Jacob."

William. She hadn't thought of William. In her mind's eye, she only envisioned her running into Jacob's arms, kissing him passionately, and holding onto him, never wanting to let him go. What a terrible mother to think only of herself and her own needs.

Her mother continued, "I think we should all take the train to New York. We'll rent a small room for the night. William can visit his father and spend the night with us. This way, Bonnie and William can be together with Jacob. Bonnie won't travel alone, and the two can spend some time together before he goes to war."

Although she said it in a sweet, quiet tone, her eyes were steel. Her mother wasn't asking permission, but simply telling her father how things were going to go. She had never seen her mother take charge like that before and was grateful to experience it now.

Her father deftly turned the conversation around so the trip was now his idea and began making the appropriate arrangements. They decided not to tell William why they were going in case something didn't work out. Instead, they would tell him they were taking a trip by train for his upcoming birthday.

Bonnie wondered how many times this flip-flop of roles happened without her noticing. She had always seen her father as stern and gruff, always the head of the household. But this evening, her mother took the reins before allowing her father to take the credit.

With the knowledge that she would see Jacob in a few short days, time, once again dragged by, each day slower than the last. Finally, it was time to get on the train.

Although they would be traveling at night, they didn't purchase a sleeper car. The cost was too prohibitive. Instead, they sat in the passenger car, the lights flickering by the window, until one by one, they all fell asleep, propped on each other's shoulders, the side of her father's face pressed onto the hard, cold window.

Chapter 38

BONNIE AND JACOB: January 1945

As trees blurred by in the morning light, Elaine pulled some bread and jam out of a sack for breakfast. William hopped from one foot to the other, excitedly pointing out the window. "Look! It's a lake. I see a boat. Two boats!" Although his initial response had been more reticent, his last experience with trains being the day his father left for war, he now buzzed with enthusiasm. "I want a train of my very own. I'll keep it in my room with my cars and firetruck!"

Bonnie did her best to maintain a calm, steady exterior despite her elation, managing not to jump up and down and cause a scene. Unlike William, she understood the destination ended in Jacob's strong arms. Though she was glad William would be able to see his father, selfish thoughts often crossed her mind – she would rather have the 24 hours with Jacob completely to herself. Nonetheless, she planned to make the most of the time they had together.

Their train pulled into the station at 9:45 am, and there, on the platform, stood Jacob in his uniform, scanning the windows of the train. Bonnie saw him through the window, but Jacob had yet to see her. He was leaner than when he left, but looked, if that were possible, even more muscular. Although unlikely, she had the distinct impression he had grown taller as well.

He strained at the glass, desperate to catch a glimpse of her. She pressed her hand to the window, the way they had when he departed, and his eyes caught hers. Time slowed down and halted as they stared at one another, soaking in everything they missed during the last year.

William looked up at his mother's face, not understanding why she was smiling so broadly. He tried to get her attention by pulling on her coat, but she didn't hear him. He climbed onto the seat and put his hands on her face, but when she still didn't respond, he followed her gaze with his. In a flash, time moved forward again as William screamed, "Daddy!!!!!!!!

Crying, kissing, hugging, and laughter all mixed together like a hearty beef stew put to boil for a Sunday family gathering. William could not be persuaded to let go of his father, so Jacob hoisted the child into his right arm and swung the duffle bag over his left shoulder, using his left arm to pull Bonnie tight. Mother and Father Phillips flanked either side of the happy family as they made their way to the tiny hotel lobby.

For the next several hours, Jacob regaled them with

tales of army life in Arkansas, while Bonnie and William peppered him with questions. Bonnie, too, happily provided the tiny details of their life in Connecticut that rarely made it into a letter.

After dinner, when William could barely hold his eyes open another moment, Jacob tucked him into bed, said his goodnights to his in-laws, and whisked his bride into their waiting room. He was so happy to be with family again, but these next 12 hours were hers and hers alone. He didn't want to make small talk. He didn't want to put on a brave face. He didn't want to do anything other than hold his wife close, whisper in her ear, and let his fingers explore the length of her body.

Though Bonnie slept fitfully on the train, she was not tired. All she could think about was Jacob, his muscular body pressed against hers. By the end of the evening, she was having trouble keeping her hands to herself, despite the disapproving looks from her parents. Jacob had barely closed the door when she fell into his arms. The kiss was one suspended in time – one that each had dreamed about so often they both wondered if they would wake up to find it wasn't real.

They made love quickly and hungrily, unwilling to hold back their passions. Then they talked long into the night. In the dark, with Bonnie pressed to his side, he told her of his fears. Of his hatred. Of his longings. She reciprocated with her own secrets. Neither was shocked. Both simply took the words and tucked them away, helping to bridge the gap between what they had once known and what was now the truth. The war had changed them both.

Before dawn, they made love again. This time, more

slowly. Stripped of a sense of urgency, they enjoyed skin against skin, lips on shoulders, hands in hair. Bonnie secretly hoped she'd find herself pregnant. Jacob prayed fervently his seed would not find fertile ground. Each for the same reason – the fear this war would take him away and never bring him back again. Eventually, time demanded they untangle their bodies and dress, both wanting the clock to move more slowly – to give them even five more minutes.

Breakfast was far more somber than the dinner meal the night before. Although everyone painted on smiles, the conversation was as forced as the laughs. William sensed his Daddy was going away again. He clung to his arm so tightly that both had trouble eating. At 10:10, they all stood together on the platform as Jacob's train pulled in. He would take a short jaunt to Orangeburg and leave for Europe in just under a week.

If possible, this parting was more heart-wrenching than the last. Thankfully, Bonnie's parents said their goodbyes quickly, and left the three of them huddled together. William, still remembering the words of his uncle, held in the tears despite wide eyes and trembling lips. Bonnie, with no such instructions, let her tears fall unheeded, as did Jacob. The whistle blew mournfully, long and low. Jacob gave one last kiss to his family and boarded the train. Instinctively, he put his hand on the glass. Bonnie lifted her hand in response. William waved until the train was a speck on the horizon.

Jacob was heading to war.

Chapter 39

JACOB: Spring 1945

Watching Bonnie and William recede into the distance the second time was the hardest thing he'd ever been forced to do. When he left a year ago, he was headed to Indiana and then Arkansas. Although lonely, he was safe. This train ride would take him one step closer to real war.

His ship was set to arrive in France on February 14th. Valentine's Day. A day he should be with Bonnie, bringing her flowers and spending the evening within her loving embrace. Instead, he would be processed like a side of beef and attached to the Fifteenth United States Army.

While on the ship, Jacob paid close attention to his companions. Despite their loud talk and brave words, he detected the same fear that resided deep in his chest. Everyone declared the right words. Everyone wanted to win the war. But the unsaid words suggested these men weren't sure they were the right soldiers to make that happen. Nonetheless, like Jacob, they signed papers stating they would, indeed, fight to win, and were now headed to prove their mettle.

Their arrival in France corresponded with the arrival of a cold front that, to William, seemed to last the rest of the winter. Though France always sounded so romantic, the devastation from the last year of fighting left the countryside desolate. France was now devoid of German forces, due in large part to the Allied invasion that began in June, but the cities and towns were a jagged collection of rickety, burned-out buildings with occupants more akin to skeletons than humans.

Food was scarce, worse than it had been during the Depression. True, Jacob had rations, which was more than many could say. He thanked God above that he was given something to put in his belly every day. Even so, as in his youth, his hunger was never fully satisfied.

One day after a long march toward Nuremberg, he and several companions spotted a skinny, old chicken running between some bombed out houses. He took it upon himself to capture the bird, pluck the feathers from its scrawny body, and cook it on a spit for dinner. Despite the divine aroma of juices dripping into the fire, the meat was sinewy and stringy.

Jacob choked several times as he forced himself to swallow. Because of his hunger, he pushed in unpalatable bite after bite, before finally heaving into a narrow ditch by the side of the road until his stomach emptied. From that day forward, he never again wanted to eat chicken. Each time he tried, the meat would stick in his throat and his memory, causing a reflexive gag.

Jacob worked hard to keep his spirits up, looking for the positive in his situation. He was hungry, but at least had rations. He was cold, but at least had a wool coat and a blanket. He was in a war zone but was not in any real danger. This last blessing was the one for which he was most grateful.

The fighting in this area of France had ended. His unit's job was simply to clean up and keep the peace.

A few of his buddies experienced a skirmish here or there with a rogue Kraut hell-bent on going out in style, but luckily, Jacob was always occupied with some grunt work when it happened.

Rumors flew around camp like bullets. "Did you hear? We're going to be attached to another unit and be part of some real action" was in complete opposition to "Did you hear? The war is almost over. The Krauts are ready to surrender." Jacob prayed earnestly for the latter rumor to be true. He wanted the war to end before he engaged in a true battle. Unfortunately, on April 17, his division was reassigned to the Third United States Army and entered Germany two days later by crossing the Rhine at Mainz. They were heading straight to the front.

On their way, Jacob's unit went through Massenbach, his ancestral hometown, a tiny village with white houses and red roofs. A large church stood atop the hill surrounded by a cemetery. Except for the loaded guns and uniforms marching through the streets, Massenbach looked untouched by the war and likely as it had when Grandpa Mattias left decades ago.

German women and children peered at them from behind ragged curtains over broken windows. One little boy escaped from his mother and ran out into the yard before she could drag him back behind the shoddy wooden door. The boy, about the same age as William, bore a strong resemblance with his dark hair and dimpled smile. Jacob's hard-fought battle within his mind to view the German soldiers as his enemy crumbled like dust to the ground.

That boy could be William. The mother rushing to his side and dragging him back behind the safety of the thick door could be Bonnie. He imagined the woman's reaction to her son disobeying her orders to stay inside and the tears on the boy's face as her fear put him in his place.

Swiveling his head from left to right and back again, Jacob took in the reality of the town. House after house was shuttered up tight against the advancing American soldiers. Winter gardens were devoid of leaves, and spring gardens were going to seed. No one collected water at the well. The church bells did not chime the hour. No laundry hung in the warming spring breeze.

Massenbach, a town that once was his own, was a ghost town. The ghosts were not spirits, but women and children living in fear, starving, and wondering if they would live to see the end of the war. The men were gone, fighting on some front if they were lucky. Dead if they were not.

He was the enemy here. It wasn't the Krauts these women feared. It was Jacob. Jacob the German American who chose his new homeland over his old one. Jacob who believed Germans were vicious and cruel. Jacob who blamed the Germans and their need for power for the war. Jacob with his rifle as his best friend.

Bile rose uninvited in Jacob's throat. He barely made it behind a tree before he heaved, tears falling unheeded onto his shirt. He quickly wiped his eyes. He could easily tell his companions the food hadn't agreed with him. It was true. But he wouldn't be able to explain the tears. How could he tell those who counted on him in battle that he wondered if the Germans were any more the enemy than they were?

His angst, however, was short-lived. Within hours, bullets began flying over his head. His enemy was no longer the Krauts. Or the Japs. Or the thoughts in his head. His enemy was any gun pointed in his direction. He shot at guns, stuffing the humanity from Massenbach down deep. Guns. He would shoot at guns.

From Nuremberg to the Isar River to Wasserburg to Indorf, they fought their way through the final days of April. Shooting by day, muddy, wet, cold foxholes by night. Those Jacob had grown to love died at his feet, bullets whizzing by his ears so closely he swore he felt the breeze on his cheeks.

After the first real day of battle, Jacob slumped into the foxhole to take his turn at sleeping in the deafening noise. Despite the nightfall, his companions' faces lit up with each explosion, illuminating the anger or fear or defeat, depending on the face or the moment. Jacob pulled out the crumpled photo of Bonnie and William. He had come to view this photo as his lucky charm. Certainly, it was the reason for what he was doing and the catalyst for making it home.

Stuffing the image back in his pocket with the letter he had written to Bonnie in case of his death, he pulled his helmet down over his eyes. In what seemed like mere moments, a hand shook his shoulder. It was his turn to watch.

And so it went, the fighting continuing day after day, night after night. The Germans fought with ferocity, as though, Jacob mused, they were fighting for a land they loved. Apparently, no one had yet told them the rumor that the Americans were winning the war and defeat was on the horizon.

When he could, he tried writing to Bonnie to let her know he was alive. However, the raging battle kept him busy, and even if he'd found the time to write, the mail service was spotty at best. Jacob rarely heard from her now that he was no longer in the United States. Because the letters that made it through to the front were months old, he had no idea if she was receiving his posts. She must be worried, but there was nothing he could do to comfort her. He simply prayed she would feel his presence and know he loved her more than life itself.

William turned five while he was aboard the ship to France. Then Spring arrived without much fanfare, but he imagined the apple trees in bloom near their home in North Canton. How had an entire year passed with only one brief visit to his family? How many more years would pass before he held them in his arms again? More importantly, would he ever see them again?

When he did manage to write, he tried to keep his letters upbeat and positive, but there wasn't a lot to say. He wasn't going to tell her about companions in his foxhole being shot mere moments after he ducked for cover. He couldn't explain the sheer magnitude of the noise. He didn't want to worry her with his incessant hunger or the cold rain. But this was his current reality.

He looked around at the men who had become his brothers. Haggard men, streaked with dirt and unkempt hair, smiles that didn't always reach their eyes. They had seen too much and lost too many.

Stew was shot through during their first full-scale engagement. He crumpled in the field, falling first to his knees as a red circular stain spread across his back. Then, he unceremoniously fell forward without a sound, face planting in the dirt – and there he remained throughout the day as bullets whizzed overhead. It wasn't until nightfall that they were able to bring what was left of him back to safety. It was Jacob who had reached into his pocket and rescued the letter penned to the man's mother 'just in case.'

Then, last week, they lost Bullseye. The day had been long and cold, the fighting non-stop. William loaded, locked, aimed, and fired in an endless procession, until, finally, Bullseye relieved him.

"Go on, Mule. Grab a bit of grub and try to catch a little shuteye. It's time for a professional to take over." He grinned broadly as he pulled the rifle to his shoulder, giving Jacob a playful jab with his foot. And then his smile disappeared, along with half his face. Some Kraut had gotten a bead on him mere seconds after he and Jacob exchanged places.

No, these were not the stories his dear Bonnie needed. He refused to burden her with his doubts and fears.

Because of this, he tried to look for some funny story to retell. Even in the midst of such total devastation, he found a bit of humor poking its head out warily to see if it might be appreciated. In one letter, he talked about the state of his boots and how his toes were thankful to be liberated from the uncompromising leather. In another, he wrote about his buddy's girl back home and how she would cover his envelopes in red lipstick.

There were other funny things he saw and heard, but they were too close to the truth to send in a letter. For instance, as they learned how to use the rocket launcher in the field, the directions read, "Aim towards the enemy." Another sage piece of advice was, "If the enemy is in range, so are you." Although he and the boys got a good laugh, he couldn't imagine Bonnie would find the humor in the situation. Of course, Jacob learned if you didn't laugh, you'd simply sit down on the cold, wet ground and cry.

His unit's goal was to reach Czechoslovakia, where the final stronghold of German soldiers remained. Here, they would work with the Russians, who were fierce soldiers known for their cruelty. In fact, in the final days of battle, entire German units were surrendering to US forces just to avoid imprisonment by the Russians. The fanatics, however, those Jacob believed were the most responsible for the war, continued to fight.

On May 6th, Jacob's division was assigned to capture the Skoda Munitions Plant in Pilsen. The battle was easier than most. Despite the fear that the ease with which they met their goal meant they were walking into an ambush, the plant was in their possession before nightfall. The next two days, the first non-battle days in weeks, were spent 'mopping up' and patrolling the area.

The silence, after so many nights of continuous battle, was uncomfortable to Jacob's ears. He detected every insect, footstep, or muffled conversation. Each felt louder than the explosions that had been bombarding his ears for days. He considered the saying that silence was deafening, finally understanding what it meant.

Two days after the battle in Pilsen marked the formal acceptance of the Allied Forces of Germany's surrender. VE-Day. The war in Europe was over. However, unlike the ticker tape parades and celebrations happening throughout Europe, soldiers on the front lines, like Jacob and his unit, were a bit slow to believe it was over. It took time to acknowledge the shooting which had come to a stop, and the silence that followed was a permanent condition.

Shortly after the surrender, General Eisenhower sent a message to his troops. Jacob read the words while looking over the shoulder of another soldier. They read: *The route you have traveled through hundreds of miles is marked by the graves of former comrades. Each of the fallen died as a member of the team to which you belong, bound together by a common love of liberty and a refusal to submit to enslavement. Our common problems of the immediate and distant future can be best solved in the same conceptions of co-operation and devotion to the cause of human freedom as have made this Expeditionary Force such a mighty engine of righteous destruction.*

Let us have no part in the profitless quarrels in which other men will inevitably engage as to what country, what service, won the European war. Every man, every woman, of every nation here represented has served to the outcome. This we shall remember – and in doing so we shall be revering each honored grave and be sending comfort to the loved ones of comrades who could not live to see this day.

It was true. The path to Czechoslovakia was strewn with friends, as well as enemies. Now that the Germans had surrendered, Jacob's hidden angst, the despair and lament he refused to allow since marching through Massenbach, came rushing forward out of the dark. The truth that each gun he killed was held by men like himself haunted his thoughts.

Once again, he pushed the thoughts down. The war was only half over. Despite his buddies talking about going home, those thoughts were premature. The Japanese were still at work. His unit had been trained to kill these enemies, and he had no doubt he would be sent to do so.

This understanding, as well as the sheer loss of lives in the European Theater of operations, tempered his VE-Day celebration. He stood on a hill looking over Pilsen and contemplated the war. In the past year alone, over half a million US soldiers were wounded or killed. But as considerable as that number was, it didn't begin to encompass the entirety of the death toll. Germans died, too. As did Poles, Czechs, French, British, Russians...not one European country was spared. The final count was well over 40 million people, half of which were women, children, and the elderly – those who hadn't signed up to die.

He was immensely thankful the war had not come close to his family. Somehow, other than the initial bombing at Pearl Harbor, the United States managed to avoid direct attack. He couldn't imagine fighting the war only to come home to find his wife and child had been collateral damage to a war they didn't start.

He said a quick prayer, thanking God his family had been spared. Then he shed a few tears for those who weren't as lucky.

Chapter 40

BONNIE: Spring 1945

Initially, Bonnie raced to the mailbox every day upon arriving home from work, waiting breathlessly for her next letter from Jacob. Eventually, she gave up asking about letters from her true love – she hadn't heard from him in weeks.

Of course, in some ways, she was grateful. If there was no communication, then he was still alive and had not been captured by the enemy. She knew what happened when a soldier died. She witnessed it over and over as uniformed soldiers came to a home, knocked on the door, and a high-pitched keening rose up over the rooftops. The next day, the blue star on the service flag in the window would be covered by a gold star as the family mourned.

She also knew they could come knocking if Jacob were captured because this is what happened to her friend. One day, a few months earlier, Collette did not come to work on Friday, and Bonnie assumed she was sick. With such close quarters in the typing pool, Bonnie felt she worked in a giant petri dish with scientists hovering to determine what would happen next. However, when Collette didn't come to work for three more days, she got worried.

After work on Wednesday, Bonnie headed to Collette's home. Although they didn't get together often after work, they had spent a few Saturday afternoons working together on different projects like canning the green beans in Collette's victory garden. Upon arrival, she found her friend sitting in the front room with uncombed hair and vacant eyes.

Bonnie knelt in front of her, concern and fear pulling at her features, and engulfed her dear friend into a hug. She had no way of knowing what had happened, but intuited it was about her husband, Robert. Collette began to cry, softly at first, and then in uncontrolled sobs that shook her tiny frame. Bonnie, now terrified, now certain that what Collette would tell her was going to rock her world, let her cry, waiting for the devastating news.

Eventually, Collette's sobs turned to hiccups and sniffles, but she was still silent. Bonnie didn't press for answers. She would know soon enough, and she was terrified at what she was going to learn. Anything that happened to Collette could just as easily happen to her.

Finally, Collette said in a whisper that Bonnie strained to hear, "Robert has been captured." Bonnie's first reaction was one of relief. Robert was not dead.

But...being a prisoner of war was not something anyone wished for. In some ways, it could be worse than death.

Collette went on, "He is in a German prison camp. I don't know anything else. I don't know if he was wounded. I don't know if he is with other men from his unit. I just don't know." And she began to cry again.

Bonnie determined that not knowing was harder on her friend than a sure knowledge that Robert had died. In her mind, her husband suffered all manner of atrocities at the hands of the hated Germans. The stories of POW camps ran rampant throughout the United States. Prisoners were left in isolation. Cells were not heated despite the bitter cold. Food was scarce, leaving many POWs to starve to death. Interrogations after deprivation, and worse yet, interrogations combined with torture. Frostbite. Missing teeth. Broken bones. It was no wonder Collette didn't come back to work for two weeks. And when she did, though she still ate lunch with Bonnie, she no longer had the quick, innocent smile or the look of mischief in her eyes. The war hit too close to home.

Bonnie, though certain Jacob was still alive, was anxious for news. Her friend Collette's suffering only intensified her yearning to know more. Since she could not count on letters from Jacob, she became glued to the news each evening, trying to determine where Jacob might be and how the war progressed. She purchased an atlas and made a mark whenever the news mentioned Europe, always wondering if Jacob had been part of the action there.

"A three-day offensive by the American Tenth Mountain Division, aided by Brazilian troops, has resulted in gains up to five miles as of yesterday afternoon and

greatly improved the Fifth Army's positions southwest of Bologna, according to today's official reports."

She hadn't received a letter from Jacob in so long she wasn't even sure what Army he was attached to. So, she dutifully listened and made a mark slightly southwest of Bologna.

"Field Marshal Sir Bernard L. Montgomery drove two armored columns toward the great north German port of Bremen and the city of Hanover today, while Gen. Omar N. Bradley's tanks, massing for a drive across central Germany, pushed steadily eastward along the road to Leipzig."

"Rolling at the rate of more than twenty-five miles a day, the United States First Army's armor under the command of General Eisenhower swung almost without hindrance tonight toward a juncture east of the Ruhr with the United States Ninth Army."

"Soviet troops, smashing as much as twelve miles through German Baltic defenses, yesterday captured the big junctions of Lauenburg and Kartuzy on the road to Danzig and split the enemy lines on the outskirts of the former Free City. The pocket in the Danzig area also was substantially reduced."

"Leaving trails of steaming vapor in their wake, United States bombers bound for Berlin bombed armament industries in and around the Nazi war capital."

She placed red X's on Bremen, Hanover, Leipzig, east of the Ruhr, Lauenburg, Kartuzy, Danzig, Free City, and Berlin. Despite listening intently, she never determined where her husband might be or what he might be doing.

Though the news told her little, she still listened every day. She cried when she learned of casualties even if certain Jacob couldn't have been involved. The tears were two-fold – tears of sadness for other families losing their loved one and tears of joy that Jacob was still alive. When she was happy, she felt guilty. When she felt sad, she felt guilty as well. Trying to reconcile her emotions coupled with guilt was difficult and often left her lethargic. Only William pleading with her to play cars forced her off the couch.

The exhaustion of waiting, worrying, and wondering was like moving through thick soup, her feet being sucked into the dredges, and her body unable to move with her former fluidity. No matter how hard she fought to release her body from this sludge, she simply could not get free.

She went to work and came home each day but felt nothing inside except anxious dread and the anticipation of one waiting for the death squad to pull the trigger. She would hold her breath as she approached her home each evening, believing that two soldiers would be waiting to give her the excruciating news of Jacob's death. Though no soldiers ever appeared, the gripping fear of imminent disaster never abated.

Her nights were no better. Instead of falling into a deep, blissful sleep at the end of a long day, she would be plagued with terrifying visions. Planes crashing. Bombs exploding. Bullets flying overhead. Jacob crumpling to the ground as a patch of red grew across his chest, grimacing in pain, mouthing the words, "I love you." She would wake in the morning more tired, if that were even possible, than the day before. She was a mere shadow of the woman who sent Jacob to war.

Then, on Monday, May 8th, the radio blared with the

news all America had been waiting for. The European war had ended. *"Throughout the world, throngs of people hail the end of the war in Europe. It is five years and more since Hitler marched into Poland. Years full of suffering and death and sacrifice. Now the war against Germany is won. A grateful nation gives thanks for victory."*

Germany surrendered. As she sat in the large room with the rest of the ladies in the typing pool, the heavy, dull blanket that had enveloped her for months dropped from her arms and legs. Her head cleared. She noted the colors of the room. She heard the laughter echoing in her ears. She was unaware that the sound came from deep within as she laughed for the first time since Jacob said goodbye in New York.

There were celebrations across America with parades and bands and confetti. Everyone with a flag within the little city of Hartford displayed it, making the roadways a blur of red, white, and blue as she drove home from work that day. In their own home, her mother used their rations to bake a cake and churn some homemade ice cream for an impromptu celebration.

Bonnie could tell William didn't know what to think. He listened to the news with the adults, but the words were too big and cumbersome for him to understand. Mostly, he pushed his cars around on the floor in front of the radio, flashing the occasional smile at his mother. He seemed to comprehend something good was happening but was unsure how it affected him.

She was careful not to say Daddy would be home soon, because soon to a child was so different from soon to an adult. However, Bonnie felt confident she'd be with Jacob by the end of the summer. It was this hope that buoyed her up and gave her an energy she hadn't experienced in months. The anxiety was gone. Jacob was safe. The war was over. Soon, the troops would come home, to waiting girlfriends, wives, children, mothers. The smile would not leave her face.

The next morning, President Truman announced the official German surrender. She stayed home from work, despite it being a Tuesday, because she didn't want to leave William. She had a strong desire to be with her family, celebrating the impending homecoming of her husband. The war, this horrible nasty war that had taken so much from them, was over.

William warmed up to the idea that something good was happening and asked if they could go to the park. Bonnie was more than happy to oblige. After lunch, she would take him to the park, and they'd fly his kite. She couldn't think of anything better to do with a free afternoon at the end of the war than watch a kite fly free in the wind.

Both her parents were home to listen to the President speak, too. Truman began:

"This is a solemn but glorious hour. I wish that Franklin D Roosevelt had lived to see this day. General Eisenhower informs me that the forces of Germany have surrendered to the United Nations. The flags of freedom fly all over Europe. For this victory, we join in offering our thanks to the Providence that has guided and sus-tained us through the dark days of adversity."

As President Truman continued to talk, Bonnie's mind wandered. She was so grateful for the German surrender. But she wasn't at all certain she was thankful to Providence. Providence had allowed the war in the first place. Providence had not kept Jacob on US soil. Providence had sent her husband and many others into harm's way. Was it really Providence who had brought the war to an end?

She had never been terribly religious and often wondered how those who lost loved ones reconciled their faith with the reality of their situation. Could a loving God let innocent people die in a war? She was pretty certain she'd never be able to believe in a God who allowed her husband to die. She had a hard enough time accepting Him now.

These kinds of thoughts, however, always left her uneasy, as if tempting fate. She was well aware she should have faith in God and worried He might be angry with her ungrateful musings. So, as she always did whenever she questioned His all-knowing nature and benevolence, she quickly bowed her head, saying a silent prayer for the continued safety of Jacob and his unit. Now was not the right time to be angry with God.

As she said "Amen," she heard Truman's next words: *"We must work to finish the war. Our victory is but half-won. The West is free, but the East is still in bondage to the treacherous tyranny of the Japanese. When the last Japanese division has surrendered unconditionally, then only will our fighting be done."*

With these words, Bonnie's stomach began to sink as if she had swallowed a large brick. It was then she realized a cruel trick had been played on her. It was then a thought as piercing as a bullet and just as deafening exploded in her head.

The war was not over.

Europe was in full celebration, as was evidenced by

the front-page stories in the newspaper this morning, but the newspapers didn't tell the whole story. The soldiers, her Jacob, would now be needed to fight the Japanese.

Truman's words echoed in her head. "Last Japanese division...Then only will our fighting be done." How could she have been so naïve? How could she have been so blind to the reality of the situation? Jacob was not through fighting. Jacob had already been trained to fight in the Pacific while in Arkansas. It was only a last-minute change that sent him to Germany.

As this realization screamed through her body, a cold sweat broke out on her brow. A wave of heat washed over her to be replaced immediately by icy cold fingers. Everything slowed down until the words on the radio made little sense.

"Oh, God, no! Please, no." Jacob slipped away from her grasp. His presence in her mind disappeared with each word uttered by President Truman. The war was not over, and he was not through fighting. Jacob is not coming home.

Bonnie now experienced everything through the veil of a monk's chant: Not coming home. Not coming home. Not coming home.

Her father said something about victory to her mother, and her mother laughed in return. It was a tinkling sound full of vibrant life. They had not yet been engulfed by the chant that held her captive. They were unaware of the true implication of the President's words. They were still under the illusion that Jacob would be coming home.

The chant continued in her head. Not coming home. Not coming home. Not coming home.

She tried to shake her head no. She wanted her

parents to understand that the war was far from over. She wanted them to feel her agony, to hold her in their arms, to cry the tears that wouldn't fall from her eyes. But no words came. Her head would not obey her mind's commands. She sat there with "not coming home" running on an endless loop.

She resorted to screaming in her head at her father. "NO! Daddy, no. There is no victory. Jacob is not coming home. This isn't victory. He can still die at the hands of the enemy." But her father could not hear the words in her head and continued to laugh and smile as though all were right with the world. And the chant continued, "Not coming home. Not coming home."

Pushing the chant aside, she began begging God, pleading with him to forget her earlier musings. "No, God, no! Please, please do not send Jacob back to war. Please let him be finished. Please let him come home. I cannot live like this much longer. I don't want to live without him." But the chant inside her head refused to be stifled. The louder she screamed in her head at God, at her father, at the world, the louder the chant became until the words boomed in her ears, overtaking all other thoughts.

She was frantic, but no one in the room acknowledged her angst. Truman droned on in slow motion, reading the formal proclamation. William pushed his cars around on the floor. Mother rocked back and forth in her chair with the mending in her lap. Her father puffed on his pipe.

"Not coming home! Not coming home! Not coming home!"

President Truman's voice sounded far away, as if

someone had moved the radio to another room. But there it stood broadcasting the news she didn't want to hear – Jacob was not coming home. "Not coming home. Not coming home."

The edges of the room were now very dark, and she could only see the radio, as if it were in the center of a long tunnel. The last words before she fainted were: *"The power of our people to defend themselves against all enemies will be proved in the Pacific War as it was in Europe."*

Chapter 41

WILLIAM: November 2016

William put the truck into park at the top of the drive but didn't immediately get out and head into the house. Instead, he gazed at the flag whipping on the flagpole – a methodical back and forth that soothed his swirling mind. He was such a proud American and could not imagine what his life might have been like had Germany or Japan succeeded. In those moments, he was deeply grateful that his father, along with other men of his ilk, took up the call and fought.

However, the little boy with the sad eyes brought back floods of emotions he successfully squelched for years, and the rhythmic flag taunted him with 'what ifs.' Throughout his life, whenever he felt a 'poor pitiful me' moment bubbling to the surface, he forced it back down with a strong shot of pride in his father followed closely by a chaser of patriotism. He wasn't going to be a whiny man, blaming all his troubles on his father's absence during what psychologists now called the formative years.

Despite all the shoving and hiding, the truth was that the war didn't just change his father and his mother. It changed William, too. Perhaps not really changed him as much as created him. Yes, created. He had been a mere child without any strong roots or understanding of the world.

His mother's tears and his grandmother's anxious fussing formed a basis for what life was and how it worked. Missing the man as tall as the trees and as strong as a bear taught him to be brave even when he was not. Well-meaning phrases like "Don't cry" or "Be a big soldier" taught him real men don't have emotions. The war created the man known to his family as William.

Today, as the flag shimmied in the wind, he finally allowed himself to feel things that had been locked up for nearly three-quarters of a century. What, he wondered, would life have been like if there had been no war at all?

William's life in Hartford wasn't terrible. He had a room of his own. He had a mother who loved him and a grandmother who took care of him each day. He had a grandfather who provided the presence of a man in the home. He had a yard to play in and toys to play with. Compared to children in war-torn Europe, his was a luxurious life.

Of course, William knew nothing about Poland or

France or Czechoslovakia. He knew nothing of bombed-out homes or orphanages. He knew nothing of Jewish death camps. What he did know was that he missed his daddy and his dog. He wanted to go home to live in the pink house with the apple trees and have Mommy with him every day instead of Grandma.

He loved Grandma Phillips. She loved him and cared for him while his mommy was at work. But she didn't sing funny little songs to make William laugh or make up silly words that were special for just the two of them. With Grandma too busy to take him to play with the neighborhood boys, his mother at work, his father at war, and Vonk back in Ohio, he was lonely.

He spent his days sitting outside talking to his cars. They became his best friends. They listened to all his secrets and his dreams. One day, he wanted to design cars like Grandpa used to do. In fact, he would spend hours drawing cars, but rarely were they seen by anyone other than the little black ants he disturbed as he shifted the dirt around with the pointed end of a stick.

Of course, to say that he spent every day sad and lonely wouldn't be true. He loved ice delivery day. Twice a week, on Monday and Thursday, Earl came riding down the street with a horse named Bugs and his wagon piled high with huge chunks of ice covered lightly with straw to keep the sun from melting away his goods.

It was unusual to see a horse on the road since most people used cars, but Earl went back to doing things the way his daddy did them during the First World War. With rationing of rubber and gasoline, he told his customers his horse-drawn wagon was simply part of the war effort.

As soon as William detected the distinct clopping sound of Bugs' hooves on the pavement, he would run to the kitchen and beg for a scrap of apple, celery, or carrot. Then he would race through the front of the house and out onto the porch, letting the door bang noisily behind him.

Out to the front yard he would go, stopping at the gate, knowing he was not allowed to go out into the street. Here he would stand guard, hopping impatiently from foot to foot, waiting for Earl and Bugs to arrive. Breaking the ice into chunks was not a quick process, so he would often have to wait for 30 minutes or more as Earl inched closer and closer to William's home.

Finally, when the excitement was at fervor pitch, and William's tiny frame quivered with anticipation, Earl would pull up to the gate, wave his hat at the grinning boy, and say, "William! So nice to see you today. I see you didn't go in to work this morning." Then he'd let out a laugh that started in the hollows of his toes, building steam until it jumped clear of his mouth and exploded into the yard inches away from William's sentry post.

William didn't understand the joke, but he loved it when Earl laughed, so he would laugh right along with him. Then he'd call to his grandma, telling her to come out because Earl was here with the ice.

Grandma would come down the walk slowly, wiping her hands on a cloth she'd put over her shoulder. William wasn't to go outside the gate until Grandma was by his side. Her slow procession down the walk seemed like an eternity as Bugs' treats became hot and sticky in his small hands. As soon as she reached William, he would push through the gate and run to the front of the wagon, talking to Bugs the whole time.

"Hi, Bugs. Remember me? William? I've got a treat for you today. It's some carrots. Grandma's making soup. I don't think you'd like soup much, but I like it, don't I, Grandma?" he'd say, flinging the last words over his shoulder at his grandma. She would smile and nod as William went back to his conversation with Bugs.

"Do you like pulling the wagon, Bugs? Is it heavy? It looks heavy. I'm designing a wagon for you that will make it easier to pull the ice. It has more wheels and is this big." William stretched his hands out to the sides as far as he could stretch, making Bugs whinny as the treats were taken out of his reach.

William quickly put his arms back down so Bugs could finish eating. When the last piece of carrot was eaten, William turned his attention to Earl. He loved how Earl cut the ice from the enormous block into something small enough to fit in the kitchen box.

Each block of ice on Earl's wagon was bigger than William's bed. Earl once told him that two blocks of ice weighed the same as Bugs. William couldn't imagine picking up Bugs, but Bugs seemed to have no trouble hauling four big blocks at a time.

Of course, William understood Earl couldn't bring the huge block of ice into the house. It was far too large and wouldn't fit in the ice box. Grandma always asked for 40 pounds of ice, so Earl would grab up his ice pick and ax and chip away at the block until a smaller block magically appeared.

Earl would grab up the new small block with a pair of metal tongs that he held in his large, heavy-gloved hands. He'd throw the block over his back, protected by a black cape that reminded William of a rain slicker, and place the ice into the box in the kitchen.

The best part, however, came at the very end. Earl would turn to William and offer him a small sliver of ice as a treat. He would suck on the cold indulgence until it melted in his mouth or down the front of his shirt, whichever came first. Earl's ice delivery was the absolute best part of his week.

Eventually, the days got warmer. Grandma didn't need to bundle him up in his coat, scarf, and mittens before heading out into the yard. In fact, most days, he could play with a light jacket or sweater. The trees turned many shades of light green, and the birds sang lovely tunes in the sunshine.

He was sitting in the yard, pushing his cars around a new road he created under the towering maple tree, when he stopped, suddenly afraid. Grandma shouted something. Then, the neighbor lady screamed. He didn't know what was happening. His hand was frozen to his car and the only things moving were his eyes, which darted from house to house.

Before long, the neighborhood, which was normally so quiet that the bees buzzing on the flowers were audible, began to hum with noise. Voices grew loud. Neighbors cried. And laughed. Suddenly, a loud noise exploded into the air as someone shot off their gun on the front porch. William, not understanding what was happening, fell to the ground and began to cry.

He wanted his mom, but no one came for him. No

one thought to tell him what was happening because they assumed he was a happy-go-lucky boy without a care in the world. The adults in his life all wished they could be him, free from worries about the war. They didn't understand his loneliness. They didn't understand his fears. They didn't understand how the war was shaping him and would be with him for the rest of his life.

Eventually, William got up enough nerve to sneak into the house, tears mingled with dirt making muddy streaks down his 5-year-old cheeks. When he stood in the doorway, Grandma was laughing. She grabbed him by the shoulders and pulled him close. It was then the radio announcer stated:""...*throngs of people hail the end of the war in Europe.*"

He wasn't sure what a throng or Europe was, but he grasped the meaning of the words 'end of the war.' Was it possible? Was the war that took his daddy away and made him leave Vonk and took his mommy to work and brought them to Connecticut and made them leave their pink house over? As Grandma continued to hold him close, William was no longer afraid. However, he was uncertain why the tears continued to fall from his eyes.

For the next several days, the radio hummed constantly. Mommy stayed home more. Everyone was happy. They even made cake and ice cream, which he hadn't eaten since his birthday, a very long time ago to a child of five.

Grandpa puffed his pipe and used words like 'victory over the Nazis' and 'God's will was done.' William didn't know what these words meant, but since Grandpa said them with the broadest smile he ever saw, he was happy.

Then Grandpa announced the President of the United

States would soon be speaking to the nation. William learned about presidents from his grandpa. They were the leaders of the country. The first president was Washington – it started with a 'W' just like William. Washington was his favorite for that very reason.

He also learned a president died while Daddy was in the war. He couldn't pronounce the name, but it always reminded him of 'rooster.' The new president called himself True Man. William couldn't understand why. He knew what the truth was and what a man was. That was easy. But he didn't understand why someone would want to call themselves that. Nonetheless, President True Man was going to speak, and Grandpa was excited.

When the president came on the radio, the room got very quiet. The only sounds were the President's words, the wind softly rustling the living room curtains, and tiny wheels rolling on the braided rug as he pushed his cars along his imaginary highways.

Although he tried to listen to the words, they made little sense. Solemn. Rooster. Eyes-in-a-Shower. Victory. Providence. Adversity. He did hear the word surrender, which Grandpa told him meant that the Germans gave up and didn't want to fight the war anymore. That was good because that meant his daddy could come back home to him.

No one said so, but he was sure that would happen. Daddy left to fight in the war. The President told everybody that the war was over. Now, his daddy could come home. It made perfect sense. So, he quit trying to listen to the words and rolled his cars around the edges of the rug, waiting for the moment his daddy would knock on the front door.

He wondered how long it would take for his daddy to come home. Maybe he could get here by suppertime. The thought made him smile.

As he sought out his mother's eyes to see if his daddy might really come home in time to tuck him into bed, his mommy fell from her chair. Grandpa and Grandma flew to her side. William stared with round eyes – a new fear entering his heart.

Chapter 42

JACOB: Summer 1945

Despite the VE-Day proclamation, life at the munitions plant continued exactly as it had before the surrender. Patrols scouted the area and stood guard, but against an enemy who no longer existed. At first, after weeks of constant noise and commotion, the peaceful days were exactly what the soldiers longed for. Eventually, however, they got bored, and when soldiers get bored, trouble seems to follow.

Looting was a real issue. It wasn't so much that the men were mean-spirited. No one in Jacob's unit ever hurt anyone to obtain the spoils of war. They simply wanted some sort of souvenir to take home to prove they'd been there. With no need to focus on survival, they used the extra energy to focus on finding the best prizes to take home to their families.

The spoils were sparse at best. The little town of Pilsen had been under siege for weeks and most things of value were already gone. However, this did not stop the patrols from sifting through the rubble and wandering into homes. One day, when Jacob was out on patrol with six other men, they decided to snoop around in a now defunct air raid shelter. Perhaps they'd find something taken into the shelter by a panicked German after a midnight siren and discarded as they quickly left the city for the last time.

As Jacob and his buddies made their way down the stairs, they found a light bulb burning in the center of the large room, the light swinging slightly from side to side. Jacob's skin came alive with gooseflesh, the hairs standing at attention. Electricity to the city had been cut off for weeks. And why was the bulb not only shining but moving? There were no birds. There was no breeze. The dangling light had no reason to sway.

"This makes no sense," he said in a loud whisper to his companions. "Why is there electricity here in the shelter? I don't think we are alone."

His companions ribbed him for being a chicken. "What's gotten into you, Mule? We've won the damned war. We are the victors and to the victors belong the spoils! It's a wonder we won with people like you afraid of a light bulb." The rest of his group laughed.

Despite his misgivings, the rest of the group began to search for treasures. Buzz located a door at the far end of the large room. What lay behind the door sent everyone into an excited frenzy. Along the walls were several SS weapons with the swastika symbol emblazoned on the butt. Several plates of half-eaten food sat on the floor as well. Fresh food. In the corner of the room crouched a young girl, trembling uncontrollably, furtively glancing at another closed door on the far wall.

As Buzz grabbed the handle, ready to jerk the door open, Jacob could contain himself no longer.

"No! Buzz, this is stupid. Obviously, someone has just been here. I don't feel right about this. I'm leaving. We all need to leave. Grab what you are going to grab and let's get the hell out of here."

Jacob's eyes were firm, and his voice was steady. He rarely gave orders, leaving everyone shocked that he did so now. Yet, one by one, they grabbed up a few of the weapons, looked back at the young girl, and walked out of the shelter, back to the munitions plant. Although the guys ribbed him for being a coward, no one stayed to determine what was behind the closed door. Jacob wasn't worried about the names because, despite their ribbing, they felt the same way. They just needed someone brave enough to say so.

Jacob was not surprised when official word came down that some soldiers would be demobilized and discharged, while others would be kept in Germany for the occupation or redeployed to fight the Japs. Who got what assignment depended on points as per the ASRS.

The point system, officially known as the Advanced Service Rating Score, wasn't too complicated. Every soldier got points for doing certain things while enlisted. If you earned enough points, you went home. If you didn't, you stayed. Jacob finally got hold of a copy of the ASRS and added up his points quickly in his head.

One point for every month of military service. He had been in the army since April the previous year. That gave him 13 points. One point for each month of overseas service. He had been in Europe for 4 months. Four more points for a total of 17 points. He had one battle star for five points, and a dependent child at home for another 12 points. Jacob's total of 34 points did not meet the required 85 to go home.

Though not surprising news, Jacob hung his head. Seeing the truth written out in black and white was tough. He began preparing for the day he would be sent to the Pacific.

He wanted to write to Bonnie but didn't know what to tell her. He imagined a letter that started with:

> *Dear Bonnie,*
> *I am 51 points shy of coming home. The fastest way to get back to you is to go into battle in the Pacific, earn some medals for combat, pray I don't get shot or captured, and be home in a year or two.*

No. That letter would have to wait. Once he received orders, he'd write and let her know what to expect. There was no need to frighten her. Of course, he had no way of knowing Bonnie hadn't left her bed in over a week with what the doctor called a nervous breakdown. Had he known, he would have written her a letter full of false hope, trying to comfort the woman he loved. Instead, he waited for his orders.

Finally, Jacob's entire unit was classified as Category II, meaning they would be redeployed to the Pacific, leaving directly from Europe. The goal was to arrive in mid-September. In the meantime, they would continue their training in the small German town of Regensburg. This city, hardly touched by the war, was in Bavaria where the Danube and Regen Rivers merged. Here, Jacob's unit would be combined with other Category II soldiers to create a new unit ready for battle.

Always looking for something positive, Jacob thanked God he would have the opportunity to stay with so many of this unit, the same men he trained with while in Arkansas. They, like he, joined the war effort late and had few points. Therefore, they would remain together.

Jacob would much rather continue the war by the side of those who had already proven they had his back, although his unit would be taking on more personnel because the original number who left Arkansas with him had dwindled. Harry, Earl, Manny, Doug, Chuck, Robert, Peter, and James – eight of the forty-two men from his original platoon, and over four dozen from the original company – were no longer with them, having given the ultimate sacrifice. However, unlike many other units, at least their core was still solid.

After leaving the ammunition plant, his unit was assigned to one of the many tent cities set up throughout Germany. Here, they were given tasks to keep them occupied and out of trouble. However, trouble seemed to seek him out even when he wasn't looking for it.

For instance, a few days after arriving, Jacob and his crew were out on patrol. Although the war was over, there were still small pockets of resistance throughout the country, and it was up to the Allied soldiers to be sure Germany knew her place.

He walked through the city with his gun to the ready, but his mind elsewhere. He admired the beauty that had miraculously come through the war with very little damage. To his right loomed the Cathedral of Regensburg. The building was over 300 years old and considered the finest example of German Gothic architecture in this region.

Up ahead soared the Golden Tower. At 164 feet tall, the tower was what was left of a castle that stood over 700 years ago. He was imagining what Regensburg would have been like with a castle when suddenly, a tremendous BOOM flattened him to the ground.

Unable to hear, he pushed himself to the side of the road, looking back behind him. Somehow, while entrenched in his own thoughts, an Allied tank rolled up behind him and shot the top out of the tower.

Eddy, ol' Razor Eyes, was a hero, at least in Jacob's book. He learned as he walked along, taking in the sights like a vacationing tourist, Eddy continuously scoured the area, front and back, side to side, eyes darting from door to window to alleyway, despite the end of the fighting. As they rounded a corner, Eddy noted a quick flash in the tower up ahead, though when he peered through his scope, nothing caught his attention. But then, he thought he saw another flash and what appeared to be someone moving in the shadows.

He quickly motioned to the driver of an idling tank, who maneuvered the machine into place, and blasted the tower, toppling the sniper to his death – just as he zeroed in on the unsuspecting Jacob. If it hadn't been for Eddy, he would be a dead man.

That was not his only close call after the war. Two weeks after reaching Regensburg, Jacob read the Stars and Stripes. There, on the front page, was a picture of 18 SS soldiers who had been captured, hiding in a bomb shelter in Pilsen. He studied the article carefully. In the shelter, they discovered what was left of an SS unit holed up with a few civilians, one a girl of about 17. Jacob's blood ran cold. He recognized the place and the girl. The door they hadn't explored would have put them face to face with a trapped enemy – an enemy with surprise on their side.

With two dodged catastrophes, Jacob was happy to receive a simple, safe job. During the summer months, when not training for battle, Jacob educated soldiers waiting to go home. Thousands of soldiers in Regensburg had enough points to be classified as a Category IV. Nonetheless, many waited for months for transportation back to the States because the war in the Pacific kept the boats and planes occupied with more important work.

While at the lumberyard, Jacob learned to draft. Since this was a skill that would be in demand once soldiers returned home, Jacob became a drafting teacher for anyone who wanted to learn. Classes were held three hours each weekday, and Jacob was given extra ration coupons for his work with the soldiers waiting to be repatriated.

It was time to write to Bonnie. He had gotten a letter from her two days ago dated from March. At that time, she had not received a letter from him since he started crossing France. Although she didn't say so, he sensed the worry in her words. He was concerned whether any of his letters ever made it her way.

Dear Bonnie,

Oh, my darling, how I miss your sweet smile and gentle voice. Although the war is over in Germany, the aftermath of war is all around. People are hungry. Women have empty eyes. Children beg in the streets for food. My compassion often overtakes me, leaving me with less to eat but a conscience that allows me to sleep at night. I think I've developed that hollow leg again I had when I was a child.

How is William? Please tell him his daddy loves him. I long to be with both of you again. But, Bonnie, my love, it may be a while longer. I had hoped beyond hope to come back home to you when Hitler surrendered, but the war with Japan is still in full swing. Each day brings news of new battles won and lost. If we don't win the war with Japan, then everything we've done, and all that was sacrificed here, will be in vain. I know you want me home as much as I long to be there. But I also know that you understand.

My unit is heading to the Pacific Theater in mid-September. In the meantime, we are training and helping occupy this area of Germany. I've been told that I cannot tell you my location, but I will tell you that the area avoided heavy bombing. Most of the city is still standing, though we are living in tents on the outskirts of town. It feels good to have a permanent bunk rather than sleeping in a foxhole.

You'll be surprised to hear that I am now a teacher! Can you believe it? Those extra classes I took while at the lumberyard are proving beneficial as I teach other soldiers about drafting. Can you imagine your shy Jacob as a teacher? The first day I

was so nervous I had to excuse myself to the bathroom three times. I couldn't decide if I wanted them
to call me Mr. Miller or Jacob. It seems my nickname
has stuck, so they call me Professor Mule. Little do
they know that you think of me as a mule, too, but
due to my stubborn nature and not my ability to
carry things like a pack animal!

For my efforts, I'm getting extra ration coupons.
I'm sending these to you in hopes it eases the burden
at home. Make something sweet and eat a little extra
for me. Be sure to describe the delicacy in detail in
your next letter. That way, if my leg gets too hollow,
I can eat your letter, which is likely to taste as good
as anything the Army is providing!

Remember the song I used to whistle when I
first met you? My Bonnie lies over the ocean, My
Bonnie lies over the sea, My Bonnie lies over the
ocean, Please bring back my Bonnie to me. I would
have never thought how fitting that song might be.

Trust me, true love, when I say I'm coming
home to you. I shall. I love you with all my heart
and soul. If not for you and William, there would be
no reason to live, but memories of you keep me
strong each day.

Give my undying love and affection to your parents.

Yours always,
Jacob

Jacob longed to tell her more, but his letters were
censored. How could he tell her he came to realize that
the German soldiers were no more an enemy than he
was? How could he explain his heart ached knowing he

had killed men with wives and children? Could she ever understand the tug and pull of his heart between his family and country in the US and his family and country in Germany?

It made little sense to him, but he felt as connected to the Germans here as he did to the Americans back home. Despite being an American, he was also one of them. How would he ever reconcile the idea that he had killed his own to save his own?

"Dear God," he thought, "please, please find a way for me to find peace in my heart. Help me find a way to make amends for doing what I had to do despite not wanting to do it."

Chapter 43

BONNIE: Summer 1945

The doctor came by each morning to check on Bonnie's condition. She complied with the doctor's requests, no more and no less. Sit up. Take a deep breath. Cough. Hold a thermometer in her mouth. Produce her wrist for a pulse. However, whenever the doctor spoke or asked a question of her, she would blankly stare with unseeing eyes.

Elaine often piped in with a few words, trying to make things seem better than they were. She loathed the doctor's diagnosis, refusing to concede that Bonnie's mind had snapped. "She ate all her chicken broth at lunch yesterday" or "I was able to coax her to sit in the chair by the window all afternoon" or "William convinced her to push around a car on her bed." Elaine proudly delivered these accomplishments to the doctor as proof.

Bonnie, though not responding to the doctor, was aware of her surroundings. She was aware of her mother's ministrations. These "good" moments were nothing more than doing what she was told, just as she did for the doctor.

For Bonnie, nothing mattered anymore. She couldn't even get up the gumption to pretend for William's sake like she had been doing for months before the war in Europe ended. Of course, he was the only reason she didn't retreat to the horrors in her mind. She wouldn't be drinking broth to 'keep up her strength' because she wouldn't have anything to do that required strength. It didn't take much strength to slip quietly away into the everlasting darkness.

But William did exist, and a tiny part inside her head, the part that sounded a bit like her mother scolding her when she was a child, still fought to live. Bonnie did her best to push that sliver of saneness deep down because living without Jacob was not something she was willing to do. However, that little spark kept her sipping broth and following commands.

Her mother came to the room and coax her to take a bath. "Sweetheart, you haven't taken a relaxing, warm bath in four days. Let me draw up the water, okay?"

Bonnie turned her head to face the opposite wall. Her mother couldn't fathom that taking a bath was a monumental task worthy of an Olympic gold medal. First, she'd have to walk down a flight of stairs to the bathroom. Then she'd have to undress. Then she'd have to heave her exhausted body over the side of the large claw-footed tub. Once there, she would have to do more than sit. She'd have to wash her hair and rinse it free from the shampoo. Next would come washing and rinsing the length of her body only to be followed by hauling herself back out over the side of the tub that grew in size each time she considered it.

Perhaps, if it stopped there, if she could lie down on the bathroom floor and sleep, she might muster the energy needed for this 'relaxing, warm bath.' But the remainder of the grueling task still loomed before her. Toweling herself dry and dressing again into fresh underthings, gown, and robe. The long marathon walk that included an entire flight of upward bound steps. The Herculean effort to launch her body back into the bed. Then, and only then, would the job be completed. Only at her mother's insistence did she make the effort every week or so.

Each daily task required the same kind of effort. Eating. Sitting in a chair. Receiving company. Engaging with William. It was all too much. She wanted to sleep and never wake up.

The doctor and her parents bandied about words like nervous breakdown, hysteria, and neuroses. Only once did she hear the word insane. Her father's voice boomed through the hallway outside her room, "No doctor is going to use THAT word" – he spat the word 'that' like a dagger to the chest – "when speaking of my daughter." The sliver in her that remained perfectly sane experienced a rush of relief, while the majority of her mind remained numb to her condition, or the words used to describe it.

Now and then, the sliver she dubbed "Bothersome Bonnie" would have the upper hand, if only for a moment. Bothersome Bonnie encouraged a smile or a nod or a low moan of approval. Once when the soup was especially tasty. Once when William told her about getting ice from Earl. Once when she had a fleeting memory of Jacob holding her in his arms.

After three weeks of what her father now dubbed 'this nonsense,' the doctor suggested an institution. "Bonnie needs too much for adequate care at home. Although sometimes these things clear up with time..." The doctor's sentence faltered to a stop. It was then he suggested the Connecticut Asylum for the Insane in Middletown. "I'm not saying she is insane," the doctor soothed, "but she has suffered a nervous breakdown. A woman in her condition needs more than soup broth and hugs."

At first, her parents were adamantly against the idea. Bonnie would remain with them and her son. She needed them. However, with a bit of time and lots of persuasion, the doctor created a crack in their resolve and helped them set a date. If Bonnie wasn't showing significant improvement by July 15th, they would transfer her to the institution.

"Bothersome Bonnie" objected as loudly as possible, but the sad, depressed, "Can't Live Like This Anymore" Bonnie remained in control. Maybe there, at an institution for those labeled insane, they'd just let her die.

July 4th came and went. There were still the occasional showers, the broth, the chair in the sunshine. Then, sometime shortly before the looming deadline, William sneaked into her room in the middle of the night. She had been lying in bed with her eyes wide open, trying to keep the thoughts of Jacob at bay.

At night, her whole body ached with missing him. When she closed her eyes, every detail of his face came into view. His deep brown eyes. His long, straight nose. His thin Clark Gable mustache. His full lips turned into a smile just for her. She felt his hands running the length of her body. Without warning, her body would arch to meet his, only to discover she was alone. It was during the night she was sure the insanity label was correct.

The door opened and little footsteps scurried across the floor. The mattress pushed down slightly on one side, and William laid down with his head pressed against her chest. She lay stiff as a board, not wanting him to know she was awake, willing him to go back to his room.

William whispered, "Mommy, I had a bad dream. I dreamed you and Daddy were both gone. I was all alone. I kept crying but no one would take care of me. Mommy, I'm afraid. Can I sleep with you?" With that, he pulled her arm around his shoulders and snuggled in closer.

She felt his warm breath on her arm and the quiet thump of his heartbeat against her side. His small fingers intertwined with hers. And for the first time since she realized Jacob was not coming home from the war, she let the tears fall from her eyes.

For hours, she held her son and let the tears fall. William was unaware that his mother was crying. He had dropped back into a deep sleep as soon as he settled in the comfort of his mother's presence. She sobbed until there was no more aching left. She sobbed until "Bother-some Bonnie" had room to breathe again. She sobbed for herself. She sobbed for Jacob. She sobbed for the little boy who lost his father and was about to lose his mother to this war. She sobbed until the tears were gone, and then she slept a peaceful sleep devoid of dreams.

The next morning, when Bonnie's mother opened the

bedroom door, she gasped at the miracle before her eyes. Bonnie, though still pale and shaky, was sitting up in bed chatting softly with William. That tiny sliver that wanted to live pushed through the deepest, darkest, scariest recesses of her brain to save her child from being left alone.

Although progress was slow, there was no more talk of the Connecticut Asylum for the Insane. Each day, Bonnie gained a bit more strength, both mentally and physically. She began sitting outside to enjoy the morning sunshine while William played at her feet. Meals and baths occurred regularly. Bonnie soon began taking her evening meal with the family.

Nonetheless, everyone still tiptoed around her, making sure to avoid any mention of the war. The radio had been removed from the living room. Bonnie wasn't sure where it had gone, but she wasn't sorry for its disappearance. Not learning about the war after every radio program was a much-needed reprieve. She did wonder about him. Where he was. What his new orders would be. But she didn't want to hear the announcer give the sordid details about the latest Japanese attacks.

By the end of July, she took short walks around the block and greeted Earl as William talked incessantly about Bugs and how strong he was to pull a wagon loaded with ice that weighed as much as two horses. It was on one of these sunny mornings she got her first letter from Jacob. It was written at the end of June, just over a month ago.

She held the unopened letter in her hand for a long time. Her mother said, "Here, Bonnie. Give it to me. I'll read it. You don't have to." As she reached out her hand to take the letter, Bonnie gripped it firmly in her fingers, holding it to her heart.

"No. No. This is from Jacob to me. I'll read it...when I'm ready."

She sat on the front porch for hours, holding the letter to her chest. "Do not bother your mother, William. She needs some time alone," his grandmother insisted. Although he obeyed, his frightened eyes remained vigilant, staring at her through the window. Everyone realized the day would come when the war intruded into Bonnie's recovery. No one knew, however, how she would handle the invasion.

When her father got home from work, he found Bonnie wrapped in a shawl on the front porch, holding her letter. He glanced at her staring at nothing and then at his wife standing in the doorway. She shook her head from side to side, so Carl put his hand on his daughter's shoulder, gave her a gentle squeeze, and went into the house to wash up for supper.

Supper was a quiet affair. Nothing but the sound of silverware hitting plates. Even William, who never stopped talking, remained silent. Bonnie's plate sat empty, as it had for weeks when she was ill, like an omen. Carl wanted to fling the plate across the room, race to his daughter, and shake some sense into her head. He couldn't bear the thought of her going back to the shell of a woman she had been.

That's when they heard her laugh out loud. Then silence before a sob escaped her throat. Carl pushed back his chair to go to her, but his wife put her hand on his arm. "Let her be. Let her read the letter and feel what needs to be felt." He sat down slowly, not sure if she was right.

William slipped from the table and was on the porch in a flash. Before they could get to the door to usher the boy back inside, Bonnie scooped him onto her lap and said, "Guess what, William? Daddy is teaching soldiers, and they call him Professor Mule."

William looked confused, which made Bonnie's eyes dance a bit. Then she started to giggle, and finally let out a large bellow that echoed across the yard. William, not sure why he was laughing, joined in. When Bonnie finally caught her breath, she said, "Daddy says hello and sends his love. He wants us to know how much he wishes we were with him, but he can't come home until his job as a soldier is done. He asked us to be brave. Do you think we can keep doing that for Daddy?"

William nodded his head solemnly. He had been a big, brave soldier for a very long time. He wished he could be a little boy again, but his Mommy and Daddy needed him.

Bonnie tucked the letter into her pocket, held William by the hand, and went inside. "Mother, Father. William sends his love AND these ration coupons." Turning to her mother, she said, "Mother, let's go to the grocery tomorrow and buy what we need to make a pie. Cherry would be good. Or apple. Really, anything." Then, without warning, she grabbed them both into a hug, with William hugging her knees, and said, "Thank you. Thank you for helping me. I couldn't have done this without you."

Chapter 44

JACOB: Summer 1945

August arrived without fanfare, though Jacob celebrated the points. He was now six closer to going home than he had been when Germany surrendered. Almost halfway home. This thought both excited and distressed him. Almost halfway was better than nothing but having to go through what he'd already been through again before reuniting with his family was daunting.

The loudspeakers throughout camp blared the radio during the waking hours of the day. The war with Japan raged forward. Despite what were losing odds, the Japanese fought with deadly force, inflicting enormous casualties on the Allied powers.

The Allies demanded unconditional surrender with the Potsdam Declaration, which the Japanese rejected scornfully, despite the threat of prompt and utter destruction. Jacob, though he wanted to hate the Japanese, understood their reasoning. Had the Allies been losing, they, too, would have fought to the bitter end. They, too, would not have stopped simply because the 'enemy' promised utter destruction.

He was much more philosophical about the war since the shooting stopped. It was easier to see other points of view when you didn't have someone's best friend aimed at your head. He didn't agree with the Japanese and still had hate in his heart that they pulled the US into the war. Nor did he understand their desire to control the world. However, he empathized with their need to prove something about their country. Hadn't he joined the war to prove a point? To prove he was American enough to be seen as American rather than German?

Despite his ability to recognize the Jap's viewpoint, he was now training daily to be part of the invasion dubbed "Operation Downfall" led by General Douglas MacArthur. The Allied air support would continue bombing Japan in the same way it had been done in Europe. Then, as with the march from France to Czechoslovakia that ended the European war a few months before, units like his would invade the Japanese homeland until they got the unconditional surrender they were after.

Because of his imminent departure, his class schedule was winding down. His unit had orders to begin marching to sea on August 16th, where a ship would take him to Japan, the first wave to hit the shores. He prayed the commander learned from the carnage on D-Day, not wanting to die on the shores of Japan the way thousands had died in Normandy.

August 6th, nine days away from his march to the sea, started like any other. Jacob got up, ate his meager breakfast, went to the makeshift classroom, and began wrapping up his lessons. He hadn't gotten as far as he would have liked, but it would have to do. He was hopeful another soldier would be able to take over and teach these men more as they waited for ships to take them home.

After class and another meager meal, it was time to clean his trusty best friend. Tomorrow, the unit would have an equipment inspection as they readied for deployment. He took his gun apart, piece by piece, wiping it clean, removing grit, sanding down rusty spots, adding a bit of oil here and there. He talked to the gun as he went, thankful he was alone in his tent.

"It's almost time to go. Are you ready? Can you do this with me again? Remember the end goal – getting me home to Bonnie and William. We can't think about anything else. We won't be able to wax philosophical about war and enemies. We'll have to be razor-focused."

Jacob was willing his humanity, his empathy, everything that made him the man Bonnie loved and William needed, to recede into the background. He prayed that when he was stateside again, he'd be able to pull it out of the rubble. The war had already created cracks and crevices he couldn't fill. He wondered if he'd even know himself after the Japanese invasion.

But he couldn't dwell on that, instead pushing himself toward survival mode. "If it comes down to me or him, it will have to be him," mused Jacob. The quiet murmur, "But 'he' is certainly saying the same thing in his tent while cleaning his gun," was dismissed and shoved away like a worn-out coat. He couldn't allow those thoughts to flourish and expect to live.

That evening, the swing music that reminded him of dancing with Bonnie was interrupted by an announcement from the President of the United States. Everyone stopped eating. Jacob had just forked a bit of mystery meat into his mouth, but it remained unchewed and forgotten as he heard these words:

"A short time ago, an American airplane dropped one bomb on Hiroshima and destroyed its usefulness to the army. That bomb has more power than 20,000 tons of TNT...With this bomb, we have now added a new and revolutionary increase in destruction to supplement the growing power of our armed forces...It is a harnessing of the basic power of the universe, the force from which the sun draws its power has been loosed against those who brought war to the far East. We are now prepared to destroy more rapidly and completely every productive enterprise the Japanese have in any city. We shall destroy their docks, their factories, and their communications. Let there be no mistake, we shall completely destroy Japan's power to make war."

An atomic bomb? Jacob had no idea what this was, but he did understand 20,000 tons of TNT. That was the same as 44 million pounds! No one could survive a blast like that. The President went on to talk about the greatness of the scientific discovery, but he quit listening. How could one single bomb do the job of over 3,000 fighter pilots dropping bombs on a city? What the US accomplished was mind-numbing. And perhaps, war-ending.

The absolute stillness around the mess hall eventually erupted into excited talk as the soldiers tried to understand what had happened, how it had been kept such a secret, and more importantly, how it affected their up-coming orders. Arguments ensued about how massive 20,000 tons really was. Others argued that the President must have meant 20,000 pounds, still larger than any-thing yet dropped in Europe or Japan.

Over the next three days, little details dribbled out. That one simple bomb, nicknamed Little Boy, was indeed close to 20,000 tons, not pounds. It left Hiroshima completely devastated. Rumors were that 90% of the city was gone and almost 100,000 people were killed instant-ly. Jacob had trouble grasping the concept. With one bomb, they did what it would take entire armies several days to accomplish. Surely, the Japanese would realize they had lost...However, the Japanese were not yet ready to wave the white flag.

Then, on August 9th, the news of a second blast arrived.

"The second use of the new and terrifying secret weapon occurred at noon today, Japanese time. The target today, Nagasaki, was an important industrial and ship-ping area with a population of about 258,000.

"The great bomb, which harnesses the power of the universe to destroy the enemy by concussion, blast and fire, was dropped on the second enemy city about seven hours after the Japanese had received a political 'round-house punch' in the form of a declaration of war by the Soviet Union."

This time, instead of awed silence, a cheer erupted from the camp. Two bombs. Two cities. The United States was single-handedly annihilating the enemy. Jacob couldn't help but feel excited and hopeful. He had no idea how many of these bombs were in existence, but certainly Japan wouldn't want to find out the hard way. Maybe, just maybe, God would keep him from fighting the Japs after all.

Amazingly, there was no immediate surrender from Japan, so Jacob's unit continued to ready themselves to move out. In less than a week, he'd be back to marching. He had a letter ready to send to Bonnie but was reluctant to put it in the post. It was as if by sending it too early, he would be sealing his fate. He determined to put it in the post the night before he marched to port.

The week went by quickly. There was much to do to ready a unit for a several week march across the country. How he dreaded the marching. The last time he came across the country, it was spring and rainy. Now it was hot and humid. Neither sounded appealing. He was thankful it wasn't cold and icy. Never being able to get warm sounded far worse than sweating.

Of course, the march this time would be substantially different, even without a difference in weather. There would be no bullets flying in his direction. No foxholes. No buddies flinging backward after a bullet caught them in the chest, staring with glazed eyes. No crazy snipers hiding in towers.

Because of this, the pace would be far more grueling. They had to make it across to the northern German port of Bremerhaven. The 475-mile trip had to be accomplished in a mere three weeks, so each day would consist of a 22-mile march. His poor flat feet would be happy for the rest on board the ship that would take them to the shores of Japan, even if his mind wished to remain in Europe.

The evening before departure, Jacob sealed his letter

to Bonnie. Before he placed it in the mailbox bound for the States, the radio crackled as a bulletin interrupted the daily news show. Apparently, moments before, in his first-ever public speech, Emperor Hirohito formally announced his country's surrender.

All eyes were on the speakers as if they held the secret to life itself. In the background, they heard a man speaking Japanese. Over his voice was a British voice translating:

To our good and loyal subjects:

After pondering deeply the general trends of the world and the actual conditions obtaining in our empire today, we have decided to effect a settlement of the present situation by resorting to an extraordinary measure. We have ordered our government to communicate to the governments of the United States, Great Britain, China and the Soviet Union that our empire accepts the provisions of their joint declaration.

The letter Jacob had been holding floated to the ground, soon joined by Jacob himself. He was on his knees, weeping. All around him, his companions cheered. Guns that had been ready to go back into battle exploded into the air in celebration.

Jacob looked up, noting the flag, prominently displayed in the center of the tent city, began to flutter, as if she were aware of what was happening around her. Without thinking, Jacob started singing "My Country 'Tis of Thee," first quietly and then with the gusto of a man who sensed he would hold his wife and child again. Within seconds, the whole camp joined in as each soldier removed his hat, put his hand over his heart, faced the flag, and sang for the love of his country and all it stood for.

In the background, Emperor Hirohito continued without being heard. That night, the night Jacob was spared from further war, would be a night he would never forget. Word came around that the morning march was on hold. Instead, units would be receiving new orders. Soldiers would be going home.

Home. Oh, how he longed for home. His bed. His job at the lumberyard. His son. His wife. Dear, dear, Bonnie. "I'm coming home, my darling. I'm coming home."

Chapter 45

BONNIE: Summer 1945

Bonnie had been cleared by the doctor to begin work again the following Monday. Although she would miss her time spent with William, she was excited to be well enough to go back to the secretarial pool, a turning point in her progress toward full health.

Those at work only knew she had been ill, and not even Collette was told the whole story. Bonnie would not discuss her nervous breakdown with others. Mental illness was not understood and often feared. People who hadn't experienced such personal stress couldn't comprehend the depth of its power on a person. Being forthright about her experiences could get her shunned or perhaps cost her the typing job.

Her doctor gave her firm instructions. She was to

work three days a week for the first two weeks. At the first sign of problems – lack of sleep, lack of appetite, not wanting to engage with family – she was to stop working and seek his counsel immediately. Getting back to a more normal life would be good for Bonnie, but there was the risk of doing too much too soon.

He waggled a finger at her. "Bonnie, we almost lost you. The stress of this war has been hard on you and will continue to be hard. You have to promise that at the first sign of distress, no matter how small, you pull back and speak to me. Without that promise, I'll have to agree with your parents and order you to say home."

She had promised. She didn't want to stay home with her parents. When they looked at her, they still saw frail and small. Her mother monitored her continuously, waiting for the smallest sign that Bonnie was regressing. They both wanted her to wait a while longer.

However, money was tight, and her missing paycheck took a toll on the family budget. More importantly, she needed something to do to keep her mind off the war. Yes, stress could be a trigger, but boredom, the total lack of anything productive to do, only let her idle mind go places it should not go.

She could now say the word war without shuddering. She and war had become unwilling roommates. Each learned to stay on their own side of the room without tormenting the other. As she learned about the different battles and bombs, wins and losses, she no longer looked up the places on the Atlas. Instead, she would acknowledge the news and do what she could do to put it out of her mind.

Truthfully, she worried what she would do when

Jacob was sent back into battle. She'd be guessing again where he was and what he was doing. Whether he was safe. Whether he was alive. She wondered if she was strong enough to endure the torment. But, in the meantime, she and war brokered a truce.

The days before she went back to work were spent taking in some of her clothes. Weeks spent in bed and her slow recovery left her smaller than before. Her skirts hung on her like sacks and her shirts could easily wrap around her half again. Thankfully, her mother had picked up enough skills to measure Bonnie's new proportions. Then Bonnie used her natural gift as a seamstress to remake her many outfits. Between the two of them, several pieces in her wardrobe were given a makeover.

Sometime during the early part of August, shortly after Jacob's letter arrived, the radio mysteriously appeared back in the living room. Bonnie thought better of mentioning it but was thankful it was back. She had missed listening to the afternoon shows and the music that reminded her of her husband. However, she was very aware that the nightly news programs were no longer part of the evening ritual.

Today, right as she was preparing to put down her needle for some lunch with William, a news bulletin interrupted the broadcast. The Japanese had surrendered.

Bonnie leaped up from the couch, the forgotten sewing falling across the living room rug. She screamed so loudly that her mother came running from the backyard where she had gone to fetch William. The look of utter terror on her son's face caused her to scoop him into her arms and begin to dance. She was laughing and crying and making no sense at all.

Both William and Elaine remained confused until Bonnie, with tears in her eyes, pointed wildly at the radio just in time to hear the Emperor's translated words:

"Despite the best that has been done by everyone – the gallant fighting of the military and naval forces, the diligence and assiduity of our servants of the state, and the devoted service of our one hundred million people – the war situation has developed not necessarily to Japan's advantage, while the general trends of the world have all turned against her interest."

Her mother's eyes widened. Japan was surrendering? Is that what she was hearing? She opened her mouth, but no sound came out. Bonnie grabbed her up with her free arm and began laughing and crying at the same time all over again. The war was over. This time it was really over.

Two weeks later, while Bonnie typed, William played with his cars, Carl met with his team about a new design, and Elaine began supper preparation, the official surrender agreement was signed aboard the US Battleship Missouri anchored in Tokyo Bay. September 2, 1945, almost a year and a half after Jacob left from the train station in North Canton, Ohio, the Second World War was officially over.

Chapter 46

WILLIAM: November 2016

Cold seeped into William's trousers, causing him to realize he'd been sitting in the truck for quite some time. Marie, his wife, would undoubtedly be concerned with his actions today. She already worried that he was becoming forgetful, so sitting in the truck until he got cold would give her a bit more ammunition than he wanted her to have.

Slowly, allowing his stiff legs to get a bit of circulation before setting off, William got out of the truck and headed for the house. It had been a difficult morning with the memories and the discovery of that portrait. Once inside, he called to Marie to let her know he was home.

Since lunch wouldn't be for another hour or so, he decided to go into the garage and tinker with one of his cars. It seemed appropriate. It was what he had always done when life was difficult, even when he was a tiny boy of four and five.

As he hoisted his '57 Chevy into the air on the red automatic lifts to bleed the brakes, he was transported again to Connecticut.

His recollection of the time between VE-Day and VJ-Day was not terribly clear. He recalled vague memories of an illness that kept his mother bed bound. But in the ensuing years after the war, whenever he brought it up, she brushed it aside like an errant piece of dust that marred an otherwise perfect shelf.

She once went so far as to deny knowing what he was talking about. Nonetheless, he was certain she had been ill. He remembered clearly sitting in her room and playing with cars while she sat unmoving and unspeaking in a chair by the window. He specifically remembered his nightmares.

Mommy, Daddy, and William would all be eating supper at the table in the pink house. Mommy had made William's favorite breakfast – pancakes with maple syrup. Then, without warning, someone dressed in black and wearing a mask would grab first his daddy and then his mommy. They would struggle and try to scream, but the men would hold their mouths closed with a gloved hand. Then, as quickly as they arrived, they'd go, leaving William alone. He'd begin to cry. No one would come to help him. He would cry until the tears woke him up, often sweaty, and often with urine-soaked pajamas.

This went on night after night. Grandma always helped him dress in clean pajamas. Mommy would just keep sleeping. Then, one night, he woke up and had to be sure his mommy was still in the room across the hall, like she said she would be on the day they moved in with Grandpa and Grandma.

Without thinking too much about it, he had gone over to the side of the bed, crawled in, and slept there in her arms. He never dreamed that nightmare again. And his mommy started feeling better, too.

He especially liked that summer because Mommy stayed home. He didn't ask why. It seemed like an unspoken rule that he wasn't to ask questions about her. He was just thankful she wanted to play again.

One day, Mommy talked with him about Daddy. The war was only part way over, she said. There were still bad people who wanted to hurt our country. Daddy was being a brave soldier and needed his son to be one, too. William nodded in agreement. He wanted to help his daddy and remembered that both his father and Uncle Otto asked him to be brave. That was something he would do.

The days all blurred into one another. His mommy would sit outside while he played cars. They would eat meals and listen to the radio. Sometimes Mommy would make treats, and William would draw pictures of the treats to send to his daddy. Mommy said he was going to eat them. William was sure she must be joking. Certainly, his daddy wasn't going to eat a piece of paper?

One day, while playing in the sunshine, his grandma came out to get him for lunch. She was telling him to go inside and wash his hands when his mommy screamed from inside the house. Grandma, without saying a word, turned toward the house and began to run, moving faster than William had ever seen her move before.

Her determined steps made William's stomach lurch. He followed Grandma into the house, but was, all at once, very afraid. Grandma was standing in the living room looking at Mommy, who was twirling around the living room. Mommy looked happy, but tears ran down her cheeks.

William looked at Grandma, who stood there with her arms by her sides and her mouth making a little circle. Then, without warning, Mommy scooped up William into her arms and began to laugh. Even so, the tears kept rolling down her face.

Gently, his mother held his face and looked at him. She said to him, "My darling boy, the war is over. Japan has surrendered. There will be no more fighting."

The war? It was over? The other half that Daddy still had to fight? Daddy was done being a soldier?

William began to cry in earnest. Unwieldy, heaping sobs. Tears he had held in check since Daddy left so very long ago. The war was over and now William could go back to being a little boy.

———————

Marie poked her head into the garage. "William, it's time for lunch."

"Okay, be there in a minute." William was thankful the car was between him and Marie's probing eyes. The memories left wet paths down his rough cheeks, tears he had stuffed as a little boy that had never fully escaped. As an old man, the crying came much easier.

He wiped his face on his shirt sleeve and mumbled into the air, "Daddy, I sure do miss you."

Chapter 47

JACOB: Spring 1946

Two weeks later, the Japanese signed the official surrender. With no more war, many more soldiers would be
finding their way home. Infantrymen, like Jacob, would
not be in high demand.

However, with limited transportation and more men
going home than ever, the point system remained active,
meaning William, though slated for the States, would
have to wait his turn. Once again, Professor Mule
brushed off his duffle bag and set to work teaching soldiers.

Regensburg was now home to the largest Displaced
Persons camp in Germany as well as a much smaller
Prisoner of War camp. As a teacher, Jacob had access to
both the displaced persons and the POWs to help him in

whatever capacity he chose. As he was setting up his new classroom, he went by the prison and asked for a strong man to help him move some tables and chairs. Although he was a mule, having another mule to help would make the job faster and easier. They let him sign out Klaus, a gigantic man with a wide grin.

Jacob was wary of the smile. Why would a German prisoner of war smile at an American unless he had thoughts of revenge? Jacob made sure Klaus saw his gun. He was not going to take any chances.

All morning, they moved furniture, Klaus telling stories of the war in a German accent that was almost too thick for Jacob's ears. Although fluent, he was used to the subtler tones spoken in America.

He didn't let on that he understood Klaus' ramblings. He had never spoken a word of German to anyone in his unit, burying his heritage so deeply that no one suspected he comprehended more than the few curse words picked up along the way. Despite this lack of acknowledgment, Klaus continued speaking.

"I spent the last several months in a Soviet prison camp." That would explain his missing teeth and unusual gait. "They beat me often. They didn't like my smile." Ironically, he smiled as he said this. Jacob kept a straight face, acting as if Klaus were speaking gibberish.

Soon, Klaus began to speak of his family. "I have a wife. Three children. Two boys and a girl. I don't know if they are alive. When I am free, I will look for them." Jacob stopped working when Klaus began telling stories of his young son. "My son was just eight when I left. Such a busy boy, always finding something in the woods." Without realizing it, Jacob nodded and responded in

German, *"Kinder sind so."* Children are like that.

Klaus looked up, straight into Jacob's eyes, staring for a long moment. Neither man spoke. Neither man moved. Klaus finally flashed a smile and looked away, continuing on about his family, never asking the obvious questions. Jacob returned to his work, once again pretending he was a regular American soldier using a prisoner of war for some needed work. However, they both recognized a friendship had begun.

For the next several months, despite the strict non-fraternization policy enforced by General Eisenhower, Klaus and Jacob grew closer and closer. Each morning, Jacob would sign out Klaus to help him with this classroom. He even used him as his butler, having Klaus give him a shave or a haircut or run a few errands.

At first, his buddies thought the whole thing was a joke, like Jacob was showing this Kraut who was boss. However, the first time one of them tried to order Klaus to do a dance as they waved their gun in his direction, Jacob put a stop to it.

Still concerned that they might view him as a traitor, he put them in their place by reminding them of their humanity. "Stop it. Stop it right now. The war is over. We have won. Only an animal continues to fight to the death. We have nothing to prove here. Nothing. This man is our prisoner, but he is still a man. Would you write home to your wives? To your girlfriends? And tell them about making a man dance with a gun pointed to his head? No. No, you would not. You should be ashamed."

And they were ashamed. One by one, they left the room. Klaus looked at Jacob, not knowing what he said. Jacob uttered, *"Es war nicht richtig."* It wasn't right.

Klaus went back to shining Jacob's shoes.

When together alone, Jacob would sometimes talk to Klaus about Ohio, Bonnie, and William. However, he was still very careful. He hadn't joined the war and become a changed man to find himself on the wrong side in the end, seen as an enemy after all. There was no way he wanted to jeopardize everything he had done to keep his family safe.

His conscience pricked each time he signed Klaus out as a servant. Despite knowing that without these duties, Klaus would be locked up in the prison cell, he believed the arrangement was wrong. The only way he rationalized what he was doing was to remember that here, with him, at least Klaus had a bit of freedom.

When Klaus would talk of the war, Jacob's humanity, the part of him he had to stifle to survive, came pouring out. Klaus, like him, fought because of his family. He had to join the Nazis or be seen as a traitor. He had no choice. He was not a political man. He simply loved his country and his family. If he had said no, everyone he loved would have been thrown into an internment camp. He couldn't do that to his family.

Jacob understood. He loved his country and family as well. He fought for many of the same reasons. No man should have to make such choices. No man could and remain unchanged.

Summer turned to fall turned to winter. Jacob still seemed no closer to going home. Another Christmas came and went. His son would soon be six. Would he remember his father? Would Jacob be the man his young son remembered even if the memories were there? He was not so sure.

He had vivid dreams. Ancestors coming to him in the night crying over the loss of family. Asking him why he shot his own. The FBI coming to his door, dragging him from his family, telling him he had been an impostor all along. An American soldier and a German soldier, each with a gun to his head, each begging to be the one to pull the trigger. He would often wake up screaming, covered in sweat.

Winter eventually turned to spring, and Jacob finally got word that he would be going home. He was to report to Bremerhaven in early May. Thankfully, he would be going most of the way by train.

He asked for and received permission to stop near Massenbach on his way to the port. He told his Captain he needed to pay his respects to a buddy he lost in the area during the long march. Though he lost friends there, this was a convenient lie. He had other respects he needed to pay.

The morning he was to leave for the train, Jacob signed out Klaus for the last time. As they did on the first day they met, they stared deep into each other's eyes. Klaus smiled expansively, saying, *"Ich werde dich vermissen, Jacob."* I will miss you. Jacob's eyes filled with tears.

Then, he surprised Klaus by handing him his overcoat. He put it on the large toothless man, and though the sleeves were a bit too short, it fit him enough to be useful. Then, Jacob rummaged in his sack, handing over some German food ration coupons, a handful of Marks, and some tins of food. He grabbed him in a hug and said, *"Ich liebe dich mein Bruder. Geh und finde deine Familie."* I love you, my brother. Go and find your family.

With that he turned on his heel and left for the

station without signing Klaus back into the prison.

He wanted to believe he was a good man, but Jacob knew he let Klaus go for selfish reasons. He needed to be the man Bonnie sent to Germany, and he was terrified that man was gone. Letting Klaus go free, helping him on his way to find his own family, was symbolic.

He was American and going home. He was German and sent a German home. Two men, brought into a war with something to prove were both going home. They would both have to work hard to start living again.

Jacob needed his last acts in Germany to be ones that honored his heritage, the heritage he worked so hard to hide as a boy, as a young man, as a father, and finally as a soldier. Letting Klaus go home was one of those acts. What he would do in Massenbach was the other.

He had been thinking about this since the day he heaved on the side of the road when he realized his presence frightened those hiding in the small cottages. He needed to go back to the town of his heritage and help someone in some way. He needed to connect his past with his present, to be seen for who he was. To stop hiding and start living.

As he got off the train, six miles from town, he hesitated. He could hop right back in his seat and head straight to Bremerhaven. No one knew he was coming. He wouldn't be missed. He didn't have to do this thing.

He began to think he was crazy. He was going to waltz into town, announce he was a German American there to help, and the people were going to what? Shower him with gifts? Give him a parade with confetti and a key to the city? The Germans had just lost bitterly to the Allies. He was still the enemy. He could get shot.

Imagine that. Losing his life at the end of the war as he tried to do something right in a world that had done so much wrong. It was crazy. There was no doubt.

But he couldn't turn back. He placed one dusty boot in front of the other until he the old church on the hill stood before him. It was the only church in town, so that is where he headed. As he neared the front doors, he stopped. This was an old church, probably the same one that stood here when Mattias was a boy.

He stepped closer and touched the stones, running his fingers over the rough façade. Mattias, the man he was named for, once stood in this very spot. The connection was so strong that Jacob wouldn't have been surprised to see him standing in front of him. He was shocked, however, to find a boy of about six peering at him from behind a short stone wall.

"Hallo," said Jacob, smiling and holding out his hands as he would to a stray dog come to sniff him. Then, in perfect German, he said, "My name is Jacob. I have some chocolate. Would you like some?"

The boy looked at him with interest but didn't move. "It's okay. I won't hurt you. My family is from Massenbach. Long, long ago. Many generations. I just needed to see this place." He held the chocolate out, and the boy, dressed in something no better than rags, tentatively reached out his hand and grabbed the chocolate.

"Ich habe einen Sohn. Sein Name ist William." I have a son. His name is William. "He is about your age. He just turned six."

The boy smiled. *"Ja, ich bin sechs Jahre alt."*

Jacob nodded. "Six years old is almost a grown man." The boy nodded enthusiastically.

"Where do you live? Near here? Do you live with your parents?"

The boy looked down. "*Nein*. No, my father is dead. My mother is sick. We live in the house at the end of the road." He pointed to a little house on the main road.

Jacob blinked at the house, the very same one that sent him to the side of the road. The woman who had screamed he was the enemy must be ill. The family, who without knowing it, had dragged his humanity from the depths of his soul, causing him to see, for the first time, the realities of war, had crossed his path again.

He knew better than to go to the home. This woman would not want to speak to a man who represented those who took her husband. So, he reached into his duffle bag and pulled out the gift he brought from camp.

"*Bitte*, please take this to your mother. It is some food. Some clothes. A bit more chocolate. Tell her that Jakob Mueller pays his deepest respects. Can you do that? Jakob Mueller."

The boy took the bag and ran off. American Jacob Miller and German Jakob Mueller. Two personas living in one body. A body that was finally ready to go home.

Chapter 48

BONNIE: May 1946

The letter arrived on May 10th. For months, she had known the letter would eventually come. The war was over. VE Day had been a year ago. VJ Day happened a few short months later. But Jacob was still a ghostly presence in their home – talked about, thought about, but entirely missing from their lives.

She understood how the point system worked, and both cursed it and revered it. The men coming home now were those who joined at the bombing of Pearl Harbor. They had seen the war in its entirety. Months upon months of battle. Hunger to the point of starvation. Deprivation beyond what folks in Hartford could begin to understand. Wounded limbs. Scarred souls.

If Jacob had joined then, he would have missed his

son's second birthday and all the ones in between. William wouldn't even understand the concept of Vati – Daddy. Jacob wouldn't understand the concept of sohn – son. Instead of two years, he would have been gone for four. Four long years for Bonnie to live without her husband's caresses, his lips on her throat, his hearty laugh. Two more hard years in which he could have died or come home with a mishmash of broken parts intermingled with metal extensions.

Whenever she felt the urge to curse the system, to wish Jacob had enough points for immediate transport home, she remembered the price he would have paid, the price they would have paid. Still, she wished him home with all her might.

That's why, Friday after work, when she came home to a letter from Jacob, she was happy but expected nothing new. He had been telling her about his classes, about some children he met, about a man named Klaus who was a German prisoner. He complained about the food and the bugs. He told her he missed her and William. He always put in warm regards for her parents. But each letter for the past several months could have been interchanged for any other.

This time, however, the news was what she had not dared to hope for. Rather than his typical start like 'Dearest Bonnie' or 'My Darling,' Jacob went straight for the heart of the matter:

I'm coming home!! I'm leaving from Bremerha- ven Germany on May 12th. I don't know exactly when I'll get home. Once in port, they will send me to muster out and then I'll make my way to you. It will be early June at the soonest, the last of July at the latest.

My darling, Bonnie. Just a few short weeks, and I'll be home. In your arms to stay. I'll head home to North Canton. As soon as you can, pack up William and go home – to our home. I'll be there as soon as I can. As always, give William a hug from me. Tell him I love him. Tell him I'll be hugging him in person soon.

I love you, Bonnie. I have loved you from the first moment I saw you standing in your tiny apartment that day I delivered your groceries. I can't believe how lucky I've been to have you by my side.

All my love to your parents.

Jacob

She didn't realize she was crying until she tasted the salt on her lips. She read the letter again. In two short days, Jacob would be on a ship headed home – to their home.

She whirled around, running to the kitchen at full tilt. "Mother! Mother!" She was as breathless as if she had run a marathon.

"What on earth..." her mother trailed off as she took in the look of ecstasy on her daughter's face and the letter in her hand. "He's coming home?"

Bonnie quickly nodded, flinging herself into her mother's arms. There, in the kitchen, she sobbed like a small child while her mother rubbed her back, brushed her hair back behind her ear, and murmured, "So happy. Oh, so happy."

Carl came in from work a few minutes later to find them still standing in an embrace in the kitchen. He wasn't sure what he was seeing. Was Bonnie okay? Was she having another breakdown? But when she looked up at him and said, "Oh, Father," the joy on her face was evident.

He moved to them and held them both tightly. This damned war was over and his son, yes, Jacob was indeed his son, was coming home.

Chapter 49

WILLIAM: June 1946

William had been creating an imaginary city in the backyard under the trees on a warm spring day. He was reluctant to come inside for dinner, but now that his grandpa had pulled into the drive, supper wouldn't be far behind.

He entered the kitchen through the backdoor but froze before letting go of the screen door that would signal his arrival. His mother and grandparents huddled together, whispering in soft voices. He could not move back to the yard, to the safety of his cars, nor could he move forward to the safety of his mother's embrace.

Hugs and tears could mean so many things. Vati leaving. Mama sick. Vati still needing to be a soldier. The end of the war with Vati nowhere in sight. What could this be? Was Vati dead like the soldiers from the picture show so many years ago? Had Vati decided never to come home again? Would Mama get sick again?

As these thoughts raced through his mind, he kept reminding himself that he had to take care of his mama. Daddy had said so. He had to be a big man despite being a little boy. But he still couldn't bring himself to walk further into the kitchen.

His mother looked up to see her small son with the grave eyes, searching their faces for clues. She gave him her broadest smile, urging him toward her. Though still wary, he relaxed a bit. Smiles, in his experience, had always meant good things, unlike hugs and tears, which were very confusing to a child of six.

Mommy crouched down and held out a letter. It was from Daddy. He had learned the J for Jacob. He scoured the letter for his part, the part with William. He found it with practiced ease. He could also pick out the words hug and love. He didn't find the word kiss this time, but he found hug twice.

Questioningly, he ran his finger along his words. Daddy wanted Mommy to hug him. Daddy loved him. But what was this hug? Did Daddy want to hug William again? He looked deep into his mommy's eyes. She was not just smiling with her mouth, but her eyes were twinkling.

He dropped the letter and put his small hands on his mommy's cheeks. "Mommy? What did Daddy say?"

He didn't know why, but he had tears running down his face. He looked deep into her eyes as she said, "He will hug you in person soon."

The next days were busy. They packed his toys into

boxes. Put clothes into suitcases. Stripped beds. Made food for the trip. Then, early one morning, they loaded everything into Grandpa's car and drove back home to the pink house.

It was a bit spooky with everything covered in sheets, but before long, as Mommy removed the covers, the house he remembered started coming to life. The kitchen table where he and Mommy and Daddy ate breakfast every morning. The sofa with the tiny pink flowers. The big bed in Mommy's room that held him on nights with storms. His tiny bed that was almost too small for him now that he was six.

He ran outside to hug Vonk, but the doghouse was not in its place in the yard under the crab apple tree. Maybe Mr. Schneider hadn't gotten word that they were coming home.

He went to his grandpa and said, "Please, let's go get Vonk. I've missed him!"

Grandpa looked away. Grandma turned around quickly, busying herself with something in the trunk. His mother came out of the kitchen and bent to him. "Darling. I'm sorry. Vonk isn't here. I mean...well...Vonk is..."

William pulled away. "VONK! VONK! I'm home! I'm home boy! Come on, Vonk!" He began running down the lane toward the farm, toward the man who was going to keep Vonk safe for him during the war. Tears were rolling down his cheeks as he screamed, "VONK! VONK!"

His mother caught up with him and put her arms firmly around his middle, murmuring in his ear. "William. Vonk is gone. He...he isn't coming back home..."

"NO! NO! VONK!" And the sadness of the last two years coursed down William's face. His dog. His best friend. The one he had been forced to leave behind so that he could be a big soldier and take care of his mommy. Vonk was gone.

He cried until there were no tears left to cry. No more tears for his daddy. No tears for Vonk. No tears for his mommy. No tears at all. Then, and only then, he let his mother lead him back into the house, where he curled up in his too small bed, held onto Brelli, and closed his swollen brown eyes.

He didn't eat dinner that night. He was so tired from crying that he slept through until the next morning. Although he didn't mention it the next day, he still hoped his mother was wrong. Maybe Vonk was just missing. Maybe he would come home to him. But the day ended with no Vonk.

For days, William sat outside and waited. Hoping. Grandma and Grandpa left for Connecticut with promises to return mid-summer after Jacob settled in. Still, William sat – waiting for a dog that would never come.

One morning, very early, before his mother got out of bed, he went to sit in his waiting spot, a place where Vonk was sure to find him. But this morning, as he looked down the lane, he saw a person, not a dog.

The man was very tall. Tall as the trees. He was whistling a tune that William remembered from a long time ago. The words came floating into his head, "My Bonnie lies over the ocean. My Bonnie lies over the sea."

William stood up. He began walking toward the man who was now running toward the house. William began to run, too. He flew into his daddy's arms, who swung around and around and around. Daddy kissed his head, his face, his arms. The beard on Daddy's face was scratchy and his clothes had an odd odor, but William didn't care. His daddy was finally home from the war.

Chapter 50

BONNIE: July 1946

Those first hours together again as a family had a dreamlike quality. Several times, Bonnie reached out to touch Jacob, checking if he were truly home. She noted that William, too, needed to be close, often sitting on his father's lap or at his feet on the floor. They talked. They laughed. They hugged. They cried.

Eventually, Jacob rang up his mother and invited her to dinner at Bonnie's suggestion. She still hadn't forgiven the woman but had enough compassion to understand how much she must have missed her son. She was willing to be magnanimous this one time.

Elisabet, who had grown considerably older in the months they were away, arrived shortly after 4 o'clock. She clung to Jacob as her entire frame shook with shuddering sobs. Jacob stroked her back, murmuring, "It's okay, now, Mama. It's okay. I'm home now. It's okay." The reunion caused Bonnie to clutch her own son as tears rolled down her cheeks.

Eventually, Elisabet turned to Bonnie, pulling a covered dish out of an oversized cloth satchel. "I brought some pflaumenkudhen. It was one of Jacob's favorites as a child. I hope you don't mind." She glanced at Bonnie and then toward the ground.

Bonnie quickly took the dish, stammering, "No. That's perfect. Thank you."

Although the two women did not speak again, the evening was not strained or contentious. Each listened to Jacob talk of Germany while William played quietly, pretending not to be tired. Finally, Jacob said he would take his mother home, and Bonnie tucked William into bed. It was only when Jacob returned that Bonnie finally had the man she loved to herself.

Years floated away as Bonnie and Jacob touched. Softly at first and then more urgently, a starving man set loose in an expansive buffet of fine delicacies. It was only two years, but it seemed to be forever. A hand lifted to stroke a side. A finger traced a jawline. Fingers. Hands. Feet. Shoulders. Moans. Two people becoming one again, like before. Before the war tore them apart. Before the war changed them, making them harder, sadder, more jaded.

All night, Bonnie and Jacob touched, stroked, connected. Sometimes sleep would cloud their senses until they drifted off, only to wake again when one or the other would reach out, simply to check that the mirage had not faded.

As the sun began to rise over the horizon, Jacob

began to talk. He needed Bonnie to understand things he hadn't been able to put in his letters. Those things that he censored for fear it would scare her away or prove that he had changed beyond reason. Or that he was not a real man or real American.

He spoke quietly as he buried his head in her shoulder. He talked of God or the lack thereof. He talked of fear. He talked of death. He talked of enemies. He talked of war. He talked about change. He talked until there were no words left to say.

He lifted his head and looked Bonnie in the eyes, afraid to find anger or disgust. He had killed men. He had terrified towns. He had been scared. He was sure he had been less than a man. But all he saw in Bonnie's eyes was love. Love for him – all of him. Even the ugly parts that left him scarred, never to be quite the man he was before. He put his head back down and let two years of tears and fear fall from his eyes.

Bonnie just stroked his hair. She, too, had things to say, but realized she would leave them unsaid. He had seen things that no man should see. He had experienced death, caused by his own hand. He had endured fear, hatred, and hopelessness almost beyond his ability to bear. He didn't need to know her own grief, pain, heartache. He wouldn't be able to move forward knowing that the war had changed her, too.

So, in the deep sleep that followed his purging, Bonnie stroked his hair and thought her thoughts. She silently told him about her sickness, about dying inside. She told him of her fear that he would never come home again and that she would never survive. She told him of the days without knowing where he was. The days of pleading with God to spare him, to bring him home. When she was done, she looked down at his sleeping face, grateful he was home.

She was sure there would be difficult days ahead. Jacob would need time to adjust to being home. There was the issue of his mother to resolve. There were the children she still wanted to bear. Through it all, she would be there for him, steadying him, being the rock he needed, keeping her own war locked deep inside.

Chapter 51

WILLIAM: November 2016

Exhaustion overcame William as he readied himself for bed. The day had been a long one. Veteran's Day was one of the many difficult days. VE Day. VJ Day. His father's birthday. The day of his death. Each time, memories overcame him and left him aching inside for the boy he had been and what the war took from him.

Today, however, something was a bit different. Seeing the painting, knowing what his father had carried with him into war, seeing for a brief moment inside his father's memory. Feeling the love that was there until his father's death.

His father once told him that war changes soldiers. William always wanted to say, "It changes those left behind, too. It changed your wife. It changed your son."

But he never did. It was as if he didn't want to make his dad hurt worse than he hurt every day of his life.

The painting. The sad little boy eyes. The child trying to be a soldier with no tears falling but sadness leaking from his eyes, nonetheless. His father had known all along.

William stared into the bathroom mirror. It was the knowing but not saying that had separated them. His father knew the war changed his son but couldn't bear the thought. The son knew the war changed his father but didn't want to acknowledge that truth.

"Vati," William whispered. "I understand. I didn't then, but I do now. War changed you. It changed me. It changed Mama. But you had to do what you had to do. You loved your family and country enough to fight for us. You had a choice to make, and you made it. Yes, it changed me. But look at the man I've become. A husband. A father. A grandfather. A patriot. A man. Just like you."

William crawled into bed and gave Marie a squeeze. "I'm getting up early tomorrow. I gave Christopher a call this afternoon and took him up on his offer to go fishing." Marie's eyebrows rose slightly as she looked into her husband's eyes. "I just figured it was time," he said with a shrug, then closed his eyes.

War had indeed changed him, and he was grateful for the sacrifice his father made to allow it to happen.

ABOUT ATMOSPHERE PRESS

Atmosphere Press is an independent, full-service publisher for excellent books in all genres and for all audiences. Learn more about what we do at atmospherepress.com.

We encourage you to check out some of Atmosphere's latest releases, which are available at Amazon.com and via order from your local bookstore:

Dancing with David, a novel by Siegfried Johnson

The Friendship Quilts, a novel by June Calender

My Significant Nobody, a novel by Stevie D. Parker

Nine Days, a novel by Judy Lannon

Shining New Testament: The Cloning of Jay Christ, a novel by Cliff Williamson

Shadows of Robyst, a novel by K. E. Maroudas

Home Within a Landscape, a novel by Alexey L. Kovalev

Motherhood, a novel by Siamak Vakili

Death, The Pharmacist, a novel by D. Ike Horst

Mystery of the Lost Years, a novel by Bobby J. Bixler

Bone Deep Bonds, a novel by B. G. Arnold

Terriers in the Jungle, a novel by Georja Umano

Into the Emerald Dream, a novel by Autumn Allen

His Name Was Ellis, a novel by Joseph Libonati

The Cup, a novel by D. P. Hardwick

The Empathy Academy, a novel by Dustin Grinnell

Tholocco's Wake, a novel by W. W. VanOverbeke

Dying to Live, a novel by Barbara Macpherson Reyelts

ABOUT THE AUTHOR

Born in Athens, Greece, as an Air Force brat, Teri M Brown came into this world with an imagination full of stories to tell. She now calls the North Carolina coast home, and the peaceful nature of the sea has been a great source of inspiration for her creativity. Not letting 2020 get the best of her, Teri chose to go on an adventure that changed her outlook on life. She and her husband, Bruce, rode a tandem bicycle across the United States from Astoria, Oregon to Washington DC, successfully raising money for Toys for Tots. She learned she is stronger than she realized and capable of anything she sets her mind to.

The ride was the impetus for publishing her first novel, *Sunflowers Beneath the Snow*. Teri is a wife, mother, grandmother, and author who loves word games, reading, bumming on the beach, taking photos, singing in the shower, hunting for bargains, ballroom dancing, playing bridge, and mentoring others.

CPSIA information can be obtained
at www.ICGtesting.com
Printed in the USA
JSHW031350120922
30260JS00002B/7